MCKINLEY ELEMENTARY SCHOOL

S0-AXI-818

"The author has created an incredible eleven year-old character that surprises the reader at every turn of the page. You cannot get enough of Slater and that makes it impossible to put the book down!"

—*Dr. Maggie MacIsaac, Superintendent, Burlingame School District*

"Book 3, oh boy, oh boy! I am impressed at how Shaffer is showing the maturing of Slater as we watch and wonder if he has finally turned a corner. Loved, loved, loved camp. I could totally feel the boys' sheer exhaustion and unwavering commitment to winning. Boyhood in full fever pitch. This book is a page turner! Surely one that will be an absolute delight to readers of all ages!"

—*Daina Lujan, Principal, Millbrae School District; Vice President, South San Francisco Unified School District Board of Trustees*

"In MENACE, book three in the adventures of Slater Hannigan, the sixth-grade trouble-prone kid is back—and so are the tricks! This time Slater may have met his match when he is sent to Elmer Woods. It's another exciting episode in the drama-filled life of our mischievous hero, by author Stefania Shaffer."

—*Penny Warner, best-selling author of over 60 books for adults and children, including the Agatha Award winning middle-grade mystery series, THE CODE BUSTERS CLUB.*

"MENACE allows you to relive your childhood and learn from the power of imagination, friendship and good ole' fashioned mischief. This is a book that all kids can see themselves in and connect to. Whether you're a kiddo with a taste for trouble and adventure, or one who is a good friend looking to lend a hand—and don't mind getting those hands dirty—or just a parent looking to read a book with your kids that you can enjoy too, MENACE has something for everybody."

—William Anderson, M.Ed.,
The Manual High School, Denver

"Stefania Shaffer quickly engages the reader in the adventures of a mischievous middle schooler who continues to push the limits while learning life lessons that mold his character. Rich with vivid dialogue that creates clear imagery in one's mind, MENACE prompts the reader to ponder life's choices, all the while wondering how it's going to turn out for these characters. More than just a "good read," MENACE pushes many issues to the forefront that young adolescents must constantly deal with."

—Ron Rammer, Principal, McCaffrey Middle School,
Galt Elementary School District

Menace

BOOK 3

Menace
Copyright © 2017 Stefania Shaffer

Pressman Books
PO Box 456
San Carlos, CA 94070

All rights reserved. No part of this book may be reproduced (except for inclusion in reviews), disseminated or utilized in any form or by any means, electronic or mechanical, including photocopying, recording, or in any information storage and retrieval system, or the Internet/World Wide Web without written permission from the author or publisher.

Printed in the United States of America

Menace
Stefania Shaffer
www.StefaniaShaffer.com

1. Title 2. Author 3. Fiction

Library of Congress Control Number: 2017948358
ISBN 13: 978-09772325-43

This is a work of fiction. Names, characters, places, and incidents either are the product of the author's imagination or are used fictitiously, and any resemblance to actual persons, living or dead, business establishments, events, or locales is entirely coincidental.

Menace

—— BOOK 3 ——

Stefania Shaffer

"There are only two kinds of children in the classroom: those who are at the center of trouble and those who are on the sidelines watching it brew."

—*Madame Elsa Wilson, retired teacher, 5th grade,*
Esther Bookman Elementary

"It's been bloody awful today. But tomorrow three things will be waiting for you here: a clean slate, a fair break, and another chance to get it right. The choice is yours."

—*Mr. Mortimer Blackwell, Social Studies and Language Arts,*
6th grade, Everly Middle Grade

"Sometimes adults fail to understand—this is not one of those times. Many great people have learned that doing what is right is not always popular; and what's popular is not always right."

—*Mr. Gino Pastorino, Social Studies,*
6th grade, EMGATS

For all of my twenty-seven hundred former students who are now teachers with their own class, or married, in college, or high school, I carry with me only the fondest memories of our time together. I *never* taught a student I believed would ever fail—childhood is meant for *learning*.

This book is for you. —*Stefania Shaffer*

Men-ace: a person or thing likely to cause harm; a threat, or danger

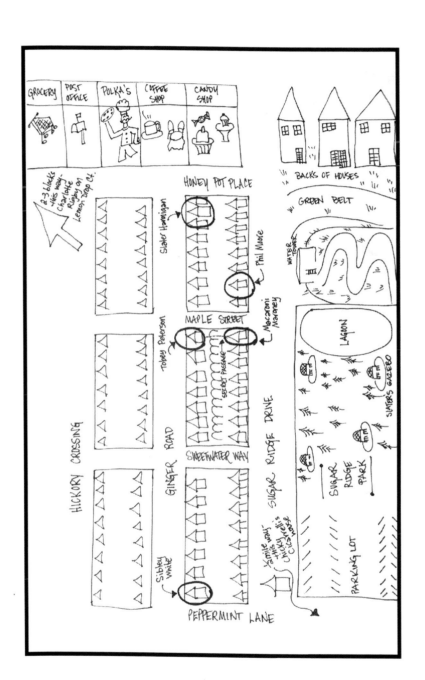

Acknowledgments

Throughout my writing career, sturdy friends have offered me as much support as anything I might depend on if I were adrift on a raft at sea.

My first readers outside of my home are these dependable logs that help me stay afloat, ensuring my foundation is set for the voyage ahead: Jenene Nicholson and Daina Lujan. Thank you for finding the right words to say and the right way to say them. My writer's heart is safe in your hands.

For the ties that bind and buoy me, I thank Evona Panycia, Kathy Nelson, Cheryl Tyler, Joyce Walter, Penny Warner, Barry Saide, Daniel Cullen, William Anderson, Earle Peterson, Judy King, Patti Smith, Maria Ribera, Martha Sutton, Fran Platt, Pam Kefer, Bronia Whipp, Heather McLean, Angela Ambrosio, Lucretia Whitener, Laura Afshar, Mary O'Neil, Amelia Ramos and Heather Polcik for your moral support. Losing oars in the water is bad, but hearing encouraging cheers from the shoreline to keep paddling by hand is always good.

The compass is never wrong. Thank you to my enthusiastic beta readers for providing the navigation I needed when the last draft was complete. To the children and adults across the country who read Menace first, your special suggestions are etched within these pages.

For holding the binoculars to my work, I thank these San Francisco Bay Area professionals for their consulting on fires, and juvenile law: Administrative Fire Battalion Chief, Kent Thrasher, Management Analyst, Matt Lucett, Police Captain, Patrick Halleran, and Retired District Attorney, Robert H. Perez.

To my harbormasters, I thank my district of professional administrators and Board of Trustees for granting me this time to voyage, and for keeping the path home lighted.

For my North Star, I thank the family and, especially, my sweet husband for supporting all of my dreams—you are my eternal reassurance and have been a constant bright source on this journey.

Without life preservers in publishing, one would be dead in the water. I am so grateful to my team: Erin Tolbert, Linda Lee, RaeAnne Betzelberger, and Rick Chappell. Your excellent work has readied Menace to set sail.

Contents

CHAPTER 1

A Proper Apology

"Slater, who was that just now at the front door?" Lynn Hannigan asks, eagerly rushing down the stairs hoping to catch a glimpse of whoever was waiting on the other side for her son.

"Mom, it's nobody," he replies with falsehoods and a bowed head. His mother has no idea what just happened.

"Well, it couldn't be just *nobody*. I am pretty sure I heard a knock," she says curiously as she stops him from shutting the door completely. She walks outside into the dark night air with her hands bundled in the pockets of her sweater to do a sweep of the street. She looks to the left and then to the right without seeing a sign of anyone around. After returning inside, she gives her sixth-grader a long, hard stare. "So, who was it?"

1

"Mom, I already told you, nobody important," Slater says, staring at the door that is now being dead-bolted by his mother.

"Hank, come down here to help me with your son," Lynn calls upstairs to her husband, Slater's father.

After a light jog down the steps leading to the front entry, Hank Hannigan senses another stand-off between mother and son, a regular occurrence these days ever since Slater got kicked out of his middle school only six months after he started.

"Well, I can tell I'm not here for my opinion on decorating the front entry; looks like we've already got two statues in place," he says trying to get his family to loosen up a bit.

"Hank, someone just came to visit Slater, and he won't tell me who it was," Lynn starts.

"Dad, it's no big deal, that's all," Slater says resigned to the interrogation he is certain will come next from his father, the district attorney.

"Well, son, if it's no big deal, then who was it? Was it Chicky?" Hank asks, referring to Slater's newest partner in crime—or sixth-grade friend—depending on who is telling the story of events that have already taken place.

"No, it wasn't Chicky. He's at his house, I'm sure under lock and key by his grandma," Slater mumbles under his breath showing some resentment for the mess they are both in right now.

"Slater, I'm tired of these little games. From now on, when I ask you a direct question, I expect a direct answer. *Who* came to the door looking for you?" Lynn says without a shred of patience left for her son after the year she has had with his mischief and mayhem. "Look, it was Sibley White, okay? No big deal, all right?" Slater says in a huff as he makes a move toward the staircase, hoping he can run up it as fast as he can to get away from the third-degree about why she was here. If only he still had a door on his bedroom to slam shut, then he would be able to fully express his frustration over how his life has been completely ruined.

Before he can even put one foot on the first step, his father puts a strong arm across the banister as a barrier to block him. "Not so fast, Slater. Come sit with us in my den for a minute." His father extends his other arm to show Slater into his office off the front entryway.

"Man, not this again." Slater has taken a dislike to the parental chats he has found himself on the receiving end of too many times these past several months.

"Slater, again, less attitude. All your mother and I ask is that you treat us with a little more respect. You should be more grateful for what we have done for you. Some kids are not as lucky," Hank says as a not-so-subtle reminder about the differences between how he and his friend Chicky are living.

"Gee, Dad, I think I hear that enough from Mom," Slater says stopping himself short before that mouth of his gets him into any more trouble.

His words are met with a sharp look from his father. The narrowed eyes beneath furrowed brows always come before a pointing finger begins wagging in his face. His mother stands next to his father with her hands firmly planted on her hips, the same matched expression on her face.

"Why was Sibley White here?" Lynn asks, knowing full well that smart little girl was probably demanding an apology—and rightfully so.

"She just, oh, I don't know, she didn't say much," Slater says hesitantly trying to process the shock of seeing Sibley on his doorstep after she has been ignoring him at school for months.

"Look, here's what I think happened. Sibley knows you stole her work, plagiarized her report, and put your name on it to get a sweet grade so you wouldn't fail Mr. Blackwell's class. And now that you've been transferred to EMGATS—in the third trimester of sixth grade, might I add, you couldn't even make it one full year without trouble—she's pretty sure you owe her an apology. Am I close?" Lynn lays it out exactly the way she would have played it had she been in Sibley's shoes.

Slater can't even believe his mother's uncanny ability to read minds and see through doors. He knows she was upstairs for the whole five minutes Sibley stood on his doorstep screaming at him, but how could she know *exactly* what had happened?

"Well, maybe," Slater offers, hoping this is enough of a confirmation for his mother to have some sympathy and leave him alone.

"Okay, then, here's what has to happen next. You need to write an apology letter to Mr. and Mrs. White for stealing their daughter's intellectual property and promise to accept whatever punishment they believe will restore their faith in you. This is not a situation where you can claim to not have known any better, because you have known not to copy other people's work since you were in third grade," Lynn says, without any regard for how embarrassing this might be for her son.

"Are you serious? You want me to write to her *parents?*"

"Oh, but I'm not done yet. Then, I want you to write a letter apologizing to Sibley for switching reports and taking advantage of your friendship—"

"But, Mom, we're not even friends," Slater protests.

"Clearly. No true friend would ever go around pretending to pass off his superior work by cheating his friend out of getting the grade that should have been *hers,* not *his.* You will never have any of the right kind of friends if this is how you treat people, Slater," his mom continues with her ire.

"I can't even believe the things you make me do!" Slater shouts.

"The things I *make* you do? Slater, I do not *make* your choices; *you* do. I do not *make* your messes; *you* do. I do not *make* amends for the wrongs you have done; *you* do. Got me?" She finishes with her hands now at her sides, brushing invisible lint from her tailored pants as if she has just brushed off this topic and is ready to move on.

"Son, your mother is asking you to do what is respectable. We have raised you better than you have been behaving this past year, and we expect for you to start acting like someone who values the things we have taught," Hank says, rising from his chair, satisfied that his wife didn't need his help after all. "I suggest you go upstairs and begin your penance."

What can he say? Slater feels awful that Sibley has one more reason to be mad at him. No matter how many times he tries to explain his way out, he always seems to land in some kind of new trouble just waiting for him.

"I'm going," he says dejectedly before he turns to ask over his shoulder, "Hey, when can I get my door put back on my room?"

"Bad timing, bud. I don't think your mother is in any kind of mood to have this conversation right now," Hank says without even having to look at his wife to know he is right.

As Slater shuffles up the stairs through the shower curtain hanging in his doorframe, he plops down on his bed to think about how to start a letter to Sibley's parents.

"Whatchya doin'?" Graham, his fourth-grade brother, pops his head up from beneath Slater's bed to surprise his brother.

"Gra-ham! You scared me! What did I say about sneaking into my room when I'm not here? Stay out of my space and leave all my things alone," Slater snarls out of frustration.

"Well, it's not like you had your *door* shut. Oh, maybe that's because Dad took it off since you got in trouble," Graham says gloating.

"Dude, I'm being serious right now; get out," Slater says through gritted teeth.

"Okay, I'm leaving. I just wondered what Mom and Dad said to you downstairs. And anyway, who was that girl at the door?" he asks, smiling like he knows more than he is letting on.

"She's nobody. I don't want to talk about it and I don't want you in my room. I wish I had a door so I could slam it really hard after you leave!" Slater shouts.

"Graham, come down here, honey," Lynn calls from the kitchen. She can tell when the ref needs to call penalty on the play, and Graham's sneaking around freely in Slater's business is only making things worse.

"Hi, Mom, I'm here," Graham says after running down the stairs and cozying up to his mom with a big hug.

"Bud, I need you to do me a favor," Lynn says, looking straight down into her little man's face while he beams up at her with a big crooked smile. "Can you give your brother some privacy for the next few days? He's a little bit on edge and has a few things on his mind he needs to work out in peace and quiet. You understand, don't you, buddy?"

"Yeah, Slater's in trouble because a girl yelled at him, huh, Mom?"

"Well, I'm not sure about *all* of that, but he needs to make some amends with his schoolmate, and I think he can do that better without a little brother underfoot, okay?" she says running her fingers through his mop of hair.

"Okay, Mom, I can stay down here with you," he says pleasantly. "But that girl sure was mad. She even told Slater she hates him," Graham says, grinning.

"Well, sometimes friends get into fights, and I am sure Slater is

going to figure out a way to make it up to her. But we don't need
to bug him about this anymore, do we, bud?"

"Don't worry, Mom, I'm not going to start a fight with my brother.
He needs all the friends he can get," he says with a twinkle in his
eye.

"Dear Sibley," Slater starts off his letter with the most appropriate
term of endearment he can think to use.

He doesn't want to call her his *friend* and he certainly can't start
an apology off with *Dear Sworn Enemy.*

> *"I am writing to tell you how sorry I am that I stole*
> *your work and put my cover on your report. I didn't*
> *think it would matter so much because your grade is*
> *already so high in Mr. Blackwell's class, and besides,*
> *he said he wasn't even going to grade your extra credit*
> *because you didn't even need it. Me? Well, I need as*
> *much help as I can get. Not everyone is as smart as*
> *you, Sibley. I wish I knew half the stuff you have rolling*
> *around in your brain. But, that's beside the point. I*
> *shouldn't have been so sneaky, and I guess I'm really*
> *sorry. Don't you think you can understand why I did*
> *it and forgive me? You are a stubborn girl. I've been*
> *working really hard to try and tell you my side of things*

and you don't even give me half a chance to explain.
You just like being mad—and friendless. Because
that's what friends are supposed to do for each other,
Sibley. They are supposed to stick up for one another.
And I know you say I did a bad thing, but it's not like
I ruined your whole grade in Mr. Blackwell's class,
Sibley. You're too smart—nothing can pull down your
grade."

"Oh, Slater," his mom yells up to him from the stairs below, "don't forget—I want to read that letter of apology *before* you put it in the envelope."

Aw, man, Slater hisses under his breath while he scratches out his entire draft and then crumples it up into a tight little wad using all his might as if he were squeezing the life out of the paper ball shaped like someone's little head—*whose* head he is imagining is not quite clear.

"Dear Sibley,

I am writing to tell you how sorry I am for being such
a bad friend—even though you probably still don't
consider me your friend on account of all the times
you tell me you hate me—but, I still would like to be
your friend if you ever change your mind. I know I've
done some terrible things, but I never thought you
would ever know about any of it, so I—"

Slater slams his pencil down hard and then decides to just snap it in half. It feels so good, so he opens the entire box of new Ticonderogas stored in his desk and starts breaking them all, sometimes in clusters of five or six, just to see if he can. It takes all his strength, but when they crack like little twigs and he has nothing left in his room to destroy, he decides he needs to get out of the house.

He runs down the stairs faster than he can call out to his parents, "I'll be back in ten minutes," then doesn't even bother slamming the front door behind him. He just runs. He runs across the street without even looking twice, like he has been taught to do ever since he was old enough to discover that his house was nearly kitty-corner with the candy shop on Honey Pot Place. He runs across Sugar Ridge Drive, straight into the park, where he can find solace inside the gazebo that has always been reserved for secret meetings with his friends.

He sits down low on the floorboards inside the white lattice structure to be sure no one can see him alone in this park, where no one else seems to be today, surprisingly enough. He rests his head on his knees and thinks about what he really wants to say to Sibley White.

He doesn't have a clue. Nothing comes to mind. He just feels awful that she is so mad, but he doesn't know what he's supposed to put in a letter that will make her feel any better. In this moment, he realizes he doesn't have to put it in a *letter*. It's only been an hour since Sibley came to his door. Maybe she's had dinner by now, but it's still not too late. Slater springs up from his seat on the wood floor and bolts from the park, this time running toward the opposite end of Sugar Ridge Drive from where he entered.

He runs past Maple Street and Phil Moore's old house, which sits near the corner, and he runs the distance of the next block, where Sweetwater Way reminds him there are only ten more houses to go before he reaches Sibley's street—Peppermint Lane.

Slater doesn't even slow down to take in the view of her disheveled home and weedy front yard. He's seen it before. He takes pounding sprints up the brick steps leading to Sibley's front door and raps as loudly as he can, unafraid of who might be there to greet him.

There is some commotion behind the door with a gruff voice asking *who on earth would be at our door tonight?* From out of view, only one small child might actually know and secretly, she is crossing her fingers tight that she might be right.

All the night air swirls into the front entryway when Mr. White's urgent swish of the front door opens violently, as if he resents this neighborly intrusion. "Young man, state your name and your business here," Mr. White says standing sternly in the doorframe.

"I, um, I am sorry to disturb your household, Mr. White, but I am in Sibley's class at school. My name is Slater Hannigan, and I um, I wanted to—"

"Slater Hannigan, I have heard quite a lot of your name recently. I am not sure I like the context that comes before this introduction." Mr. White looks firmly at Slater, while Slater holds his gaze, trying not to be intimidated into looking at the ground.

"I, um, I'm sure you have heard about a lot of rotten things that

I have done, sir; but I, um, well, I, um, wanted to speak with you and Mrs. White to apologize properly, if that's all right," Slater says, finally finishing the first thought he organized in his head on his run over here.

"Well, young man, if you are sure you'd like to come in to face the fire, I want you to be prepared. There are two very unhappy ladies in this household tonight," Mr. White says while gesturing with his hand that Slater is welcome to come into the living room.

"Sidra, Sibley, we have company," Mr. White calls to the kitchen where he is sure they are already eavesdropping against the swinging kitchen door.

"Mother, I do not want to go out there," Sibley says in a hushed whisper while Mrs. White wonders what that boy means by coming around here after dinnertime.

"You stay here, then, I'll see what he wants." She tosses the dishtowel to the counter where pots and pans are left to dry and walks slowly toward her guest while untying the apron bow behind her waist.

"This is Sibley's mother, Mrs. White. It seems as if Slater is here to offer us an apology," Mr. White says in a slight accent that Slater doesn't recognize.

"Slater, what is on your mind that you had to rush over here after the dinner hour?" Mrs. White begins without an ounce of warmth or hospitality, making this difficult scenario even more excruciating for poor Slater.

"Well, ma'am, I'm sorry if I'm coming at a bad time. My mom

told me to write you a letter, but I'm really bad at writing and my thoughts kept getting jumbled, and then I thought of something that maybe I could say in person," Slater begins sincerely.

"All right, Slater, we're listening." She sits with her arms folded tightly across her chest, the expression on her face not softening.

"I want you to know that I consider Sibley a friend, even though I don't think she wants to be mine. I am sorry for switching my report cover with hers, and I know how much her work and her education mean to her. I really didn't expect this to be such a mess, but it's all my fault, and I am prepared to do whatever you think I should to fix it in your eyes. I've already been punished by the school, and I am on restriction at home, but I want you to know that I am willing to make this right to your family. I feel bad," Slater says with just the right amount of moisture beginning to well in both of his eyes.

Mr. and Mrs. White have no idea what to make of him. They never expected to see this boy in their home, and they never imagined he would be the type of child to make amends for his wrongdoing. They look at one another and then quickly back to Slater before Mrs. White speaks. "Well, Slater, I do appreciate your words here, but I am just not sure this is a situation that can be remedied. It is more of a character issue for us, and we are not sure we want our daughter making friends with people who, well, people who—"

"I understand. You don't need to say it. I'll be going now, but I just wanted to say that if you thought you could use any gardening help, or painting shutters, or something, I'd be willing to work off the same number of hours it took for Sibley to do all the research on that report of hers," Slater offers thoughtfully.

Again, Mr. and Mrs. White both look to one another unsure of what to do, while Slater gets up from their couch upholstered in tortoise green colored velvet and slips out the door before calling loudly over his shoulder, "I wish I could take it all back. I'm really sorry, Sibley."

As fast as Slater ran toward Sibley White's house just minutes earlier, he now runs away from it at a breakneck speed back to Sugar Ridge Park—to his spot in the gazebo, still vacant—waiting only for him. He curls right into a little ball on the wooden floor behind the lattice fence and sobs as hard as he can where no one can hear him.

He doesn't even know why he is so upset. He just knows how awful apologizing in person felt.

He hears quiet murmuring outside of his private getaway before solid footsteps enter his sacred hideout. When a firm hand is placed upon his shoulder, he looks up blurrily through wet lashes.

Standing tall above him is Mr. White who squats down low to kneel beside Slater. His only words are warmer this time. "Let's get you home. I'd like to tell your parents about your offer." With that, Mr. White hoists Slater off the floor in one swoop, and just when Slater wipes at his eyes one more time with his elbow sleeve, he finds Sibley standing just outside of the gazebo's opening.

She cannot believe that Slater Hannigan has been crying—over her. She looks at him bashfully. He wears a stunned expression, completely mortified by her presence. It is obvious he wants to run away through the tiny gate that her father is unwittingly blocking. It seems like punishment enough that Slater knows she saw him crying, so she offers him the only thing she can with the sincere hope that it will make everything better tonight. "I accept your apology."

Before the Whites can escort Slater across Sugar Ridge Drive on their way toward his home, they run into his father who is already looking for Slater in the candy shop on Honey Pot Place.

"Son, there you are," Hank calls from a distance.

When the two families meet face to face, it is Mr. White who makes the introductions. "I am Giorgio White, and this is my daughter Sibley," he says while extending a hand to shake Mr. Hannigan's own. The two men stand there together as if they have known each other for longer than this minute, but they have never met before—Hank Hannigan is sure of it. They are both of the same brawny build that has them standing head and shoulders above their own circle of friends. Their firm grip in each other's clasp is something they do not normally feel when greeting other men whose mitts are usually smaller.

"It is a pleasure, a real pleasure, to meet you, Seymour," Hank says while smiling warmly before naturally asking the obvious question. "How did you all come upon each other tonight?"

"Well, your son came to our home to apologize to my wife and I directly." Mr. White looks brightly at Slater. "His sincere offer to work off the same number of hours it took for Sibley to do the research on her report made us realize he was truly showing great character," Mr. White watches while Hank Hannigan looks pleasantly surprised at Slater. "Before we could accept, he had already disappeared out our front door. We finally caught up with him and wanted to bring him home so I could tell you personally that it is obvious you and your wife are doing a sincere job raising him up to be a fine young man," Mr. White says while stroking the back of his daughter's hair as she stands right beside her father.

"Well, his mother is going to be so happy to hear this bit of news. Slater, shall we bring the Whites over to meet Mom?"

"Oh, no, Mr. Hannigan, that would be too much trouble. Better that the wives meet each other when we are guests in your home," he says with a very formal accent, perhaps European.

"Yes, you're probably right. What is Slater committing to doing for you?" Hank asks, wrapping his long arm around his son's shoulders.

"Well, Dad, I offered to do gardening, or painting—whatever Mr. White needs," Slater says looking up at his father for his approval.

"Fine, fine…then when should I send him over?"

"We are very humble people, lecturers for the university—" he says, a fib he has practiced often, "—so we spend most of our time inside our books rather than managing the weeds out front. Sibley says it took her twelve hours to do all the research necessary on her report, so if you agree that twelve hours is a fair exchange, then we have many chores that we could use Slater's help on in keeping up the outside of the house."

"We are perfectly agreeable. His new schedule at EMGATS means he has school now until 6 p.m. every day, but Fridays he is out earlier and weekends we can make him available," Hank says encouragingly.

"Why don't we expect Slater on Saturdays from 8 a.m. until noon for the next three weekends?"

"We guarantee he will be there." Hank Hannigan shakes Mr. White's hands good-bye and Sibley looks over her shoulder as she walks away with her father.

Slater stands there for just another minute to give a final wave in the air and then walks the span of four shops on Honey Pot Place before he and his father arrive home.

"What took you so long?" Lynn asks when she sees her husband and son coming up the walkway. "I was beginning to get worried."

"Your son found some work." Hank smiles at Slater. "It seems he went straight to the Whites to apologize by means of offering to do yardwork as a form of his punishment."

"You did?" His mother seems dumbfounded.

"Yeah, Mom, I didn't like my letter," Slater says looking more relaxed now than he felt a half hour ago.

"Well, tell me all about it. I want to know every single detail; don't leave anything out." With this, Lynn pulls up a stool at the kitchen counter and peels a tangerine for herself and one each for her husband and son, while she stays glued to his story wondering all the while how he got the courage.

When Sibley White goes to sleep, a wide smile crosses her face knowing Slater will be her houseboy for nearly a month—and that *does* seem like punishment enough.

CHAPTER 2

Field Trip

Every Monday morning begins the same way at the Everly Middle Grade Alternative to Traditional Scheduling—forever known as EMGATS. Mr. Pastorino announces to his social studies class any important information the assistant deans want shared with his sixth-graders, usually about a special speaker invited to give an assembly once a month, or internships available to students in eighth grade. The only reason why sixth-graders are told about professional opportunities is to keep them motivated to stay at EMGATS for the following two years. Roll is taken and then the kids are given twelve minutes to sort their backpacks for assignments expected to be turned in before tomorrow.

After all the morning's business has been organized, and he has regained the attention of his class, Mr. Pastorino adds the very comment EMGATS students eagerly anticipate hearing all year long. "Class, we have just gotten permission to attend the Exhibit of the Gods. We'll go to the Henry Archer Museum in downtown Clifton." As he continues talking about the date and details, Slater turns slyly in his seat, throwing his head back to catch Chicky's eye in the last row—both of them sharing a knowing glance. "Field trips are one of the perks of attending a smaller school, and part of our aim is to make every class feel like a science lab, because when you are hands-on with your learning, you will remember things for a lifetime, well beyond the next test." Mr. Pastorino sees a lot of enthusiasm spark among his students who have all raised hands in the air about the big day.

"Mr. Pastorino, I have a question," Tony Jefferson says. After getting the nod from his teacher, he begins, "Are we taking one of those old, yellow school buses, or are we carpooling with parents?"

"I was about to cover this; good question. We don't have the funds for the bus. Besides, it'll be way more practical for us to take the train since it's so nearby and only a twenty-minute ride. Sound good, everybody?"

A few more hands shoot into the air. "Yes, Marilyn." Mr. Pastorino is already anticipating Marilyn's question and decides to save her the embarrassment of asking how much money she will need to buy food. "Oh, before I let you begin Marilyn, let me just remind the class of another very important part I left out. Since this will be an all-day field trip, EMGATS is planning on providing lunch as usual. The cafeteria will also pack a hot breakfast burrito along with a cold sandwich for each student. You may pick two snacks from the fruit baskets before we leave the classroom, but you should plan to fill your water bottles in the cafeteria before checking in with me. Marilyn, do you still remember your question?"

Well, now she needs to switch gears quickly because that's exactly what she was wondering—how would she be getting all the extra money she would need to buy food downtown? Her mother only provides their suppertime meal and counts on her kids to be taken care of by the school or by the kindness of play-date moms. "Um, yeah, Mr. Pastorino, I was wondering if we should bring our backpacks with us, or if the museum has a rule about that like some of the stores do?"

"Another good question. I think you should bring a backpack to carry your water bottle and maybe a sweatshirt in case it gets really cool inside the museum. Also, bring a notebook since there will be time to sketch the statues and write down some of the things you learn while the ideas are fresh in your mind."

When the class has spent the better part of another ten minutes asking every other question they can think of to throw off Mr. Pastorino's lesson time, they are surprised when he stops teaching. Instead of lecturing today, he puts them into groups to interview each other as if they are the gods and goddesses they have been studying the past few weeks during their curriculum on Ancient Greece. After the friends scramble across the room for a rare day of unstructured groupings, Chicky and Slater make sure to land together.

"I want to be Zeus," Chicky says, the first one to claim being the ruler of everything.

"Well, then I want to be Poseidon," Slater chimes in with the next most powerful god he can remember.

"Um, usually it's polite for us to take numbers before we just begin shouting out, you guys," Marilyn complains. "But, I guess if that's how you're gonna play, then obviously I am taking Athena. See if you mess with me and my fierceness," she says giving each of them a look like she means it.

Marilyn definitely appears stronger than Slater, but she is not nearly as tall as Chicky. It is rumored that she is in charge of four younger brothers at home while her mom works two jobs. Her older brother is always training with his coach *after* he's done playing sports—his only strategy for getting a college scholarship. Every single time she cleans her room, the youngest ones sneak in to mess it all up again. Marilyn wishes she could be the one to go to work instead of staying home with all her brothers to make their dinner, read them stories and mop floors after bath time. She hates boys.

"Have you been on any field trips here before?" Slater asks Chicky, talking over Marilyn, who listens while they largely ignore her.

"Yeah, my first week. It was pretty cool; they let us go to a police station to see what it's like to get fingerprinted and locked up. We were supposed to be learning about social justice, but the cops were telling us stories about some bad things that happen on the job and it made me think that maybe I could be a cop. I'm totally tough enough," Chicky says out loud.

"Dude, *you* a cop? Why do I not see that?" Slater says, rolling back his head to let out a snort.

"Hey, Slater, like *you* could be a cop, either." Marilyn comes to Chicky's defense.

"No way, man, I don't want to be in law enforcement. I'm sick of that rat-your-friends-out stuff. I don't want anything to do with it; I've seen enough," Slater says, shaking his head while leaning way back on his chair until it teeters almost by itself without Slater having to hold onto the desk for balance.

"Yeah, I wasn't even serious anyway. I was just saying the dude had some good stories," Chicky retorts, feeling sorry now for sharing a thought he sort of liked.

"Well, anyone can be anything if you get a mentor," Marilyn says, like she's some kind of expert on the situation.

"Yeah? How do you know so much?" Slater says snidely as if he is sure she has no idea what she's talking about.

"Because last year I was in this Junior Achievement program where I got to work with a pastry chef who showed me how to bake and decorate so I can sell wedding cakes someday," Marilyn says with pride.

"Then what are you doing here at EMGATS if you're so smart?" Slater says rudely.

"I am only here temporarily, new kid. Unlike *you*, I have a plan and I don't need to tell it to you. You're stupid, anyway. You have no idea how to get what you want. You didn't even know about J.A. until I mentioned it. You're just one of those kids wasting his days, am I right? I know your type," Marilyn says with real confidence as she pushes back from her table to go talk to the teacher.

Mr. Pastorino looks over at Chicky and Slater who are both wondering what Marilyn just said about them.

"Boys, are we reviewing the traits of *all* the gods and goddesses or just your favorite ones?" Mr. Pastorino knows that groups sometimes tend to get off track when there are strong personalities in the mix.

Marilyn Washington is not one to mess around in class, and when other kids aren't holding up their end of group work, the teacher knows she will come and tell him.

"Let's do a little speed round. I'm going to hold up this deck of cards, so let's see how many each of you gets right. Tell me the name of the god or goddess *and* what they rule over." Mr. Pastorino unsnaps the rubber band from around the deck he pulls from his pocket. He sets a timer for one minute and quickly begins showing the face cards from the deck of gods.

"Um, um, it's Aphrodite," Chicky says quickly.

"Aphrodite, goddess of love, Mr. Pastorino," Marilyn continues with the *full* answer.

Mr. Pastorino puts the card in front of her signaling she has just earned this point.

The clock keeps ticking. Mr. Pastorino shows a picture of a man holding a pitchfork next to a dog with three heads.

"Oh, it's Hades, lord of the underworld, ruler of the dead," Marilyn says before the other two even have a chance to spit out their first "um."

Mr. Pastorino puts a second card in front of her growing pile.

This little game continues until Marilyn has correctly identified ninety-percent of the gods and goddesses, collecting eighteen cards, leaving Chicky with two and Slater with zero. The only one Slater really knew was Poseidon, and Chicky beat him to the punch when it came time for calling out.

"I think the goal is to study these better so when I swing by your group tomorrow, Marilyn will not be the only one with all the correct answers," Mr. Pastorino says, nodding to Marilyn who is sitting upright confidently, despite avoiding putting her full weight upon the flimsy chair beneath her for fear it might give way. Even though this is an embarrassment she has never suffered, it is the worst fear she can imagine so she always stuffs her heavy backpack beneath her seat so it can offer some kind of support, just in case.

"I told you—anybody can do anything with a mentor," she says with a positively glowing smile.

The bell rings for lunch and Chicky and Slater are ready to be away from Marilyn and her efforts to shame them.

"That girl thinks she knows everything. She's almost as bad as Sibley White, but I doubt she's even half as smart as Sibley was when Sibley was in kindergarten." Slater laughs easily at his own joke.

Chicky is not so sure he wants to encourage making fun of Marilyn. She has been pretty cool to him since he first started at

EMGATS in January. It's been three months now and he kind of likes it here and he's met some nice kids, Marilyn included.

"Oh, I don't know, she's not that bad once you get to know her," Chicky says.

"Get to know her? How well do you *know* her, Chicky? Come on, you can tell me," Slater says, goading Chicky like he might have a crush or something on big Marilyn.

"Dude, I'm just saying she's cool, so don't hate on her."

"Aw, somebody must *like* somebody," Slater says, trying to bait Chicky.

"I'm not playing, besides I think she has things kind of tough at home, so be cool, okay?"

"Yeah, okay, I'll be cool," Slater says, backing down.

There is something different in Chicky's voice—something *protective* when he talks about Marilyn—even *he* can tell. But, it hardly makes sense since he barely knows Marilyn. It's just that she reminds him of someone and he can't quite place it yet. Ever since his first day at EMGATS, he has had the haunting sense he *knows* this girl.

The next day in class brings a new focus for Chicky and Slater—this time it has nothing to do with gods or Marilyn Washington.

"Class, if I didn't make it clear yesterday—but I thought I did—you do not need to purchase your own tickets on the Pinehurst line," Mr. Pastorino says half-way surprised that some kids like Darryl Skully and Trevor Fink thought this was what their parents were supposed to do. "The *school* is purchasing the train tickets to get you as far as downtown Clifton, so don't go to any added expense. We are also providing breakfast burritos and then cold sandwiches and a few snacks. Everybody clear?" Mr. Pastorino waits for any other clarifications he needs to make even though his instructions seemed so obvious to *him*.

While the class gets back to taking notes on the formulation of Greek states, Slater writes a note and slyly tosses it back to Chicky.

"Pinehurst?" Only one word is necessary to convey all the conversation Chicky and Slater can have silently between them in their heads right now—and boy, oh boy, what a way to get their imaginations running wild.

Pinehurst is the town two hours away where Phil Moore moved to go live with his mom and her new husband. He thought he had until the end of the school year to hang out with Slater, Macaroni, Tobey and now Chicky, their newest friend to the group, but when he got the bad news before winter break that he wouldn't be returning to Everly Middle Grade, he broke down in front of all his friends on that late night at the basketball courts.

The guys all promised they'd come and visit him until Phil reminded them he was moving two hours away by car—and none of them even knew how to drive. Oh, it was awful. Poor Phil, crying like a baby, then Tobey crying, too. These guys have known each other since the beginning of elementary school at Esther Bookman; couldn't Phil's mother take that into consideration before ripping them apart?

When Slater hears the mere mention of Pinehurst, Chicky knows exactly what Slater is thinking: road trip.

"Let's do it," Chicky sends his response up the row to Slater, who happily begins plotting the events that will take place Friday, the day of the Gods Exhibit field trip.

It's not until lunch that Slater and Chicky can get any privacy to begin making their plan.

"Dude, there's a lot that could go wrong, but man, we're gonna be so close, we gotta just go for it. Phil doesn't have any friends and we gotta go check on him," Slater begins, knowing he doesn't need to convince Chicky of any off-campus escape. Chicky's probably already had experience with this kind of stuff.

"You got some money? 'Cause the way trains work is we gotta have a Pinehurst ticket to show the conductor or they kick us off," Chicky says between bites of his hot meatloaf provided by EMGATS.

"Yeah, how much you think it costs to go two hours away?" Slater wonders.

"Well, technically, we're only going from downtown Clifton, 'cause that's where the school is taking us, then it's about another hour and a half to Pinehurst. We gotta do some research; you be in charge of that when you get on the computer tonight," Chicky says, laying out their jobs.

"As far as I see it, Mr. Pastorino's gonna make us buddy up on Thursday, so you and I will obviously be partnered. It'll be harder for anyone to miss us if we're *both* gone. Especially when they do these multi-class field trips, there's gonna be like a hundred kids going to this thing, so we have a pretty good chance of flying under the radar," Chicky says, laying out the first part.

"So, we pick up our food and tickets from Pastorino to get to Clifton, but when everybody gets off, we gotta stay out of sight in the bathroom or something, right?" Slater says, thinking this through.

"Yeah, there are bathrooms in different cars, so we gotta scope that out pretty fast. Clifton's only a twenty-minute train ride from here. Then when we're *'stuck on the train, oh no!'* we'll just play it cool like we know we belong, and I think we should pretend to be sleeping so nobody bugs us, but we gotta have our ticket in our hands while we're asleep or they'll poke us and wake us up and then throw us right off the moving train."

"For real?" Slater asks in disbelief.

"Well, they do that in the movies, but all I remember is my grandma said I always had to have my ticket ready for the conductor or we'd be escorted off at the next stop."

"Okay, so then, we wait it out. We eat our burrito while we're riding to Pinehurst, then we get there. Do you know what's lucky for us? Phil's school is only a block away from the station. We don't have to take a bus or anything," Slater says relieved.

"We might be arriving around recess time or maybe they'll all be in classes. What does Phil say about that school? You think we could sneak onto campus, hide out in the boys' bathroom? You think Phil will ditch to come meet us somewhere? It's just that we gotta be kind of invisible in town. What if a cop spots three kids out of school when it's not even a holiday?" Chicky says, starting to worry about this part of their plan.

"I think we should sneak onto campus. It makes a lot more sense than us trying to blend in with all the adults around. Even if we gotta wait it out in the bathrooms, it'll be worth it when Phil sees us for lunch," Slater says excitedly.

For the next three days, Slater and Chicky try to imagine every scenario their eleven-year-old brains can concoct so they can be prepared. They decide that Slater will have to buy the train tickets to Pinehurst ahead of Friday because it will be too conspicuous to wait in line while the teachers are sorting all their field trip rosters. Imagine how that would look: a whole lot of kids bustling around to find their teacher's line while old Slater is just standing at the train ticket window, all by himself, handing over money to purchase a two-hour trip *away* from Henry Archer Museum.

The boys also agree that Slater needs to use his savings to pay for Chicky's ticket until Chicky can find the money to pay him back. Thirty dollars for each round-trip means Slater has to empty his shoebox full of cash beneath his bed. It barely leaves him anything left for comic magazines or ice cream from the truck after school, but having Chicky along will make the trip that much more fun and besides, he knows Chicky would do the same for him if the tables were turned.

The final messages Slater received from Phil last night firms up all their plans. "Meet at 11:30 a.m. Seventh wing boys' bathroom."

"Hey, what's Plan B?" Slater knows only too well that sometimes administrators lock bathrooms after they have been destroyed by a paper wad fight—or worse—at recess.

"Then, hide behind building nine where nobody ever goes until I come at lunch."

So, with this cryptic plan in place, Slater and Chicky put all their faith in the gods—and not the ones they are supposed to be seeing on Friday's field trip.

On Friday morning, with spring weather melting the snow into dirty piles of slush, Slater walks to school with Tobey and Macaroni. "It's happening. I got the tickets already," Slater whispers to his friends even though no one else is around to overhear.

"Dude, are you sure about this? What if you get caught? I don't even want to know what the punishment from your mom will be then," Tobey says sort of worried and sort of impressed.

"Getting caught? Ha! What about getting *lost?* Did you ever think about that?" Macaroni says, nervously pulling on the strap of his backpack repeatedly, a habit he is completely unaware of. His friends can tell he is beyond worried when the shredded strands from his bad strap are tugged at feverishly while Macaroni walks at a faster pace than usual.

"Hey, Macaroni, are you going to give that strap a rest?" Slater asks while giving a friendly bump up against him with his own backpack to remind his friend nothing bad is going to happen to him.

"I just—I just…well, I don't have a good feeling about this, Slater. How confident are you that you guys can pull this off?" Macaroni frets.

"I think it's gonna be easier than you think. There are so many kids to look out for, they're not gonna even miss me and Chicky. There are going to be kids way worse than us they gotta keep a better eye on, so you don't gotta worry so much, Macaroni," Slater says tenderly hoping this will finally put his friend at ease.

"Okay, if you say so, Slater."

"One thing's for sure though, Macaroni, you gotta not be all nervous in front of your parents when you get home from school today," Tobey says on behalf of Slater. "Just play it cool, or else your mom will break you down and get you to tell her what's got you so nervous."

"Yeah, for sure, dude, don't even give me away. I got this. I don't need your mom calling my mom," Slater says hanging his arm around Macaroni for a quick second to reassure his friend that everything's going to go according to plan. "When we make it back, I'll send you guys a message, so just wait for it."

"Cool," Tobey says with very little worry about Slater's little adventure.

"Cool," Macaroni says with a lot less enthusiasm.

Slater leaves the boys to walk onto Everly Middle Grade's campus while he walks to the lower south building that houses the Everly Middle Grade Alternative to Traditional Scheduling, forever known as the EMGATS campus. He sees Chicky waiting for him out front as usual and right away both boys begin grinning at each other as if they know a secret no one else does.

"Did you remember to bring them?" Chicky asks, making sure the train tickets are in Slater's pocket.

"Yep. Should we go to the cafeteria to fill up our water bottles before check-in? We gotta do everything we were told just so it looks like we're real innocent when we *accidentally* get left behind on the train."

"Are you feeling like you wanna chicken out?" Chicky asks, double-checking that Slater is really up for this kind of rule breaking.

"Why? Are *you* having second thoughts?"

"Me? No way, man. Just making sure you aren't gonna back out at the last minute."

"Well, I spent most of my stash on buying *two* tickets, so I hope I didn't do that for nothing," Slater says evenly as if he can't be pegged for being a chicken.

"Okay, cool. Pinehurst, here we come."

Just as Slater and Chicky expected, all the teachers who are participating in this Gods Exhibit field trip are busily distracted keeping almost a hundred students in order at the train station. There are a lot of excited kids. Some are running around, some are not standing with their buddies holding hands the way they have been taught to do since kindergarten. By now, these not-so-fresh sixth-graders have been away from kindergarten for a very long time.

Slater and Chicky find that everything is going according to their plan. In fact, things are turning out even better than expected since Mr. Pastorino has to pull a switch with the inexperienced sub. Poor Mrs. O'Reilly had no idea the job she accepted for today would be to chaperone a field trip. She only imagined the sixth-grade assignment would perhaps include showing a movie or having the children do silent reading for most of the day. She never, ever would have agreed to be responsible for managing a middle school field trip, of all things.

When Mr. Pastorino realizes the difficulty she is having just trying to take roll using Ms. Bateman's outdated roster, he decides he better step in since he knows these kids pretty well, and he also knows Ms. Bateman does not leave behind sub plans with any real rules or procedures to follow. It's not like she wanted to miss out on today, it's just that her youngest came down with the stomach flu at dawn when the entire household was awakened to violent sounds of vomiting in the hallway bathroom they all shared.

"Welcome to EMGATS, I see you've got your hands full," Mr. Pastorino greets Mrs. O'Reilly warmly.

With tears beginning to well in her eyes, she quickly shares with her new colleague all she hopes her new students will not grasp. "I don't have enough information here. There are too many kids and not enough names on this roster, unless some of these kids are supposed to be in another class," she asks hopefully.

"No, I think it's just that sometimes we get a couple new kids a day and some busy teachers don't update their sub folders right away," Mr. Pastorino says with a soft smile. "Look, why don't we switch classes? My kids are all over in that little cluster, and I've got a great student named Marilyn who can help you with anything you need to figure out. She's very responsible and very mature. Also, I like to be organized, so my *updated* roster and all the field trip permission slips are together in the clipboard pouch," he says, looking at her sympathetically while she dabs at her eyes and gratefully takes him up on his offer.

"We got the sub," Chicky says beneath his breath to Slater as both eye the transfer of power.

"Oh, this is going to be so much easier than I imagined," Slater says overly confident.

"Everybody, let's get with our buddies so we can board the train. Sit where you like, but stay in the same train car as your teacher so you can await the signal for getting off at Clifton," Mr. Pastorino blares through his cupped hands around his mouth.

"After you, Chicky," Slater muses politely, allowing his friend—and partner in crime—to step aboard first.

"Yes, sir, you are so kind." Chicky pretends to be an English gentleman with a very poor British accent.

The two carry on like this for the next fifteen minutes while the train conductor collects the Clifton group tickets from each of the teachers. Anxiously determined to be the first ones off the train, a pile of kids bundle themselves around the metal doors where they are not supposed to wait as the whistle blows and the train comes to a stop.

During all this commotion, Slater and Chicky slip unnoticed toward the caboose where they stow away in the bathroom—a tight squeeze for even *one* adult. While Slater stands on the toilet and Chicky holds onto the tiny wash basin to balance himself, they wait the interminable passing of four long minutes until they are sure no one has noticed them missing. *Choo-choo, chugga, chugga, chugga. Choo-choo.* The train moves again. Next stop: Pinehurst.

CHAPTER 3

Pinehurst

"Dude, how long are we supposed to stay in here?" Slater asks, hoping his friend will know.

Since Chicky is so much taller than everyone else in sixth grade, Slater mistakenly thinks Chicky must know what to do. Sometimes the other kids think of Chicky as an adult with all this worldly experience. But, the truth is, even though he has seen a few things he shouldn't have and has been to a few places no one knows about, he is still only eleven years old. How is he supposed to have all the answers when he's really just a kid like them?

"I've only been on the train a few times with my grandma and I remember the conductor knocking on doors to be sure no one missed their exit or forgot to pay," Chicky says officially.

"So, is it safe to leave yet?" Slater whispers. "Could they turn us around here and send us back to Clifton?"

"No way, man, we're going too fast for that. Listen to the whir of the metal wheels hitting the ties in the track. They're not slowing down, not even for us. Besides, the map showed nothing but a whole lot of land between Clifton and Pinehurst. So we can relax, dude," Chicky says expertly. "There are no other stops before we get off."

"Okay, if you say so, that's good enough for me," Slater says, bracing himself while Chicky slides open the door lock, slowly poking his head out.

"Coast is clear," Chicky says, pulling the door fully inward this time so they can move into the corridor. They look for two seats together on the upper deck, hoping to be as far away from the conductor as possible.

"Hey, Chicky," Slater says, while they both begin unwrapping their breakfast burritos provided by EMGATS, "did you mean it when you told Marilyn you wanted to be a police officer when you grow up?" He tears off an enormous bite from his burrito that hardly allows for him to close his mouth fully to chew.

"Dude, you're gross," Chicky says, wincing and looking away.

"What?" Slater says opening his mouth even wider to reveal all the mashed egg bits mixed with soft potatoes and white tortilla chunks dangling from his lower lip.

"Sick, man," Chicky says trying hard not to smile.

This only encourages Slater's ill behavior even more as Slater begins to breathe heavily in and out through his mouth, pushing the flap of tortilla strand forward and then sucking it back in again like a New Year's Eve noisemaker.

Once Slater finishes chewing all his food, he swallows hard and resumes his questioning. "Seriously, is that what you want to be?"

"Dude, how am I supposed to know anything about what I want to be when I grow up? I'm only eleven, same as you," Chicky says still a bit stung that Slater dismissed his idea when he brashly shared it out loud. "Why, what do *you* want to be when you grow up? If you don't choke right here on that burrito first," Chicky says with another wide-eyed expression for how much Slater can stuff into his mouth at once.

It's almost like watching a cow chew his cud—he chomps freely, oblivious to the unsightly spectacle he is to onlookers who cannot turn away. When Slater is finally able to breathe and talk without a mouthful, he takes only a moment to think through his final answer. "I want to be famous."

"Makes sense," he says, even though Chicky was expecting Slater to say what kind of a job he thought he would be doing. "So, how do you get to be famous?"

"Every fool knows you only need one thing," Slater says, holding Chicky's interest captive, "and it's not talent," Slater snorts.

"It's not talent? Well, then it must be mentors, like Marilyn said, people you already know can help you," Chicky says, racking his brain.

Slater scoffs at his reasoning. "No way, that could take so many years, and then you gotta give all your money away to all those people who helped make you who you are. No way, that's for chumps."

"Then what's the thing you need to be famous?"

"Outrageous!" Slater says with a confident beaming smile and a devilish twinkle in his eyes. "Seriously, think of every kid our age and how they are making all this money from their videos. I'm gonna do that. Just as soon as I get something outrageous to put out there. That's how I'm gonna make my money. Just watch, Chicky. I'm gonna be famous and you're gonna remember we had this conversation right on this here train. All when we were only eleven years old."

"How long have you been thinking about this? Seems like you have it all figured out," Chicky says in awe.

"I'll put it this way, it's the only thought I've ever had."

Suddenly interrupting the boys from their deep conversation, a bellow can be heard from the next car as it quickly approaches. "Coming through. Have your tickets ready," a deep voice calls loudly through the metal door slats closing with some effort behind him. Gusts of wind can be heard, along with the roar of the ferociously spinning wheels. Iron clanks upon iron as the interlocks beneath the cars that bind them together move rapidly with the rhythm of the train. "Pinehurst, forty-five minutes ahead. Have your tickets out, folks."

"Got the tickets still?" Chicky asks, hoping this is not where their entire plan falls apart by losing their escape route.

"Right here," Slater says as he pats at his jeans pocket and pulls one out to hand to Chicky. "Conductor's coming by; he looks mad," Slater says nervously.

"They always look like that. Just relax and act like you belong here," Chicky says smoothly.

Slater slouches back in his leather coach chair and pulls his hoody over his eyes. He tugs at the strings around his neck, tightening them just a little more than usual. He lets his arm dangle on the rail while clutching the ticket to Pinehurst within his fingertips. He watches the men in the chairs three rows ahead do the same and they look like they have done this before, so it must be right.

"Tickets, have your tickets ready," the conductor blares loudly. Any of the passengers who might have dozed off are startled by his collection attempts. He nudges one gentleman who is snoring loudly. "Sir, I need your ticket to Pinehurst," he says, while poking the man once in the shoulder.

"What? What? Where are we now?" The older man seems disoriented for a moment longer than it should take for him to realize he is halfway through a long nap on his way to visit his grandchildren in Pinehurst.

"Ticket to Pinehurst, sir? Sorry to disturb your rest. We're about halfway there and you can go right back to dozing as soon as I clip your ticket," the conductor says with more compassion this time.

"I've got it right here somewhere. Oh, yes, I put it inside my wallet so I wouldn't lose it," he says, reaching inside his coat pocket. He swiftly pulls the ticket to be punched by the conductor's special tool and then returns to his nap.

Slater and Chicky keep one eye on the old man and one eye closed. They know the conductor is just inches from asking for their own tickets to ride.

"Boys? You headed to Pinehurst?" the conductor asks, giving them the full weight of his stare.

He is a piggish looking man with a chubby face, pink in color. His eyes squint in the same manner a detective's would while interrogating a criminal, bending over him with a floodlight flashed in his eyes. His large stature complemented by his dark navy conductor jacket and suit pants make him appear very official, very powerful, and very scary.

"Yes, sir, here are our tickets," Chicky says, handing his downward while Slater's arm dangles just above the conductor's hat with his ticket still in hand, waiting to be punched.

"Why aren't you boys in school today?" the conductor asks while they both look at each other.

"We're going to see my grandma; she's pretty old and needs our help," Chicky blurts out. For some reason it sounded way more convincing in his head than it comes out sounding now.

"Well, that's pretty thoughtful of you," the conductor says through those beady little eyes of his. "That explains one of ya. What about the other?"

"Who? Me? Yeah, well, I am coming along to offer moral support," Slater says real fast like it's a pretty big responsibility.

"And where are your parents in all of this?"

"Oh, well, they're already there, at grandma's house, and they're just waiting for us," Chicky offers, sounding more believable this time.

"I see," the conductor says as he stares at them just long enough for the boys to get the impression he is memorizing their faces.

Both boys begin to perspire while they work very hard at trying to look cool and relaxed.

"Have a safe trip, then," the conductor says as he continues on through the next car where they can hear him faintly calling, "Tickets, have your tickets ready," as the screeching of the metal tracks can be heard before the vestibule doors slam shut.

"Man, that was close," Slater says with a big sigh of relief.

"Yeah, that dude scared me for a minute. He's, like, 'What about you?'" Chicky says, pushing his face real close into Slater's and imitating the beady-eyed stare down.

"I know, dude, I did not expect him to be asking me questions. Was I convincing? He never talked to any of the other passengers about their business in Pinehurst. What's up with that?"

"Nosy old guy, I guess," Chicky says as he leans back into his chair after taking a few swigs from his water bottle. "Let's take a nap for a little while. Suddenly, I'm really beat."

"I was thinking the same thing."

While the boys enjoy the rolling motion of the train charging down the tracks at over 80 mph, they are quickly lulled to sleep as if they have not a care in the world. Soon enough, they are going to be reunited with their life-long friend—well, Phil is really only *Slater's* life-long friend—and enjoying their cold ham and tomato sandwiches with extra Swiss cheese at John F. Kennedy Middle School in Pinehurst.

They haven't given a second thought as to what they might be missing out on at the Exhibit of the Gods field trip, nor have they considered the possibility that *someone* just may have noticed by now that two hooligans have gone missing. They certainly never suspected that certain someone might be Marilyn Washington, who is right this minute contemplating what Chicky and Slater might be willing to pay in exchange for her silence.

After all, it was just after the crowd of students charged off the train onto the downtown Clifton platform that Marilyn turned back to see who was still inside the passenger car she had walked away from only a few seconds earlier. When she saw Chicky rushing with Slater the *opposite* way from the exit doors, she knew right then and there that Chicky wasn't about to be getting off at this stop.

Somehow, he must have felt her gaze because in that same moment, Chicky made the fateful mistake of looking through the window where he saw Marilyn's mouth gaping wide open. The only thing he could think to do was to hold his finger up to his lips as if to say, *"Shhh, please don't tell,"* as he also pleaded by putting his palms face together as if to pray for her silence and not rat out her friends.

For their entire train ride, Chicky never says a word about it to Slater. Why worry the kid when he is already nervous enough?

Once the conductor is safely out of earshot, he radios the dispatcher at the train yards. "We have two unaccompanied minors Pinehurst-bound, estimated time of arrival is twenty-two minutes. Check EMGATS for missing students. Over," the conductor relays his succinct message to the dispatcher. They have seen this from time to time. What kid doesn't fantasize about running away on the train? Unfortunately, these two somehow got this far without anyone realizing they were all on their own.

"Confirm *em-gats?*" the dispatcher says through a crackly connection.

"That's affirmative, dispatch. Two minors wearing school sweatshirts with bold letters reading *Echo-Mike-Golf-Alpha-Tango-Sierra*. Over." After spelling the Alpha-Bravo-Charlie alphabet used in every military unit and police emergency call central, the dispatcher now has the phone number coming up on his screen monitor for Everly Middle Grade Alternative to Traditional Scheduling.

"Good morning, EMGATS. Patricia Davison speaking," the secretary says in a sing-song voice after picking up the telephone on only the second ring, thanks to a very slow day at Everly Middle Grade Alternative to Traditional Scheduling.

After a bit of static on the line, she hears a far-off voice crackling through her receiver. "This is Dispatch at the Remington Train Yard and we've been notified there are two unaccompanied minors on board our Pinehurst line; estimated time of arrival at platform is 11:08 a.m. Are you, by chance, missing two male students?"

"Oh, good grief, let me get you Assistant Principal Amanda Hiller right away, please hold." She lets her fingers dance across her telephone dashboard as she quietly pauses her caller and connects to Ms. Hiller. "Amanda, we've got a potential missing students situation, a gentleman calling from the train yard for you," she says with urgency.

"You're kidding me? Release the call," she says firmly to Mrs. Davison and in the same breath greets her caller in her all-business tone, "Amanda Hiller, assistant principal at EMGATS. I understand you have our children on board?"

"Ms. Hiller, I'm Skip Ridge, dispatcher at the Remington Yards. We've got a report coming in about two unaccompanied minors headed to Pinehurst, due at the platform at 11:08, about ten minutes from now, and they seem to be wearing your school's monogrammed sweatshirts." He pauses to let her absorb this information before he gets to the real question, "Ma'am, are you missing two students today?"

She presses her fingers to her temples to rid herself of the headache she can feel coming on while cradling the phone receiver in her neck. "I sure hope not, Mr. Ridge."

He only half-chuckles. It would be wrong to laugh any harder in a situation as potentially dangerous as this.

"Do you have any descriptions? I've got a hundred kids out on a field trip today who were taking the Pinehurst line only as far as downtown Clifton." She begins unwittingly tugging fistfuls of hair at the nape of her neck. She pulls hard to relieve some of the tension building in her shoulders. Right now she is the only one with the responsibility of making sure all her students return safely.

"Let me put you on hold while I ask the conductor," Skip Ridge says quickly.

As the head secretaries, Patricia Davison and Carmelita Jones, stand by in her office, she gives them marching orders. "Who is missing? Take roll! At the museum! Now!"

She hasn't even figured it out yet, two students missing, and she doesn't have a clue. She can't even be bothered to double-check that I took roll accurately. Mr. Pastorino would not be happy about this at all. Marilyn Washington is thinking through how this mess is going to turn out for Chicky and Slater. Her teacher Mr. Pastorino got stuck babysitting a different class and she got stuck with the oldest sub in the universe who happily put Marilyn in charge after Mr. Pastorino's glowing recommendation. So, here she is with the teacher's clipboard and the sacred knowledge that Chicky and Slater never stepped off that train.

Stupid boys. How dumb can you be? And then you have the nerve, Chicky, to think I should be the one to keep your little secret? I don't owe you anything. Marilyn can feel herself getting all worked up in her head. She keeps staring at this clipboard. The only question she needs to answer is *Do I report you before—or after—they discover you missing?* She gives herself time to think it over and after ten more seconds, she realizes the only person she needs to worry about is herself. If she loses Mr. Pastorino's trust, she might be losing a future letter of recommendation when she resumes Junior Achievement next year, if all goes according to her plan.

"Mr. Pastorino, can I talk to you for a minute?" Marilyn asks politely over the ringtones now erupting from the phone in his pocket.

"Marilyn, just give me a second and I'll be right with you," he says, looking at the school's phone number appearing on his screen.

"Final stop for Pinehurst, train ends here. Please gather your personal belongings and be considerate about taking away any of the trash or newspapers you brought aboard. We thank you in advance for helping to keep Country Pride Railways ready for its next passengers. Have a safe and pleasant stay in Pinehurst," the conductor finishes cheerfully.

Chicky and Slater are way ahead of him, though. They have already managed to collect any evidence that they were ever on board and skedaddle down to the caboose bathroom where they hid out nearly two hours earlier so they could avoid detection at the Clifton platform. Just as soon as the train comes to a screeching halt, they will bolt.

"Gino, we need an emergency head count from every teacher within the next three minutes," Mrs. Davison commands Mr. Pastorino. "There's a report saying two students never got off the train bound for Pinehurst." She speaks quickly to convey the seriousness of the matter while Assistant Principal Amanda Hiller finishes her call with the dispatcher, Skip Ridge.

His worst fear has finally come true. Losing students on a school field trip is the only thing that gives him nightmares. "Oh, Patricia," he says with a heavy voice, knowing how much trouble this is going to cause for the school, "let me call you right back with the numbers. Do we have any other information? Why do they suspect it's our kids?"

"They are wearing EMGATS sweatshirts," she offers matter-of-factly, "Amanda's on the line trying to get their descriptions now." She wants to sympathize, but right now she is anticipating all the phone calls she will be fielding from the angry parents who won't already be lined up in front of her desk demanding to talk to the assistant principals just as soon as word of this gets out.

While Gino Pastorino puts his phone back into his pocket reaching instead for his whistle, he hears that steady voice calling his name once again. "Mr. Pastorino, I already know what you need. It's Chicky and Slater; they never got off the train," Marilyn Washington dutifully reports.

Does it count as doing the right thing if she is only *one* minute too late? It sure could have saved Mr. Pastorino a whole lot of embarrassment if he had been the one to *initiate* the report instead of looking like an irresponsible teacher who can't keep track of his own field trip.

"Why do I have a feeling you've known about this for a while?"

"Ma'am, the only description we were able to get from the conductor is one male, tall, with red, curly hair, and second male Caucasian, other details unknown because his hoody was pulled down low around his face," Skip Ridge relays.

"Mr. Ridge, thank you so much for calling. We'll handle it from here," Amanda Hiller says gratefully.

"Yep, you're welcome. These boys made it a little farther than our policy would normally allow. It's against train rules for kids this age to travel this kind of distance without a guardian. Good luck, and if there's anything you need, give me a call back."

Skip Ridge is grateful he is not dealing with a worse problem right now. It could be the police contacting him to ask why Country Pride Railways sold tickets to minors in the first place.

As the train pushes into the Pinehurst platform and the pressure from the air brakes is released in a loud hiss, the doors open, allowing the waiting passengers hovering in the vestibule to shuffle down the stairs patiently.

Only two eager passengers push their way through the crowd, skipping freely once they are through the platform, then jogging toward John F. Kennedy Middle School just blocks from the train station.

"Hey, man, see? No problem, just like I said." Chicky grins at Slater.

"Yeah, that was really pretty easy. We should do this again

sometime for spring break or something. I'm not going anywhere this year on account of my restriction for, you know, plagiarizing." Slater says it real low like he still feels shame in talking about it. But, he is not telling Chicky about his punishment to do chores at Sibley's house. No way. Some things are too unbearable to speak out loud.

"Hey, there's the school. Wow, I thought for sure it would be much bigger. It looks just like our old elementary," Slater says wondering how difficult it will be to blend in on such a small campus."

While Marilyn holds her composure in front of Mr. Pastorino, he holds the phone to his ear, impatiently willing for someone to pick up the line. He listens to the first ring of the office phone, before speaking rapidly over Patricia Davison's greeting. "Good morning EMGATS, Pat—"

"Patricia," he interrupts, "I just learned that the two missing kids on that train are Chicky Cicarrelli and Slater Hannigan. Can you put me on with Amanda?" Mr. Pastorino has a silent conversation with Marilyn as they exchange heated stares while she observes how he handles this emergency.

"Gino, are you sure it's Chicky and Slater?" Amanda Hiller asks eagerly.

"Yes, we had a mix-up with a sub this morning and I had to

switch classes, so I am only just finding out about this, but I am positive it's them. What do you need me to do for you right now?" He is dreading that he already knows the answer to this question.

"Don't lose anybody else."

Amanda Hiller will need to schedule two meetings for each family to meet separately with Mr. Pastorino—as soon as the parents first confirm how they would like to collect their children. Two hours away is still quite a distance for any law enforcement agency to travel outside of the Everly or Clifton jurisdictions. It certainly is not going to be feasible for the administrators of EMGATS to abandon their school responsibilities—not now when a hundred other children are expected to return from a field trip in a few hours. And quite frankly, Amanda Hiller needs to bring her Co-Assistant Principal Maureen Templeton up to speed as this will likely become *both* their problems to share as they prepare to inform the superintendent together.

"Amanda, I just got Brady Johnson to cover my class, and I've worked out which teachers will cover your afternoon classes, so I'm here. Let's get this mess figured out," Maureen Templeton says, charging into the office they share.

"We need to call the parents. Who do you want to take, Chicky or Slater?"

"I vote not the D.A." Maureen says smiling widely. "Besides, you were here first."

"I knew it," she offers a tired smile in return. "Okay then, let's agree to keep the script simple: there was a mix up at the field trip, the boys took the train to the end of the line at Pinehurst. Just the facts, get the parents to come in for a face to face before we release any more info about the train conductor having to call our attention to our own missing children, because I'm sure Delcia is going to want to be involved," Amanda Hiller says while looking miserable at the idea of what might happen to each of them after a debacle like this. Delcia DeMarco-Bradley, the superintendent of Everly School District, takes child safety and parent concerns very seriously—obviously, she should. But so do the teacher involved and, clearly, both of the assistant principals.

"Hey, which bathroom wing did he say for us to wait in?" Chicky asks Slater.

"Wing seven. I count ten buildings only, so it should be easy enough to find. Let's hide in those bushes until all the kids get out of class," Slater says hoping Chicky agrees.

After what seems like an hour, the bell rings for lunch only a few short minutes later with doors bursting open and dozens upon dozens of kids racing to find their place in the cafeteria line. "Let's go, this is us," Chicky says, jumping the hip-high gate blocking the driveway from cars entering campus.

They easily blend in by sprinting to keep pace with the other kids.

"Here's building five, we're close, let's go left," Chicky offers.

They walk right into the boys' bathroom in wing seven and greet their old pal Phil who is already waiting with a huge grin on his face, "What took you so long?"

They actually hug it out and high-five each other and then move on to hide behind building nine where Phil knows they can be alone to eat the lunches they all carried in their backpacks.

"So how is it really, being here with your mom's new husband?" Slater asks, wondering if Phil will even answer this in front of Chicky.

"Well, the dude buys me lots of stuff. I guess he's trying to make it less miserable. My mom is all about rules as usual. But when I see my dad on weekends, he totally takes me places like pizza and camping and stuff. It's not as bad as I thought it would be, I guess."

"Yeah, well, not much new with me, still in trouble with my mom. Probably be that way until I die, or move out of the house, whichever comes first," Slater laughs, but the other boys know he means it.

While the phone rings at the Hannigan household, Amanda Hiller is just about ready to hang up to try a different phone number listed on the emergency card when she hears a breathless voice. "Hello? You still there?"

She takes a single deep breath. "Mrs. Hannigan, this is Amanda Hiller, the assistant principal at EMGATS," she says without a hint of nerves in her voice. She braces herself for the rest of this call.

CHAPTER 4

Busted

"Is there a problem, Ms. Hiller?" Already, Lynn Hannigan has snapped her focus into full mama bear mode. She is feeling annoyed that these schools have very little to offer in the way of monitoring students and protecting her son from getting caught up in classroom antics. *What could be the trouble now?* She doesn't really want to find out.

"Mrs. Hannigan, there has been a mix-up with our field trip to the museum." She does not pause long enough to allow Slater's mother to interrupt. "Slater never made it off the train, which pulled into its final destination at the Pinehurst station twenty minutes ago. We can assure you he is safe, but the two-hour distance from Everly means the police in Pinehurst will need to hold him until a parent can pick him up." There, she said the hardest part. She spat it right out and now it's over. Well, nearly over.

"Whaaaaat?" For the next minute, Lynn fumes and accuses, and screams and berates, until she finally ends with the worst words of all. "You do know that my husband is the district attorney?" With that, she slams down the phone before the connection is cut.

Amanda Hiller covers her face with both of her hands and pushes her fingers hard through her scalp over and over again. When her co-assistant principal, Maureen Templeton, pops in from where she had been making her call to Chicky's grandmother in the conference room, she sympathizes. "Oh, Mandy, let me guess: that did not go well."

"It's even worse than you think. I have to call her back because I didn't get a chance to tell her that the police have not *found* Slater yet because they haven't even been informed he is *missing*."

"Okay, first thing we've gotta do is get you a comb. You look like a crazy woman with what you've done to your hair here." Maureen Templeton opens the closet that houses all the confidential student records to angle the door with its full-length mirror so Amanda Hiller can see for herself the wild, deranged look most people could expertly create using a garden rake.

"Oh gosh, nervous habit," she says, trying desperately to smooth it down with one of the new lice combs she unwraps from its plastic seal. There's no luck dragging those fine teeth through her snarls. "Forget it, I'll just deal with this later. I've got to call her back. Right now. She's probably already on the phone with her husband, the D.A.—or worse, she's probably on the phone with Delcia right now."

The panic is beginning to set in. She dials the Hannigans' number again while her fingers tremble. She has never lost a child, not even on the field trips she organized when she was a full-time teacher. But a problem like this has never happened before at EMGATS. Now she has to be the one to take the lead in fixing it all. At age thirty-three, she still hasn't had the kind of life experience to train her for what is likely going to be a parent lawsuit against her for her personal negligence. *Somebody put me out of my misery,* is all she can think while she listens to the phone ring.

"Yes, this is Lynn Hannigan," she is greeted by a completely different sounding voice than the first time Mrs. Hannigan picked up her phone. Gruff and curt now, Amanda Hiller should not have expected anything different.

"Mrs. Hannigan, Amanda Hiller again. Update for you, we have not alerted the police that Slater is missing because we wanted to first ask you if he has any connection to Pinehurst. Someplace, or someone, where we might have the officers check first?" *This was good, sounding like I'm in charge. Hold it together, Amanda.*

"Let me get this straight, you really have *no idea* where my son is right now? He could be wandering around Pinehurst for kidnappers to snatch him up off the streets? Do you know what happens to little boys when they are left all alone in the middle of some godforsaken place, lost, with no money, no idea how to get home? I am just adding these complaints to the list that will be presented in the lawsuit, Ms. Hiller." Lynn Hannigan is seething.

"I know, Mrs. Hannigan, but please, I need you to work with me here before I call the police. They are going to want to know where to start looking first. Is there anything that holds significant meaning for Slater in Pinehurst?"

A pause on the other end of the line is long enough to worry Amanda Hiller that the connection has been broken, regrettably requiring her to call back for a third time. "Hello? Mrs. Hannigan, are you still there?"

"Pinehurst? You said Pinehurst, right? I think I do know where Slater probably went. One of his best friends just moved there a few months ago; he left over winter break. Find the middle school where Phillip Moore is enrolled. I am sure that's what's happened here. Slater has gone to visit Phillip," Lynn Hannigan says, without shouting this time now that she is stringing together bits of the whole picture.

"This is a very big help. And if it's any assurance to you, Slater is not alone, Mrs. Hannigan. He was on that train with another student. I probably should not be releasing the other child's name at this point, but he does have company," Amanda Hiller says evenly.

"Let me guess," Lynn Hannigan snarls into the receiver, "is it Chicky Cicarrelli?"

"Hank, Slater is with Chicky. They went to go meet Phillip Moore. That's the likely explanation," Lynn says, filling her husband in on the newest update in her fourth phone call to him within the past ten minutes.

"I told them that if I ever caught wind they were cutting school, I would go see the juvenile court judge myself. Lynn, this is out of control, even for him. We need to start taking some drastic measures, and I'm not just talking about taking away his birthday party extravaganza, or whatever you usually call those over-the-top circus events you pride yourself in putting together every six months."

"Hank, look, taking your frustrations out on me is not going to help us right now. I think it's time we look into those options we discussed if Slater ever got to a certain point. I think we're there now with this little stunt. He just doesn't get it. He has no idea how dangerous the world can be," Lynn says before she hears a beep on her line signaling there is another call waiting. "Hank, let me see who's calling, hold a quick sec," she says without waiting for his response. "Lynn Hannigan here."

"Hi, Mrs. Hannigan, this is Delcia DeMarco-Bradley, superintendent of Everly School District. Your information was very good. There is only one middle school in Pinehurst, John F. Kennedy, so it was easy to confirm that Phillip Moore is currently enrolled there as of January sixth this year. We have involved the authorities and the local school administrators, and they are conducting a campus sweep right now. Lunch is expected to end in a half hour;

if they are not found in the next five minutes, their principal will trigger the alarm for an emergency drill requiring all homeroom classes to meet for attendance. It won't be hard to flush out two visitors once they pull Phillip Moore into the office to ask him a few questions." She is concise and unemotional. "It might not even come to that, but this is the plan if we don't get any word in the next four minutes from now."

"I will be waiting for your next call. Thank you for keeping me updated. When this is over, I would like to schedule a meeting—"

"Are you available to come into my office Monday at 4 p.m.? Mr. Pastorino and both assistant principals, Ms. Hiller and Ms. Templeton, will be there as well. We want to understand how this happened." She stops herself here to keep her suspicions to herself that these boys did some advance planning of their own to be sure it was no accident they were left on that train. "We also want a portion of this meeting to include Slater, so please make sure he knows to wait at the district office after school." Without leaving room for Mrs. Hannigan to interrupt with loud screaming outbursts the way she had earlier when speaking with Amanda Hiller, Delcia DeMarco-Bradley excuses herself to take another phone call.

With half of lunch recess still remaining, the boys talk about their old memories together at Slater's Halloween Haunt and laugh about the fun they had up until the night when Phil told them he was moving away.

"Hey, glad you guys came," Phil says while he leans against his backpack to catch some afternoon sun.

"Yeah, it wasn't really as hard as I thought it might be. Right, Chicky?"

"Well, there is only one tiny problem, but I didn't want to worry you about it because you were already so nervous—you should have seen him Phil, totally sweating it when the conductor asked him why he was going to Pinehurst," Chicky laughs while tipping his head backwards.

"Hey, what *little* problem?" Slater says not laughing one bit.

"Dude, be cool, it's all right. It's just that on our way back to the caboose, Marilyn was standing on the platform and I saw her through the window—and she saw me—and I sort of gave a her a sign like *please don't tell*. She's pretty cool, though; we don't gotta worry about her," Chicky says as he folds his hands behind his head and lies back upon his nearly empty backpack like a wilted pillow.

"Well, dude," Slater says, while watching a group of adults convene a distance away on the west lawn. They are speaking into walkie-talkies, signaling with hand-motions for the others to follow them in a slow-motion jog toward building nine. "I don't think you know Marilyn half as well as you think you do."

With the sun's rays resting on his belly, Chicky offers a sleepy response, "You worry too much." His final words are met with a long shadow cast over him as he opens his eyes to find a fully uniformed officer blocking the brightness of his sunshine.

"Hank? How are you, buddy? Haven't heard from you in a few months—ever since the move. What's new?" Paul Moore enthusiastically greets his old friend's phone call from out of the blue. He has been so wrapped up in his new job and spending time with Phil that he hasn't reached out to many of the people he left behind.

"Buddy, love to catch up, but wish I had better news than what I'm about to lay on you now," Hank Hannigan starts in directly. It's the only way he knows how to deliver earth-shattering reports. Like ripping off a Band-Aid quickly—it only stings for the first minute.

"Oh no, something with Slater? You and Lynn? What's up, Hank?" Paul Moore has no idea how to brace himself.

"Would you believe Slater and Chicky had the guts to ditch a school field trip today that was supposed to be in downtown Clifton? Instead of getting off the train, they rode it to the end of the line. Give you one guess where that took them," Hank says more than exasperated.

"Are you saying they're in Pinehurst now? Geesh, what is it with these kids?" Paul Moore knew one more benefit of making the move from Everly would be keeping his kid away from Slater's increasingly bad influence. That hill fire at the neighborhood

Fourth of July celebration left Paul Moore with the sneaky suspicion that Slater—not Phil—was the one who called the shots during that little catastrophe.

"Here's what we know. The principal at J.F.K. Middle School is conducting a campus sweep right now, but it's lunchtime. So, if they can't find all three boys in the next few minutes, they'll do an emergency drill for homeroom attendance. The Pinehurst cops are on campus to help with the sweep. They are bound to find the boys together—all three of them—because there is no other reason for Slater to want to be in Pinehurst except to see Phil." Hank reels off the details quickly, bringing Paul Moore up to speed.

"This is just great," Paul says sarcastically. "I'll head over to the school right now. Are you thinking you want me to pick up Slater and Chicky and hold them at my house until you get here—or, do you want the police to hold them downtown to teach them a lesson?"

"Yeah, this one's a real bonehead move. Lynn's already pulling out brochures for discipline camps she researched last summer. Ideally, I'd love to grant my permission to release Slater to you so we can pick him up this afternoon. But, Chicky's grandparents also have to make the same call to the school and I haven't even spoken to them yet to know how far along they are on this. Will you do me a favor and let me know what's going on when you get to the school?" Hank Hannigan understands he is asking a lot of his old buddy. Having a son like Slater poses its challenges, including the threat to long-standing friendships—adults and children alike.

"Hank, I'll do it. I don't love the idea of it, but I understand, you probably want to keep this as quiet as you can. I don't know how fast news travels from Pinehurst all the way back to the law offices of the Everly District Attorney."

Hank sighs heavily into the phone knowing that was meant as a jab. "Sorry to put you in this position. I wish things were different. Thanks, man," he says, sounding like he has the weight of the world on his shoulders.

"Mrs. Hannigan, we have found all three boys together on the JFK campus. The principal there just informed me they were hiding behind a building when they were discovered during the campus sweep. What are your plans for collecting Slater?" The superintendent speaks authoritatively, a mode she has been in all day between calls with the school district's own team of attorneys to prepare for a possible lawsuit.

"My husband just phoned me with the plan. We know Phillip Moore's father very well, so he has agreed to keep Slater at his house until we get there, and my husband has already asked the school to release Slater into Paul Moore's custody. We are happy to drive Chicky home too, but I'm not sure if I should make this phone call to his grandparents, or if you would prefer to do this yourself?" Lynn Hannigan seems much calmer right now. Maybe this is a good sign.

"Is it fine with you if I ask the other student's guardians to make arrangements with you? Once I get their permission to share their son's name, I will call you back and then you may coordinate the pick-up with them," Mrs. DeMarco-Bradley states cordially.

After everyone is in agreement, and especially after Chicky's grandmother expresses her gratitude to Mrs. Hannigan for offering to bring home Chicky, Lynn Hannigan picks up her husband from his office as they head out of town together. "Where's Graham going after school?" Hank Hannigan asks after slamming the car door and buckling his seatbelt.

"I called Janice Hamigachi, and she'll keep him overnight so he and Jason can have some fun. I called the school to give my permission, so we're good," Lynn says to her husband.

"This is going to be a really long drive, Lynn. I don't want to lecture the boys on the way home, especially not with Chicky in the car. I think we need to cut them off from seeing each other. When EMGATS took Slater, did they say for sure he could transfer back to Everly?"

"They certainly did give me every impression that EMGATS is only temporary until Slater can pass his classes and, truthfully, he is smart enough, he just didn't want to do the work at Everly. He's lazy," Lynn says completely unsure how Slater turned out so differently from what she expected when he was just a baby.

"Look, what do you think? You want him to stay at EMGATS where he goes to school until 6 p.m. most days, or do you want him away from Chicky? You know that hill fire started well before

Chicky ever came into the picture," Hank Hannigan says carefully, hoping his wife can see what he is getting at.

"Hank, I know, I know. But Slater is not in charge of the world. His friends were just as much to blame. The only other option is to finish out the year home-schooling him. I don't think I want to take that on, but I suppose we could hire some tutors and the school would have to offer a teacher to make sure he gets the curriculum. What do you think?" Lynn is contemplating all sorts of scenarios she has never considered before.

"I think we need to hear what the school has to say first. Maybe they have another solution we haven't thought of. Can they separate Slater from Chicky's classes? They've only got another two months left; how hard could that be?"

"I've been on the phone with the superintendent already a few times today and we're meeting Monday after school. Can you leave the office? I think it's really important you be at this one; the weight of the D.A. and all that will probably mean they'll have their legal team there as well. I was pretty angry with Amanda Hiller and maybe got a little carried away with my threats," Lynn says knowing how she can be sometimes.

The boys never even had a chance to try and run before the officer snuck up behind them. "I'm Officer Mendoza. Which one of you is Chicky Cicarrelli and which one of you is Slater Hannigan?" He reaches out his hand to offer them help up from where they had been sitting. "Let's go."

CHAPTER 5

Trespassing

The silence is deafening. Slater and Chicky do not utter a word as the Pinehurst police escort them to the school's front office. Officer Brooks—who was searching for missing kids inside the bathrooms—has caught up to his partner, Officer Mendoza, and stays in rhythm with Chicky, just in case anyone has the bright idea to bolt.

The walk through campus during the last few minutes of lunch recess would normally be filled with sounds of chaotic play from kids chasing each other over a ball, or music blaring while a gaggle of seventh-grade girls sings along to the newest pop song. But, there is no noise coming from the onlookers now who watch Phil Moore flanked by the principal, Verna Deerborne, and the assistant principal, Jerry Bryant, along with two police officers accompanying two young strangers. They walk urgently in the kind of quiet that can only spell one thing: doom.

Phil Moore is mortified to be at the center of this attention from the friends he has just made and other schoolmates who haven't even learned his name yet. They all gawk, wondering what could have happened to bring the Pinehurst police to campus. He knows the rumors will start swirling. Sadly, there will be no more transfers to other schools for him because this town is in the middle of nowhere. Unless his mom and her husband—and his dad who would surely follow—agree to relocate one more time so Phil can start another new life free of embarrassment, then he is going to be stuck at John F. Kennedy Middle School for the rest of the year, and for all of seventh grade and eighth grade following. How will he ever survive?

Chicky Cicarrelli cannot believe his bad luck. *Did Marilyn do this?* He wonders what his grandma and his gramps are thinking. He is not supposed to be causing them any trouble while they take care of him. He never would. He loves them. But who ratted on him? That's what he wants to find out.

Slater Hannigan can only hear his father's words play over and over in his head. *Don't let me find out that you two are cutting school, or I'll be visiting the juvenile court judge myself.* He wouldn't really turn in his own kid. Slater will just apologize and sound like he means it this time. He will add an extra "really" when he says how sorry he is. What can his parents do? *It's not like they're going to kick me out of the house.*

When they reach the backside of J.F.K.'s administrative building, Officer Mendoza holds the door open as everyone shuffles through the hallway leading to the principal's conference room. At least Phil is spared this one additional humiliation of not being paraded through the front of the office. It never fails that some parent is waiting in the lobby to pick up their student early for an appointment, or some sick kid is sitting in the nurse's office on the leather cot, or a few of the student council kids are supposedly doing office work, but really they are paying closer attention to the office gossip told in their presence. He doesn't feel like running into anyone today.

But, if he had been brought through the lobby—seven minutes from now—he would have seen his father rushing through the front office doors to greet him with open arms, quickly taking him out of there to bring him home.

Once everyone is seated around the longest conference table at the school, Phil, Chicky, and Slater take a big gulp. It doesn't look much like the schools they've ever seen, or even inside any of the principal offices they've ever been. Despite the familiar flag stands and school award plaques at the front of the room with quotes boldly carved out of metal that say, "Teachable Moments Happen Here" and "Progress, Not Perfection," something about the presence of police officers is making them feel awfully uncomfortable.

Verna Deerborne takes a long look around the room and then begins, "I don't believe we've been properly introduced. I'm the principal, Mrs. Deerborne, and this is our assistant principal, Mr.

Bryant. You have already met our Pinehurst police, Officers Brooks and Mendoza. We have reached your parents, who are on their way here. Before they arrive, tell me what is the reason for your visit to J.F.K. today?"

She is calm, seeming the type to not be flustered by anything. Not a room full of wild kindergartners during craft time, or even her own collection of young grandchildren groping at her for a lick of the batter spoon before she puts cakes in the oven, can jar her nerves. She has seen it all. So, she is not surprised when she hears the cockamamie story about being *accidentally* left behind on the train.

"Well, my friend Chicky and I were on a field trip when the train pulled out of the station before we had a chance to get off," Slater begins with his version of what all the adults expected to hear.

"Yeah, we were stuck in the bathroom. The door was jammed and we couldn't get it open in time and—" Chicky trails off when the principal slaps both of her palms against the table top.

"Boys, let us begin another way. The truth shall set you free—now Slater, would you like to start over?" She keeps her hands flattened, her eyes drilling into him as if she might leap across the table if he gives her another nincompoop answer.

"Well, once we realized we were on our way to Pinehurst, then it occurred to us that Phil was a student here and we thought we could at least check to make sure he's doing okay," Slater tries again slowly.

"Yeah, we haven't seen each other since Phil got transferred mid-year, and it can be hard making friends when you're the new guy," Chicky says tenderly.

"What kind of crock is this? Do I look like I fell off the turnip truck yesterday?"

Any ounce of sympathy they thought they might be able to wring from this old lady with their sad little sob story is completely blown out of the water.

"Officer Mendoza, can you please tell these young men why they are in trouble and what the charges could be?" Principal Deerborne says invitingly, as if she is going to enjoy this part of the meeting.

Chicky and Slater look at each other nervously. "Charges? We didn't do anything wrong, officer, I swear. We were just riding the train, that's all. We didn't hurt anybody or destroy anything, just riding, right Chicky?" Slater says, looking around to see if there is one adult in that room who is willing to believe him.

"Yeah, just riding, that's all. We didn't bring harm to nobody. We were just checking on our good friend and then we were going right back home, that's all," Chicky adds hoping he has done his part to make a convincing case.

"Boys, you do realize you are deliberately cutting a school field trip? You are legally required to be in class," Officer Mendoza begins.

"No, but, you see we were *left* on the train, sir," Slater repeats weakly.

"Son, I think we all know that just wasn't the case." Officer Mendoza continues, "and until your parent or guardian can collect you, I'm afraid we're going to have to hold you at the juvenile detention center."

"But we weren't even—" Slater is cut off before he can offer another word from his ridiculous lie that will land him in even deeper trouble.

The door opens abruptly with Ms. Gibson peeking her head in. "Mr. Moore is here, Mrs. Deerborne."

"I'll come get him myself," Mrs. Deerborne says eyeing Slater. "The facts are going to come down hard on you, young man. We know more than you think." With this mysterious exit, Slater worries what is going to happen to him in Pinehurst and hopes for the first time that his own father will be here soon to protect him.

When Mrs. Deerborne leaves the room for merely a brief instance, the eyes from each guest dart back and forth. It's as if there is a secret code language being discussed, yet the silent conversation Chicky and Slater are having is nothing like what the adults are telepathically communicating.

"Can I go to the bathroom?" Slater asks demurely.

"Um, yeah, I need to go too," Chicky chimes in, thinking there's no way he wants to be left in that room by himself.

"Boys, why don't you wait one minute for Mr. Moore? I'm sure he'll have some instructions for you," Officer Brooks says while writing something in his pocket-sized spiral notebook.

"What does the embossing on your sweatshirt mean?" Officer Mendoza asks, passing the time.

"EMGATS stands for Everly Middle Grade Alternative to

Traditional Schooling," Chicky says, spouting it off easily. He knows it as well as his name and address.

"What is the *alternative* to traditional schooling? Are you learning something different, like at homeschool?" The officer is genuinely interested now.

"It's just a way longer school day, like until six at night every day and then our classes are really long, too, like two hours. They offer us hands-on learning experience in four core subjects. We don't have electives or anything like that." Chicky summarizes the parent brochure.

"Wow, that is a pretty long day. Is that why you guys wanted to get out of your field trip today?" Officer Brooks joins in.

"Nah, we just wanted to come see our good friend, Phil, here," Chicky says again.

"Yeah, I had no idea these guys were coming until a couple a days ago. I said that sounds cool. We were just planning to eat lunch together, that's all. It's not like I was gonna be cutting school or anything. We didn't want to go off campus 'cause, like, none of us really knows the area very well," Phil says.

"Yeah, and if this school wasn't so close to the train station, we probably wouldn't have even come since we didn't want to be getting lost or anything in a strange town," Chicky says, reassuring the officers that they really meant no harm.

"What was the field trip you missed?" Officer Mendoza asks.

"About the Greek gods and stuff at the museum in downtown Clifton. We've been studying them for a few weeks and the teachers wanted us to see the statues up close," Slater says, trying to inform the officer what their school is like.

"So, what do you think your dads are gonna do when you go back home?" Officer Mendoza asks genuinely.

"I don't know," Slater says, lowering his head like he really does know but just doesn't want to say.

"I don't have a dad, but my gramps is probably going to be real surprised and my grandma is going to be real worried," Chicky says slowly, thinking for the first time about their reactions.

"My dad's not gonna be that mad because, like, I didn't plan for any of this, and I never left campus, so I don't think I'm really gonna be in any kind of trouble," Phil says, rationalizing out loud why it would be preposterous to think of his situation in any other way.

"Well, Phil, we'll see about that when we get you home," Phil's dad walks in on the tail end of his son's comments.

"Hi, Dad." Phil gets up to go stand with his father.

"Son, not so fast. We're all going to sit down to have a nice little chat about contributing to the delinquency of a minor, or in your case truancy."

"Mr. Moore, I want to thank you again for sharing the details of Phillip's plan to entertain uninvited students outside of our district while they visit him on our campus. According to the messages you found on Phillip's phone, the boys planned to meet inside the bathroom of wing seven before hiding out during lunch behind building nine," the principal begins making her case so all in attendance know the facts.

Phil's mouth drops so fast that he has to use his fist to rest his chin upon so he doesn't come across as this surprised again.

Slater and Chicky are glancing sideways at each other now, anticipating what the principal is going to reveal about *their* role in all this.

"Evidently, Slater, you and Chicky were not simply *abandoned* on the train, as you say. According to the depot records, you pre-purchased two youth tickets yesterday to travel from downtown Clifton to the end of the line in Pinehurst—specifically so you would not arouse any suspicion by traveling as un-ticketed passengers. Unfortunately for you, the conductor was right to be curious about two unaccompanied minors riding a train far away from the destination where all their other fellow students—wearing the same identical school sweatshirts—had already gotten off.

"Tell me, where am I wrong on any of this?" Mrs. Deerborne leans forward imagining she could wheel a bowling ball at them, successfully knocking them down in one strike because they are scrunched so close together.

Slater and Chicky look immediately to each other's sweatshirts. They never considered in all their careful planning that the uniform shirt they had been wearing every day for many weeks now, months in Chicky's case, would be the most obvious clue that would give them away. *Stupid, amateur move,* Slater thinks.

"It seems as though your odds of slipping away unnoticed increased when the EMGATS substitute took over your teacher's class—yes, let me see, that would be a Mr. Pastorino, right?"

Chicky has a sinking feeling. He thinks back to when Slater's dad yelled at both of them and said if any class cutting occurred—or anything like it that went against school learning—he'd be visiting the juvenile court judge himself.

"Ma'am, if you are done here, I have received written permission to take Chicky and Slater into my custody until Slater's father comes to get them." Paul Moore is ready to wrap things up here. "I am also checking out Phil for the rest of today and I have consent from his mother if you want to give her a confirmation call." Mr. Moore is constantly following the rules of his custody hearing—when it comes to school, he and his ex-wife agree to keep each other completely informed about *everything*.

"Mr. Moore, before you do go, we would like to remind you and Phillip that being new to our school is no excuse for not understanding our rules and their consequences if broken. Today's escapade does not technically fall under the category of *cutting class or truancy;* however, *harboring unregistered students* does seem like something we are going to be adding to our handbook," she says matter-of-factly.

"I assure you, we understand. Don't we, Phil?"

"Yes, sir, yes, ma'am," Phil says with his head bowed.

"You boys are very lucky to be missing out on a stay at juvy. I highly recommend you avoid that place at all costs in your future," Officer Mendoza states officially as he stands up with a straight face. His leather belt weighs heavily around his lean waist and makes a crinkling noise when he moves to shake hands with the other adults in the room. Both Slater and Chicky get a closer look at his holster and gun, bullet slips, tazor and handcuffs.

"Yes, sir," Chicky says, standing too, hoping he will be seeing his gramps very soon.

"Sorry, we didn't mean to cause so much trouble," Slater says out loud not sure if he should be addressing the principal, the officers, or Phil's dad.

"All I will say is that if you are trespassing on this campus again, we will have you arrested and the officers will have no choice but to detain you in the juvenile correctional facility," Mrs. Deerborne says without mincing words. Some grandma she turned out to be. There is nothing sweet about her.

The short drive to Mr. Moore's house means he has only about ten minutes to deliver a good strong lecture of his own.

"Boys, I know you've been missing Phil and he has sure missed you guys, too. But, you cannot just pick up and take off on trains to come see him, not like this, and never when you're missing school. I am worried about you three. Whenever you get together, it seems like there's trouble brewing. That fire this summer was scary enough; you're lucky nobody got hurt and that no property damage was done—"

"I wasn't there, was I, Mr. Moore?" Chicky asks humbly, hoping this will jog Mr. Moore's memory. The last thing Chicky needs is to be accused of more trouble than what he's actually really and truly done.

"You're probably right, Chicky, that was before your time. But I think you've been involved in a few shenanigans with these guys, so I am not leaving you out of this scolding, okay?"

All Chicky can do is sit there and take it like the rest of them. Once Mr. Moore has had his time to say what's on his mind, he finishes by pulling into the local ice cream store, empty for now until school lets out.

"What are we doing here?" Phil asks, confused after getting the harshest lecture he's heard since he wedged his army man down the bathtub drain.

"Well, since your friends did go to some trouble to say hello, seems only proper that we buy them some ice cream. Mind you, I am not rewarding what you did here today. I'm just saying, it's hot out and I'm hungry and this place is open. Got it?"

"Got it," Phil says with a wash of relief coming over his face as he nudges into Slater and Chicky in the back seat, each boy pulling off his seatbelt excitedly.

Phil, Slater and Chicky will get to spend most of the afternoon together catching up until Hank and Lynn Hannigan come for them. Unfortunately, the Hannigans won't be stopping to get them ice cream, or anything else light and fluffy on their long drive home.

Solitary confinement and hard time is more their style.

CHAPTER 6

Purgatory

The hum of their engine idles as Lynn and Hank Hannigan sit in front of Paul Moore's apartment building. With her hand on the keys, ready to pull them from the ignition, Hank goes over the plan one more time. "Chicky sits in the way back, Slater in the middle. They are not to talk or even look at one another. Are you sitting next to Slater, or up front?"

His wife turns to look at him, worry lines deepening around her eyes. The two-hour drive from Everly seemed to fly by; certainly, the thermos of coffee helped. "Oh, I am sitting right next to Slater. Are you okay to drive? You're not getting tired, right?"

"Oh, father warrior never tires," he says with a renewed vigor, lurching into his he-man pose like a gorilla. "These guys have to feel scared, Lynn. That's the only way we can prevent this from happening again. They have no idea how many different ways this could have gone down. They are just lucky—this time."

"Ready then? Let's go get them," she says, unclicking her seatbelt and slamming the door harder than usual behind her just to be sure her boy hears her energy loud and clear from across the street.

Bzzzz. Bzzzz. Bzzzz. Bzzzz. Bzzzz. Lynn Hannigan's typically impatient demeanor has now ratcheted up a few hundred notches. *Bzzzz. Bzzzz. Bzzzz.* Her annoying trigger finger on the buzzer is over eager, anxious for the door to open the same way a five-year-old awaits trick-or-treating goodies he has come to expect.

"Lynn, hi. Come on in," Paul Moore reaches out to give a weak hug to his old neighborhood friend before extending his hand to greet her husband. "Hank, good to see you."

There is a different vibe in the air than how they used to be toward one another when they were together for all those years as parents of elementary children. Attending plays, cheering on their teams, and celebrating victories with pizza parties at Polka's, owned by their other good neighbor Jim Peterson, Tobey's dad—done now.

A lot has changed in the eight months since the hill fire last summer. Even more has been altered in Phil's life after having to pick up and move to this new town away from everything familiar—friends, Everly Middle Grade, and the best house he ever lived in—including the Sugar Ridge Park right across the street.

Paul Moore has a lousy new job but it means he gets to stay close to his son. He and his ex-wife are communicating better and it seems like they agree more often than not these days when it comes to what is best for Phil. They both agree that being farther away from Slater Hannigan was one of the best reasons for relocating.

"Hi, Dad. Hi, Mom," Slater says, a ring of brown chocolate around his mouth still lingering where he hastily only half wiped.

"Ice cream? Really? Are you guys celebrating the trouble you caused today?" she says, completely perturbed that they have actually been enjoying themselves like it's just a playdate without a care in the world for all the unraveling that is about to happen.

"Well, we were hungry, and the parlor was the first place I spotted. Sorry," Paul Moore says sheepishly.

"Chicky, your grandparents want us to bring you home, so get your stuff. You're coming too," Hank Hannigan says without any sign of warmth.

"Boys, we're going to talk in the car. Phillip, it's good to see you, and I am glad that you are adjusting here. But, I want to be clear," her tone changes abruptly from lukewarm to icy, "it is not okay with us that Slater decided to come visit you on his own, and I would highly encourage you to share information like this in the future with your parents before I have to get in a car, and drive two hours to drag his behind back home. This is your responsibility too. Friends don't let friends make stupid decisions—"

Hank yanks her elbow, pulling her closer to him, a signal to back off just a little.

"Lynn, it does seem that Slater was the initiator in all of this. So, to speak harshly to Phil is probably a little overkill, don't you think?" Paul says, pushing his son to stand behind him, shielding him from Lynn's verbal bullets.

"And another thing, Phillip. How awful would you be feeling right now if Slater never made it to Pinehurst? What if someone stole him from the train? You have no idea what weirdos there are out in the world. Did that ever cross your mind when you were making these secret plans to put my son in jeopardy? Did it?" The more she goes on, the more worked up she gets.

"Mom, forget it. It wasn't even Phil's fault. I just wanted to come and check on him to make sure he had friends and stuff. Why do you always have to go so ballistic over something that didn't even happen? We had it all worked out. You didn't even need to come get us. We had a ticket home. The train was perfectly safe," Slater reels off indignantly.

"Paul, thanks again for picking up the kids. I owe you one," Hank says to his old friend who is not feeling very friendly right now.

"Hank, consider it my parting gift. Not sure when the boys will be able to get together again," Paul Moore says with foreboding, hoping that Hank and Lynn will read between the lines—his *when* should really have been substituted with *that*—but he was being polite. He hopes they understand this is not quite the friendship he wants to promote, either between his son and theirs, or between him and the Hannigan parents.

Paul Moore holds open the front door to his shabby little brown apartment. It is his gesture, signaling the unspoken words that he is also ready for them to leave.

As the minivan slider opens at the pace of a snail's crawl, Lynn reorganizes the seating chart just when Chicky tries to scoot in next to Slater in the middle bench. "Uh, nope, Chicky, you're in the back. I'm sitting next to Slater here. Put on your seatbelts, boys, this is going to be a bumpy ride." She isn't talking about the road conditions, either.

"Hank, do you want to start, or shall I?" They already have their routine down and this is part of their opening act.

"Darling, go ahead," he says from behind the wheel.

"It's not that I am mad at you and that I don't like you anymore. It's that I love you so much, you have scared me out of my mind," she begins with Slater before she arches her neck to look behind her. "Chicky, this applies to you as well. We have grown very fond of you and have always welcomed you into our home. But, I am sure you remember our conversations from a few months ago when you were first transferred to EMGATS that if you and Slater ever conspired to do something that goes against getting an education, then we would not support this friendship. You know what I'm talking about, don't you?" Lynn says sharply, reading Chicky's expression.

The view from the outside of one boy seated up against the windows, directly behind the other, might give any onlooker passing them on the freeway the impression that this glossy black van was a prisoner transport bus. Chicky and Slater might as well be shackled on their way to court because Mrs. Hannigan is judge and jury right now, laying out their new reality. She is going to punish Chicky just as hard she can—and then she's going to lay into her son.

"I remember," he says, his eyes staying locked on hers. He has heard yelling from adults before, plenty of times. But somehow this feels different. This is not some teacher he hardly cares about—or his dad in the early days before the last time he stormed out the door, which turned out to be the last time he would ever hear that shouting voice again—except for in his head, always in his head.

"Chicky, I expect more from you," and then she sharpens her focus to Slater, hardly finished with her message. "You have been full of surprises this past year, my child, but this takes the cake. I mean, what were you thinking, traveling all this way, by yourself? How is it that you thought you would get away with this? That the school wouldn't figure out that two of their kids were missing? What do you take those teachers for, dummies? You have no idea what this has unleashed, Slater. There is a huge meeting scheduled for Monday and there are going to be a lot of people sitting on edge because of the stunt you two pulled today. This is something juvenile delinquents do, when they run away, or get caught up with—" Lynn could go on for hours, but her husband jumps in to take over his part of the script.

"Boys, you have made a real mess here that your mother and I and Chicky's grandparents are left to clean up. This is not just about you—there are teachers who are worried about their jobs because you got away from their supervision. The superintendent is involved and I expect there are going to be lawyers at this meeting on Monday. There will be consequences for your poor decision-making here—"

"But, Daaaad!" Slater says desperately, "We didn't *run away*. We weren't even trying to get away from home, we were coming back before school ended. Are we, like, getting arrested, or are you calling the cops on us, or something?" Slater's eyes begin welling with tears because he truly has no idea what is going on. Yes, he knows they were supposed to be on a field trip, but they *were* coming back.

"Son, I need you to take a deep breath for me right now. You are *not* going to jail, nothing even close to that. Your mother and I are going to make sure this does not go any further. However, you have proven to us that you and Chicky cannot be trusted, so we are going to make some new arrangements to your class schedule." Hank holds his son's gaze in the rearview mirror for far longer than it is safe to take his eyes off the highway.

"Chicky," Lynn looks over her left shoulder in time to catch him wiping his face real fast with the corner of his sweatshirt hoody. "Oh, Chicky, I am sorry you are upset. It's okay, this is a big deal and it's okay to feel lousy about how it's turning out for you and Slater. But I can promise you, your grandmother and grandfather are both just as worried about you as we are about Slater. This was a scary day for all of us, not knowing where you were, or if you'd be safe when we found you," Lynn says with more compassion in her voice this time.

"I'm really sorry to make you worry. We just wanted to have

some fun with Phil, make sure he's okay. It's hard being the new kid in town—" And this is where Chicky stops suddenly because he is overcome with emotion at the idea of losing the only really true friend he's made in Everly.

He pulls his hoody down over his head, yanking hard on the strings, closing up his face so he can have privacy within the thick cotton of his fabric cave. He looks like a human sleeping bag, but Lynn understands. With only one gesture, she reaches her hand behind her, patting his knee gently to comfort him, letting him know she cares about him too. The shaking inside the sweatshirt begins. She quickly pulls her hand away, worrying that she is the cause of Chicky's silent crying inside the security of his dark hole.

Slater takes Chicky's silence as a signal that he is tired, too. Tired of hearing his parents yammering at him and tired after the long day of executing their plans that fell apart faster than the few days it took for them to make. The sun beats through the window, resting upon his shoulder. Its warmth puts him into a coma—his eyes close easily, while his head bobs back and forth.

Lynn leans in closer to her sleeping boy, wrapping her sweater in a soft bundle on her shoulder as she pulls Slater's head to rest in the crook of her neck. She listens to him breathe through the opening around his nose. He is completely out. The motion of the car has always had this effect. She looks at his hands, growing large like his father's—long fingers thickening, but still only dimples where his knuckles will grow in soon. The dirt beneath his nails along with the jagged cuticles remind her that he has always been good with his hands, good with figuring out how things work. Curious. He has always been curious.

"Lynn—" She is snapped out of inspecting her son by the abrupt sound of her husband's voice, "how about we stop, get something to eat? The worst of it is over. Let's not let the mood hang for the rest of the night. What do you say?"

"Well, they're both sleeping now, probably they can use the rest. How much longer until home?"

"About forty minutes."

"Okay then, if you see a little restaurant, we can pull over, but I don't really want fast food; I feel like soup. Maybe steak for the kids. I'm sure they're hungry."

"There's something up ahead in a couple of exits, Nino's Family Dining. Worth a try."

After an early bird dinner at Nino's highway diner, the Hannigans and Chicky talk about anything other than the events of the day and their spoiled friendship. Sports talk has everybody contributing, especially about the best athletic plays of the year worthy of highlight reels. Talk of their favorite players and whom they want to meet someday bring Chicky and Slater further out of their slump. General weather commentary is also duly noted since there are predictions for an active tornado season this spring due to the warmer than usual temperatures at the end of winter.

When the Hannigans drop off Chicky at his grandparents' house, they all walk inside together to be sure there is no miscommunication about the restrictions going forward.

Chicky puts his key in the doorknob, which has not been pulled shut, so his weight pushes the door open easily.

"Gramps," Chicky calls through the darkened living room over the blaring sounds from the TV of an opera performance in Italian. "Grandma," he continues calling through the attached kitchen behind the living room wall. The house is not big and grand like the Hannigans'. It will not take a search party to look through the two bedrooms and one bath that keep a modest family content under one roof. Simplicity is all his grandparents ever knew, so they never wanted for things so long as they could finally own their own property.

"Chicky, where do you think they might have gone?" Hank asks without concern yet. Maybe this is the time they go to the grocery store before preparing dinner. Anybody could have accidentally pulled the door only partially closed, not waiting for the familiar click to confirm the house is secure. Maybe they were in a rush. Sometimes people like to leave a TV on to signal to would-be burglars that this house is not to be disturbed.

"I don't know, they're always here when I get home from school, unless my gramps has a doctor's appointment. Wait, I need to check something," Chicky says as he sweeps back into the kitchen to look at the refrigerator. After scanning the magnetic calendar closely, he is sure there are no places where his grandparents would be expected right now.

"Hank, I know Fiorella was planning to be here. She said she would wait and it did not matter how late we were; she was going to wait for Chicky to come home," Lynn says, sounding a bit uneasy now as she repeats his grandmother's words.

"Would your grandparents leave a note someplace they were sure you would find it?" Hank starts imagining something else may be at play here.

"Either my pillow, or the bathroom mirror, if it's not on the fridge," Chicky says, while taking off to his room with Slater in tow.

There is no need for Chicky to say a word. A picture says it all. His little bed is a small mattress on the floor, stained in places, but he has several blankets he has piled on top to provide him the warmth that escapes him when the cold air seeps in through his thin-paned window. His view looks into the neighbor's alley, where the garbage cans are lined up and where he often listens to the rustling of the raccoons foraging for food.

There is no closet, but there is one small dresser. Its white veneer is peeling and the small pink roses that were once painted on the face of the drawers have become scratched over time. Certainly, this is not the furniture Chicky would have picked for himself if he were on that trip with his grandmother shopping at the used clothing store. But, his grandmother never expected to find herself appointed guardian over the little boy she was surprised had grown into a giant man-child.

"Nothing here," Chicky says swiftly as he turns abruptly, hoping Slater won't linger behind him staring at his room. He runs into the bathroom where a square yellow note has fallen from the mirror into the sink. The droplets of water have smeared its ink but the message is still clear.

Chicky,

I bring Poppa to hospital.

He took ill. I stay there with him.

Ask Hannigans please keep you tonight.

Love,

Nonna

"Oh, no! Not my gramps!" Chicky says with silent tears streaming down his face. "Do you know where the hospital is? I want to see my gramps, Mr. Hannigan." He has worried for a long time that something like this might happen during the school day. But his grandmother always tries to assure him his grandfather is getting stronger and healthier with all the new medication. He was never sure it was working as well as she said.

"Okay, Chicky, we're taking you home with us. Let's get a few things packed up in case you need to stay the weekend," Lynn says protectively. She does a complete one-eighty turnaround that surprises—and delights—both the boys who are grateful they will at least get to see each other one more day.

Hank looks at his wife who shrugs her shoulders and silently purses her lips as if to say, "What're you gonna do?" She made the right call. It's what he would have agreed to anyway, if she'd asked. But she didn't, nor did she need to. She knows her husband. Discipline is one thing, but they are not going to abandon Chicky.

"Chicky, I'm going to take you home and while you get settled, I'll make some calls to the hospitals for more information. As soon as I can locate your grandmother, we'll make a plan to visit your grandfather if the hospital will allow it. Sometimes, they require patients to get more rest and that's why they insist on keeping a person under observation. It might not be as bad as you think," Hank says gently, hoping to lessen Chicky's fears.

It will take Hank a little bit of time to finally find Chicky's Nonna. The only telephone number Lynn has is to their house line. Chicky says his grandparents don't really like all the technology bogging down family time today, so they don't own any of it—no computer, no cell phone. Maybe they will think differently when the next emergency involves Chicky.

CHAPTER 7

Promises, Promises

"Where's Graham, Mom?" Slater asks as soon as they tramp through the front of the house toward the kitchen.

"He's sleeping over at Jason's. We didn't know how late we'd be getting back," Lynn says, hanging up her coat.

"So, does that mean Chicky gets to sleep in Graham's room?" Slater smiles.

"How about we set Chicky up down here in your father's office? You know how it's supposed to be arranged since you did such a nice job for Grandpa Bruce. Grab the guest basket, bring it down here and get Chicky situated," Lynn says, looking at her husband, wondering what files he has in his office that he might not want disturbed.

"Slater, give me a minute to clear my office, all right, bud?" Hank says, knowing there are several things that should be put back in the safe, completely out of sight.

"Hey, can we sleep in the garage apartment instead?" Slater asks completely bolstered by the logic in his solution.

After Hank and Lynn exchange brief looks, his mother chimes right in, "Slater, we're going to keep everybody under one roof tonight. Chicky, if you get hungry in the middle of the night, you are welcome to help yourself to anything in the fridge. Really, whatever you like. I think we have some cold chicken, a little potato salad, and a few slices of chocolate cake leftover—oh, and there's plenty of fruit, too.

"Boys, you've got about three hours before bedtime. Slater, don't forget you've got to get up early tomorrow," Lynn continues with the rundown of the household routine.

"What? But, it's Saturday and Chicky's here—"

"Slater, are you forgetting about the little promise you made?"

"Promise? What promise are you talking about?"

"The promise that you made to a certain neighbor to do yardwork. In fact, you are expected for the next three weekends, remember?" Lynn is sure he knows what she is talking about now. The look on his face and the huge gulp of air they all heard him suck in is a dead giveaway.

"Oh, yeah, yeah, okay, that's right. I'll be there. I won't be late. Thanks, Mom," he says, totally relieved she avoided using Sibley White's name knowing that would just further embarrass him.

"Good, so we're clear then? Three hours, then lights out. Your father and I are around if you need us. You can watch a movie down here if you want, or you can hang out up in your room."

"Can we invite Macaroni and Tobey to come over? Please, Mom?" Slater asks sweetly.

She looks at Chicky whose eyes seem to spark at this suggestion.

"Well, honey, let's first see what your dad can find out about Chicky's grandfather in the next little while and then we can determine our plan."

"Yeah, I hope the hospital lets me come, but if they don't tonight then it'd be cool to see Macaroni and Tobey." He figures he might as well cast his vote even though he is not an official member of the Hannigan household.

"Is that right? No chance we can make an exception to this rule?" Hank replies into the phone, conversing with someone at the hospital who has record of admitting Carlo Cicarrelli. "When are visiting hours over? Okay, thank you so very much for your help, appreciate it."

"What did they tell you, Hank?"

"Well, Chicky, I was able to find which hospital your grandfather is staying in. He's at Everly Memorial Hospital downtown—"

"Can we go? I'm already ready. Just for a short time, please?" Chicky asks urgently.

"Son, how old are you?"

"I'm eleven, same as Slater. I know I'm big for my age, but I'm not as old as people think."

"Why, what did the hospital say, honey?"

"There is a visitor's policy that no children under the age of twelve can visit patients," he says, before turning to Chicky. "Is there a chance your birthday is tomorrow?"

"Nah, not until November. But can I see my grandma? Did you get to talk to her?" His anxiety builds with the more questions he asks.

"Lynn, do you and Slater want to come along with me and Chicky? Let's take a ride to Memorial and see if we can find Fiorella in the cafeteria or the lobby, or maybe she is still with Carlo. Visiting hours end at nine o'clock, so we still have some time to track her down."

"Thanks, Mr. Hannigan. I really appreciate this," Chicky says sincerely.

It doesn't take more than fifteen minutes to get to the hospital. But it takes longer than that to find Fiorella Cicarrelli. After searching out the cafeteria, the gift shop, and the waiting room, Lynn suggests the chapel.

There in the front pew of a dimly lit room is a peaceful image of a woman who has come to pray. There is soothing music playing so softly it is barely detectable, but it helps to drown out the whispers of the other families who had come to do the same, having left already.

"Grandma," Chicky pushes out in a hoarse voice after barreling up the aisle. He is a child in this moment, younger than his stature would suggest. He lays his head on her chest with his arms wrapped tightly around her neck. His shoulders heave up and down while faint whimpers can be heard from the back of the room where the Hannigans stand awkwardly piecing together a word here and there that they recognize as English. In any language, bad news always looks like this.

"Oh, Slater," Lynn whispers to her son while she holds his hand tightly in her grip. "Honey," her voice breaks watching Chicky and his grandmother embrace, "your friend is going to need you after tonight."

Together, Lynn and Slater both turn and lean into Hank for a family hug where they all shed tears for the agony Chicky and his grandmother are experiencing. They are not sure if the right thing is to leave, allowing them some privacy to grieve alone, or if they should move closer to hug the Cicarrellis and remind them that the Hannigans are here to help.

The church seems so empty. The two of them all alone in the front seem even more lonely now that Carlo Cicarrelli will not be coming home tonight. Lynn can hardly stand to look on for a minute longer. She leads Hank and Slater to the front so they can pay respects to the Cicarrellis.

"Fiorella, we're here. I don't want to intrude, but we wanted you to know that whatever you need to help you through this time, you're not alone," Lynn says with a few teardrops falling down her cheek.

"We're so sorry," Hank says slowly, watching Chicky's expression contort into utter devastation.

"You're such a nice people," Chicky's grandmother struggles to speak. "My Carlo, I don't understand it," she dabs at her eyes. "He say he wasn't feeling too good and he look a little gray, so I say we should come to the hospital and the doctors take a look. They say he need some help right away and they take him. I never get to see him again." She buries her head in her hands.

"Oh, Fiorella, I'm so sorry. I'm so, so very sorry, this is horrible." Lynn Hannigan reaches up from where she is squatting in front of the Cicarrellis to stroke her shoulder and help console her.

"Dude, I feel so bad," Slater says to Chicky before he swipes at his face real fast with the back of his sweatshirt sleeve.

Chicky can hardly look up. He cannot say a word because nothing will come out except for tears. So, he tries not to speak and just keeps his head buried in his Nonna's sweater.

"Can we go to the cafeteria, maybe for some hot soup? You'll feel better if you get a little something inside of you," Lynn suggests hopefully.

"I couldn't eat, I'm not hungry, but Chicky, you go," his grandmother insists.

"No, I want to stay with you."

"Hank?" Lynn is trying to telepathically convey all the thoughts she has stumbling through her mind, hoping her husband will fix this situation.

"Fiorella, did the doctor tell you any instructions?" Hank begins taking charge.

"The doctor only say to me that Carlo does not look so good and then I never see him again."

"Fiorella, did you ask any of the nurses about his progress update?" Hank probes some more.

"Everybody seems so busy and nobody comes to talk with me, and I just know it in my bones, it's not good. He look not like himself," she says, wringing her handkerchief in her hands.

Hank looks to his wife and furrows his brows. He is trying not to ask the obvious question: *Is he really dead?* The nurses aren't going to give *him* any information about Chicky's grandfather since he's not a family member.

"Lynn, why don't you take Slater and Chicky to the cafeteria and order enough food so that when Fiorella and I join you, we can have a bite. Fiorella, let's go to the front desk and get some clear idea about what the hospital knows."

As Hank walks with his arm gently around Fiorella's back, Slater and Lynn walk next to Chicky. Nobody says a word. Nobody wants to jinx a thing.

"Hi, I'm Hank Hannigan, a friend of the family. This is Fiorella Cicarrelli and we are trying to get an update on her husband Carlo Cicarrelli who was admitted here four hours ago.

The nurse looks up blankly. "Tell me the last name again," she says as she types quickly into her computer without looking up as Mrs. Cicarrelli slowly spells her last name as clearly as she can manage. "The doctor will be right with you. I think he was out here half an hour ago looking for you in the lobby. Please just have a seat," the nurse says with less warmth after saying it a thousand other times today.

"Fiorella, can I get you some water?"

"You're such a nice man." She squeezes his hand, blinking for a second too long because he wonders if she has taken to praying. But she is only clearing her eyes. "It's been a long day," she says wearily with her Italian accent that sounds as if *ah* is added to the end of every word.

"Close your eyes and I'll be sure to wake you so you don't miss the doctor twice," Hank says calmly. "It's okay, you can relax. I'm right here."

When Doctor Singh appears forty-five minutes later, he finds a snoring Fiorella Cicarrelli and a patient Hank Hannigan. "You are here about Carlo Cicarrelli?"

"Yes, yes, but I promised to wake his wife here." Hank smiles softly at the doctor while he gently nudges her, hoping she will stop her own snoring.

"Was I dreaming?" Fiorella asks Hank while he points out that the doctor is here to share his instructions.

She smooths down her hair and folds her hands in her lap, holding tight to the handkerchief she has been carrying with her all evening. The doctor sits in the chair beside her.

"Mrs. Fiorella, I am Doctor Singh. I'm so sorry to keep you waiting," he says in a soothing British accent that immediately comforts her. "I did look for you earlier, but we must have missed each other. Your husband Carlo has suffered from a mild heart attack, but we have given him some medication and it seems to be working well—"

"My Carlo is not dead?" Fiorella Cicarrelli cries harder now than she did in the chapel. "But, nobody ever tell me. I just wait and I think it must be very bad news." She wrings her handkerchief and cries some more. "Thank you! You save my Carlo! You are a good man, doctor." She reaches out for his hands and holds them to her cheek instead of hugging him. "Can I see him now?"

"He is still resting, but I will have the nurse bring you back to his room. There's a very uncomfortable chair by his bedside in case you want to sit for a while. But, please, he does need his sleep and I don't want him disturbed. If he looks better tomorrow than he did when he came in today, he can go home." The doctor winks at her and leads her to the nurse's station to be sure she does not get overlooked again tonight.

"Fiorella, this is wonderful news!" Hank says, wrapping an arm around the side of her shoulder. "I think you should go with the nurse and I will bring Chicky home with us and—"

"No, no it's too much trouble, you've been too kind. I want to go home. I say goodnight to my Carlo and then I take my Chicky with me. I don't want to be alone," she says with her eyes misting up once again.

"I understand. I'll go to the cafeteria and bring Chicky back here in about fifteen minutes, okay?"

The Hannigans are all so relieved to tell Chicky the very good news. But it takes a lot of convincing for him to accept that his gramps has not died and he will be returning home after one night's stay in the hospital. "You're serious? You mean it? My gramps is not…not—my gramps is *alive*?" Chicky hangs his head as if to pray to the floor beneath his feet because after a long pause, he finally looks up with a huge grin and tears streaming down his face.

"Your grandmother wants to take you home with her, so let's bring you back up to the lobby. She doesn't want to be alone tonight and I don't think she'll be very comfortable waiting at the hospital. Besides, your grandfather needs to sleep tonight."

The Hannigans extend their well wishes to Fiorella Cicarrelli while Slater and Chicky part ways with their first-ever hug. The night's drama certainly does overshadow the day's drama, filling everyone with renewed hope—maybe Chicky and Slater deserve *one more* chance.

CHAPTER 8

No Rest for the Weary

"Have you ever heard him snoring like this before?" Lynn whispers quietly to her husband who is still standing in the doorframe as she sits atop Slater's covers watching him sleep like a baby. He is far from the baby she once fawned over as a nervous and protective new mother—far, far away from those peaceful days.

"Gotta wake him, Lynn. Get that boy out of bed so he makes it to the White's early," Hank says, heading downstairs to start the coffee pot.

"Slater," she says in her quietest whisper, hating to have to disturb him.

His arms are tossed behind his head, one beneath his pillow. His head is cocked to the side, his cheek resting upon a warmed pool of drool spilling from his mouth. His opened mouth hangs down as bursts of air from his nose become shallow sounds purring through his throat, creating a rhythmic pattern his mother watches trancelike.

"Lynn, is he up yet?" an enormous voice booms through the house. No need to be careful to let the other brother sleep since he is away at a friend's house overnight.

"Slater," she says in a song-like voice. "Oh, sweetheart, it's time to get up," her voice is barely registering over his buzzing and nostril whistling, so she takes to nudging him gently by pressing her lips to his forehead.

"Eww, Mom, what are you doing? Get off me," Slater says in a start.

"Gee, somebody's awfully grumpy."

"What time is it, anyway? It's still dark out! I don't have to be there until eight, just let me sleep," Slater says, rolling over to hide his head beneath his pillow.

"No doing, mister," she says, patting his bottom once through the covers. "It's time to get going. You need breakfast and I expect you to be downstairs after you've showered in about fifteen minutes. So, let's get a move on; your dad and I want to sit with you for a few minutes."

"You guys never leave me alone. I just want to sleep. Come wake me in a half hour, I won't be late, I promise."

"Darling, no," she says, tugging hard at the top quilt she yanks off the bed completely. "I am not asking you again and I am certainly not coming up here to wake you in thirty more minutes."

"Mo-om," he says in that tone she does not like.

"Yes, Slater?" She smiles, but her arms are crossed while she speaks slowly in a very low voice. He knows not to push it any further.

"Nothing, I'm up." He slides out both legs, pushing his feet into slippers, while putting his robe on around his cowboy pajamas—the ones he can still fit into from last year's cowboy-themed birthday swag.

"Fifteen minutes. I'm setting the timer. Demerit points for every minute you keep breakfast waiting," she says evenly. "Oh, and don't forget to make the bed," she says, looking at the bedspread she left in a heap on the floor. Now she smiles, wrinkling her nose as if she is having so much fun at her son's expense.

While she heads down the stairs, it's a good thing she is out of earshot before Slater unleashes some of the words he is not ever supposed to use, even under his breath.

Lynn's eggs Benedict and berry medley are synchronized to the sounds of the familiar rustling routine she listens for upstairs. Once the medicine cabinet mirror swings open and closed a few times for retrieving toothpaste, then putting it back, she cracks her first egg. After the sharp snap of steaming water being turned on and then off, she sets the table and slices strawberries into an oversized bowl of blackberries and blueberries. While the smell of Axe after shower spray can be detected all the way downstairs, she sprinkles a dusting of powdered sugar over the fruit and carries it to the dining room.

Ringgggg. The dinger announces the end to its fifteen-minute countdown just when a more energetic boy comes bouncing down the last few steps of the staircase.

"I made it, no demerits for me," Slater says happily. "Mmmmm, smells good, Mom. I'm starving, too."

"Well, there's plenty, so eat as much as you like. Don't forget, you're working four hours straight and I would not expect a snack break in between. This isn't school where you get recess," she says, reminding him of the penance he promised to do for the Whites.

"I know," he says while digging into his first bite of an English muffin. "So, what did you want to tell me?"

"Well, that's for your father," she says, hooking her finger over the top edge of the newspaper spread in front of his face while he catches today's headlines and stocks. This is his cue to begin.

"Son, I've got to go into the office today, but there are some things you can start for me before you go off to Sibley White's house. If I make it back before you get home, then I will load the truck to haul off the debris in the backyard."

"What? You want me to do chores *here* before I go do chores over at their house? How am I supposed to have time for all this?"

"Well, less arguing, more eating ought to do the trick," Hank says, a beaming smile upon his face.

"Is this why you guys got me up at six? I could have slept in until at least 7:30 a.m. and still made it to their house in time." Slater knows he is not out of hot water yet from yesterday, which is the only reason he hasn't quite said *no*.

"Son, let me know when you're finished with breakfast, then I'll show you what I need done. If you don't grimace as much, your work will go a lot faster," his dad says earnestly.

"There is something else we wanted to talk to you about," Lynn says, wiping the corner of her mouth delicately. "We agreed to a family party for your birthday celebration this year. Nothing more, nothing less." She takes a sip of coffee. "But your dad and I want to do it on a night when we will all feel a bit more relaxed. Is it all right with you if we celebrate a few days early on Sunday with a special dinner; that way we won't be so rushed when your dad's big meeting rolls around mid-week? And don't worry, when you get home from school Wednesday evening, I'll still do cupcakes for you as usual, but you will already have had your big night tomorrow, okay?"

"Yeah, I guess so," he says, trying to think of any real reason why he shouldn't approve.

"Okay, there's just one more thing we need to discuss before I show you what I need raked and pulled," Hank jumps in, already having finished his eggs. "The Everly District meeting about your little adventure with Chicky is going to be held after school on Monday. You will be excused from tutorials, then you need to walk over to the district office to meet your mother and me there by four o'clock. I don't want you to be late. In fact, I expect to see you there at 3:45 p.m., and if I don't, it is going to set a very bad tone. I expect you to take this meeting seriously and to show remorse for the embarrassment you caused to the school. I imagine they are approaching this thing as if they have a reputation to protect for *not* losing kids on field trips. You've managed to put a lot of capable teachers in a very awkward position. Do you understand me?"

"Yeah," Slater says, chewing more slowly now.

"I do not know if Chicky and his family will be at this same meeting; probably not. I think the school believes you orchestrated this whole thing since *you* purchased the tickets and the messages between you and Phil are on *your* phone. You are the guy here, Slater, not Chicky. You are the one caught red-handed, holding the bag, so to speak. You did this to yourself. You thought you had it all figured out, but it backfired. You may be smart for a kid, but Slater, you're still a kid. Every adult put in charge to protect you is going to be three steps ahead of you. It's called life experience. You think ditching field trips is new? *We* invented that and our parents before us would tell us *they* invented it before we ever got the bright idea—"

"Slater, what your father means to say is not that *he* was ditching school—Hank, we both know that's not the case; you were nothing less than a straight A student your entire life—but we want to remind you that adults are not dummies. They have seen a thing or two and you kids can't just keep pulling these foolish stunts," Lynn finishes with the scolding she started yesterday.

"So, here's the deal. We are not splitting up your friendship with Chicky, but we are asking EMGATS to rearrange as many of the classes you have together as possible. You guys can still see each other at lunch and tutorials, and of course, Chicky is welcome to come study here with you from time to time. But I want you to include Macaroni and Tobey in more of your activities on the weekends," he says determinedly.

"But, Dad, that's just like *splitting us up*. If we don't have any classes together, how are we supposed to really study together, huh?"

"Well, son, I think you will benefit from seeing how a different teacher instructs and then maybe you two boys will learn about new methods of studying." He looks over at his wife, who knows the next part is hers.

"Honey, we are making summer plans for you," she says, pouring another cup of coffee for herself and then a refill for her husband, allowing just the right amount of time for this new idea to hang in the air. "I have been collecting brochures over the past year of different places for you to try. We're not doing football camp this year. We're not doing baseball camp, either. I think you need to spend some good old-fashioned time in nature. I've signed you up for a survival camp in the woods involving a sixty-mile hike that sounds pretty treacherous, but something I think you are totally right for," Lynn says coolly, not expecting an ounce of pushback on this.

"What? You're kidding me, right? There's no way I'm doing that. Nu-uh, I'm not going. You can't make me and you can't force me to get out of the car. I'll be long gone before that ever happens," Slater protests adamantly after abruptly pushing his chair away from the dining room table with screeching noises coming from the floor where he just dug the legs into the hardwood harder than usual.

"Oh, now, Slater, I was afraid this might be your response, which is why we wanted to talk with you about it this morning; give you some time to cool down while you are raking, and painting, and picking, and pulling, and doing whatever else your father and the Whites see fit. I am sure by the time you get home this afternoon, you will have had a change of heart," Lynn says even-temperedly.

With that, Hank folds up his newspaper, tucks in his chair gently—without scraping the floor—and leads his son out back. "Come on, bud, unless you want to stay in here where I'm sure your mother will put you to work on the dishes," he smiles, charm oozing out of him.

Slater is stuck. Kitchen chores or garden work, either one is not what he wants to be doing right now. Climbing a mountain for sixty-miles is also not something he wants to be doing for his summer. But, suddenly, he has the bright idea to see if he can convince any of his friends to come along and get their parents to sign them up, too. For a kid who is told he needs to think more like an adult, he catches on quick.

As Slater pulls weeds in his backyard and rakes leaves into piles for the better part of a half hour, he thinks about what all his friends are probably doing today.

At half past seven on a Saturday morning, he knows Macaroni is still sound asleep in his feathery bed, with a breezy fan set on low. He has always needed the sound of a hum to lull him through the night, and while this used to keep Slater awake whenever they had sleepovers at Macaroni's, his friend cannot sleep anywhere else without dragging his personal fan along.

He is sure Tobey is up early, sweeping out the pizzeria floors and polishing the tables before the lunch crowd starts the long day ahead. His dad is training him on how to clean the ovens and take inventory of the ingredients in the refrigeration unit so that one day, Tobey can run the place. That's still a lot of years away.

What is Chicky doing early this morning? After such a scare at the hospital last night, he's probably sleeping in, but his grandmother has always been an early riser. She likes to bake homemade bread so the house smells like fresh dough on Saturday mornings. She usually has a list of house chores for Chicky to do, even when his gramps is at home. Chicky likes to vacuum and dust, but today he will also be helping his grandmother by cleaning the bathroom and tub until they shine, and clearing out the chicken coop, his grandfather Carlo's job.

"Honey, it's time to go. I think you can finish your chores here when you get home. You have a good start," Lynn says encouragingly.

"I need to bring my water bottle. I'm already hot," Slater says, half-complaining.

"I've got it here, with ice, so it'll stay cold all morning. It's not supposed to get above seventy-five today, so you should be comfortable enough. Your father left a second pair of gardening gloves for you in case you need them, and wear your hat, so you don't get burned. In fact, come here, I want to put some sunscreen on the back of your neck," she says, reaching for her bottle from the top drawer in the entryway dresser.

"Mom, I'm just gonna go. I'll be fine; it's not going to get that hot, you even said so." Slater moves away from her outreached hands full of goop.

"I'd feel better if you just let me put a little on. I don't want to waste all this," she insists, slathering generous dollops of paste onto his arms and then smearing the rest onto the back of his neck and ears before she sneaks in a swipe at his face.

"I hate this stuff. I can't wait until I'm older so I never have to wear this when I live in my own house," Slater huffs.

"Well, as soon as you have a job where you can pay your bills and buy a beautiful house like this one, and then have enough money for food, and your electricity, cable, garbage, and water bills, then you are welcome to live however you like, my sweet. But until then, guess what? You're mine," she says with a final stroke down his nose, satisfied that she has smeared enough white stuff onto him that he will be UV-protected until the sun goes down tonight.

"I'm leaving. I'll be back when I'm done," he says, ready to head out the door. "And, Mom, don't come by. Promise you're not gonna come check up on me," Slater says, staring her down, knowing full well she can say what she wants but she might change her mind later.

"Now, sweetie, it's so precious to me that you don't want me around. After all, I am the one who takes care of every little thing for you, and yet, you want nothing to do with me. How charming you are," Lynn says in a sickly sweet mocking tone.

"Mo-om, promise. I don't want you hanging out front; it'd be totally embarrassing," Slater says, his voice starting to go higher than usual, indicating his increasing anxiety levels.

"Well, gee, since your mother—the very same one who has sacrificed her dreams in order to give everything to you—would be some kind of *embarrassment* to you, I will try to stay hidden away in my tower here. Call me Quasimodo, sir. I'll just be ringing my bell waiting until you say it's safe for me to show myself, then," she says, laying it on thick, making her favorite comparison to the Hunchback of Notre Dame, which she loves to do whenever Slater tries to pull this *Mom, you embarrass me* routine.

"Never mind," he says exasperated, walking out in a hurry.

"The bells have made me deaf, sir," she calls loudly after him while he is crossing their front lawn. "Did you give me an *I love you* before you went away on your journey?" she says in her bad British accent, teasing him.

There is nothing he can do but smile when he turns to whisper what she wants to hear.

"Oh, he said it, the young sire loves his Quasimodo, I am blessed indeed," she says, blowing air-kisses in succession after him until he is well past the neighbor's house two doors down.

That kid, what am I going to do with him? she thinks to herself, happy she can still make him laugh.

What a complete weirdo, Slater thinks to himself, mildly amused, walking the length of twenty houses along Ginger Road with a grin on his face.

Ding-dong. He checks his digital sports watch reading 7:58 a.m. He's right on time. By the heat of the rising sun, he can tell it's going to be a lot warmer than seventy-five degrees today. The dead lawn out front already smells like hot straw.

The door opens swiftly. It's Mr. White stepping onto the porch, pulling the doorknob shut behind him so Slater cannot see into the house. "Good morning, Slater. You look like you are prepared for work today," Mr. White says heartily.

"Yeah, my dad already had me doing yardwork at our house before I left to come here," he says pleasantly, wondering if this will somehow influence Mr. White to have some sympathy for him these next few hours.

"Well, I am glad to know you are so familiar with requirements for maintaining a garden. I have big hopes for this front yard, and I imagine you are going to be the one to get it looking the way my wife has always envisioned. If I didn't have such delicate work, I would be able to get my hands a little dirtier," Mr. White says, realizing he has just said more than he intended.

"Do you want me to start by pulling weeds?"

"Yes, weeds first, then I have clippers for you to trim all these hedges. I don't need them to be in a special design, just straight across the tops and the sides, but they need to come down about two feet. The ladder is on the side of the house, so is the bucket for debris, and all the gardening tools," Mr. White says, directing Slater's attention to the corner of the house that bumps up against the neighbor's fence.

"Is there anything else you want me to tackle while I'm here until noon?"

"Here's the list my wife made. If you don't get around to straightening the shutters and painting them today, we can save that for next week. There are more weeds behind the house, but save those until the very end so I can show you myself," Mr. White says cordially, eyeing Slater as if to say *Do not go beyond this gate unattended.*

"Okay, I think I've got enough to keep me busy for at least two hours. If you want to check on my progress, I won't mind. I might be ready for the rest of the list, or maybe then you can personally show me the rest of the backyard." Slater can take a hint.

"Fine then. I'll leave you to it. I'm going to be working upstairs today, so if you need something, Mrs. White will be back from the grocery store shortly."

"My mom already made me a big breakfast and I've got plenty of cold water, so I'm good, thanks," Slater says, ready to get to work. The sooner he gets started, the sooner he gets home.

After the first hour of hoeing and raking, pulling and pruning, Slater has already finished half of his water bottle. The weatherman sure did not predict today's forecast right. Thank goodness he's got on his sunscreen because the back of his neck has been scorching all morning. *Now* he's grateful to his mother.

Slater has already made huge improvements to Sibley's front yard. In fact, he's imagining this might turn out to be an okay looking house when he gets done with it. The rim of dry, caked dirt that was full of weeds only an hour ago actually turned over some dark earth when Slater pierced its cracks with his hoe. He finds the water spigot and attaches the old brown hose, hoping that a good dousing will bring this garden back to life.

While he sprays the front patches of dirt, careful not to disrupt the twigs of his first hedge clippings, he hears a familiar voice calling him loudly from behind. "Slater Hannigan, what are *you* doing here?" Charlotte Rigby straddles the frame of her cotton-candy-colored bicycle, ringing her bell wildly to signal to Sibley that she is here. "Do you have a side business, or something?" she asks so innocently, completely shocked to find Slater Hannigan at Sibley's house. Her brain cannot connect the dots to any other logical explanation.

Slater takes this suggestion as the perfect excuse for why he would possibly be here on a Saturday morning. "Yep, that's it. I do lots of the neighbors' houses. Got a bunch. Sometimes, I do two a day. Saving for college, you know." The more he says, the better it sounds. Somehow it all makes perfect sense. Unless, of course, Sibley has already blabbed to Charlotte the secret between them and now Charlotte is just *pretending* like she doesn't know he's there for his punishment after getting caught plagiarizing Sibley's report.

But until Charlotte gives up her act, he is not saying a word.

"That's cool," she says, wrinkling her brow, wondering if she should ask the thing she has not yet found her words to ask.

Oh no, here it comes. She does know.

"Umm, Slater, what other kinds of jobs do you do?" Charlotte is already imagining how excited her mom would be to get some help with the garage and all those moving boxes that still haven't been opened.

"I do everything except for windows and toilets," he says, smiling coyly.

"I bet my mom would put you to work organizing our garage. It's been a mess ever since we moved here. She hasn't even unpacked all our belongings because she's so busy with my sister and brothers and me. You want to come around and introduce yourself when you're done here?"

Suddenly, Slater is feeling like he really could turn this ruse into a little business and start making some money for real. Maybe he *could* afford to buy a house and pay his bills a lot sooner than his mom might ever expect.

"Sure. Didn't you guys move into that blue and white house on Lemon Drop Court?"

"Yeah, we've got a huge koala bear flag out front, so we're hard not to miss. My mom has a thing about flags; we've got a welcome flag, and a 'Welcome Spring' flag with butterflies, and then, of course, there is the flag collection somewhere in the garage for every holiday season. Soon, there'll be Fourth of July flags lining the lawn, too; that is, if you can dig them out before then from wherever they've been packed away." Charlotte giggles to herself, hoping her mother's desire to fit into her American neighborhood isn't too obvious. Of course, Charlotte's Australian accent is a dead giveaway that her family is still rightfully proud of their Down-Under roots.

The front door swings wide open as Sibley stands in her entryway, motioning for Charlotte to come inside quickly. Sibley hardly knows what to say to Slater, so she just looks at him and waves politely and then turns to hide behind her door while Charlotte comes barreling up the front path, careful to not trip over the mess that Slater has made with rakes, hoes and a hose line snaking around every which way.

"See you this afternoon, Slater. I'll let my mom know to expect you," Charlotte calls back over her shoulder. "Hi, Sibley," she says cheerily as Sibley grabs her by the wrist to yank her behind the door before she shuts it fast.

"Did you just invite Slater Hannigan over to your house? Why? What for?"

"I think my mom needs help sorting our garage. He says he does lots of neighbors' houses. Pretty smart, if you ask me. I bet he makes some good money, too, if he's doing two houses a day," Charlotte says, rattling off the highlights of what Slater shared with her.

"Ha! That's pretty funny," Sibley says hardly able to stifle a laugh.

"I don't get it. Why is that so funny?"

Sibley takes a moment in her head to decide which answer to give Charlotte. Does she keep Slater's little punishment to herself or does she share the story behind it with her best friend?

"Well, honestly, I just never knew Slater to like hard work and I was equally surprised when I found out he would be coming here for a few weekends."

There, that says it without having to lie to her new friend—or rat out her old friend.

Somehow, Slater Hannigan is going to come out ahead—again. After all the trouble he brought to Sibley, now he is going to get paid by Charlotte's family for a real job. It's so maddening to a girl like Sibley White who believes that troublemakers should be punished—justice must prevail. Oh, if she could only be a fly on the wall at the Everly District meeting in two days.

CHAPTER 9

Opportunities

After the span of three and a half hours at the Whites, Sibley's father is quite pleased with the progress Slater has made to the front yard. "My boy, you are a fast worker. I am truly impressed. I think next weekend we'll have you sprucing shutters and test your skills a bit with the paint brush, eh?" he says, chuckling. "How would you like to come with me 'round back to pull at some of the other weeds? They're everywhere."

"Sure," Slater says, picking up the hoe and making sure his gardening gloves are still in his back pocket.

The yard in front is nothing compared to the back. Here, the overgrown brush stands hip-high and runs the length of the entire property, which is so big the Whites could have room to put in a pool, plus park a few cars, and still keep their four apple trees.

Slater's mouth falls open. There is no way in a million Saturdays he will ever be able to tackle this alone. But, he doesn't say anything like this to Mr. White. "Okay, do you want me to start in any certain place?"

"You're not afraid of a little hard work, I see. This is a good quality to have, young man." Mr. White pats his back enthusiastically. "Start in the right corner, carving a path, then work your way up and down each aisle, like in the grocery store. You'll see a clearing in a couple of weeks."

He walks inside, leaving Slater there to muster his energy for tackling these wild overgrown crops of weeds, only wishing he had a machete with him instead of a hoe.

"Is it weird having Slater at your house?" Charlotte asks conspiratorially as she and Sibley spy from behind the yellow curtains of her second-story bedroom window.

"Kind of," Sibley says, not sure how much to say, pretending to be more interested in rearranging her crayons and markers in color-coded paint buckets on her craft table.

"Remind me, do we hate Slater, or do we think he's cool?" Charlotte is still catching up on all the friendship dynamics her new middle school friends have and is always so flummoxed when she is told the next day that the person she was happy to eat lunch with yesterday is no longer inside their circle.

Sibley doesn't mind that Charlotte has ingratiated herself with many different groups at school. Sibley knows she and Charlotte will always be best friends. Anyway, Sibley is perfectly happy spending a couple of her lunches alone in the library where she can get back to her books.

"Well, Slater is—hmmmm," she starts awkwardly taken a bit off guard. "Slater was always very popular in elementary school, but we weren't always friends," Sibley says, choosing her words carefully. "But now," she is sorting this out in her mind quickly for an answer that will satisfy Charlotte's curiosity, "I guess you could say he is not an enemy." That ought to do it.

"He's cuter than some of the other boys, right?" Charlotte says, stating a mere observation as simply as she might say *My, what a sweet ladybug.*

A bug is still a bug—even if it is cute—as far as Sibley is concerned.

"*Cute?* Uh, Charlotte, I can honestly say I've never paid much attention," she says nonchalantly, although she can feel where red splotches are appearing on her neck and the warmth from her cheeks turning pink.

Sibley White is a serious girl. She is focused on her studies and her social life is of very little concern to her. She will not be caught dead talking about boys even with her best friend—and especially not to discuss the degree of cuteness she thinks Slater Hannigan is. Or is not.

Before the weekend finishes, Slater has made the rounds to the Rigby household where Charlotte's mother is anxious for some real help since her older sons are involved in every sports team imaginable and rarely home for a meal, let alone a chore.

Slater has shored up his work schedule and fee. He took what he overheard some of the girls charge for babysitting rates, then doubled it. Mrs. Rigby didn't blink twice when she heard he would happily be put to work for $20 an hour. She wants to be able to park her car in a proper garage.

The rest of Saturday is spent finishing his own backyard before his dad gets home. Fortunately for him, Slater is scooping the last pile of leaf raking when his dad pulls into the driveway with Graham in tow from his sleepover, along with another head bobbing beside him in the backseat. Jason Hamigachi got permission to sleep over at Graham's tonight.

The two younger boys barrel out of the car, racing through the house to put Jason's bag upstairs in Graham's room. They scream all the way, wafts of boy sweat lingering through the entry as they charge back downstairs, tearing out through the kitchen door to continue their war games outside.

"Hi, guys!" Lynn greets them for all of two seconds as they land at the refrigerator to grab some cold drinks before clearing through the French doors. She greets her husband more slowly as she meets him at the front door and follows him into his office off the entryway. "How was the day? Are you getting caught up?"

"Let's face it, no matter how many hours I spend there, I am never going to feel caught up. But, we are making some good progress on this case. It's a big one. We've got Washington watching us and I have a feeling, if I nail this down and get it right, this could mean some opportunities for me down the road," Hank says while he pulls apart his briefcase at his desk and empties his pockets of loose change, wallet and cell phone.

"Opportunities, huh? That sounds interesting. What kind of opportunities?" she says with an inviting smile.

"Remember Chet Hurley from law school? I got a call from him today, just out of the blue. He said he's going to be in town next week and wondered if we could have dinner," Hank says with a sly smile crossing his face. "It's been, what, twelve years since we were junior attorneys together before he went to D.C.?" Hank strokes his face, rubbing his chin, remembering he skipped his shave this morning.

"What do you think he wants?"

"I guess if he wants anything, I'll find out next week. You can handle the night here alone, right? I think this one is no wives," he says sweetly.

"What, dinner here alone with these hooligans? Not my first time, sweetheart. Go off on your little date, then bring me home some good gossip," she teases.

"How'd Slater do today?"

"I think pretty well. By his account, he landed a real paying job for another neighbor. He said the work at the White's was hard, and that Mr. White let him into their backyard, which was completely overrun, even worse than the front. He's got his work cut out for him," Lynn says while following her husband upstairs.

"Where is he now?"

"Showering. He just finished raking the backyard for you. He's been working all day. I think we should get him something a little extra for his birthday tomorrow. What do you think?"

"We agreed this would be simple, Lynn. It's not been a year for earning extravagant gifts and rewards," Hank says firmly.

"I know, but maybe just a *little* something. What could we do?"

"I tell you what, if he is actually lining up work, I'll pull together a carpenter's box with some of the overflow tools I don't need anymore. It's about time he had his own set of hammers, nails, screwdrivers, tape measure, and levels. He'll love it; what kid wouldn't?"

"Um, a kid who wants a bike instead?"

"Yeah, we're not doing a bike right now, are we, Lynn?" He takes in her puppy dog eyes, the same ones the boys use every time they run out of legitimate reasons, resorting to begging. "Come on—that just says *'Hey, do whatever you want, bud, we don't believe in punishments around here'.*"

"I know, I know, Hank; I know we agreed. It's just that I feel so bad for him. He's the only one of his friends who doesn't have a bike yet."

"They all walk. Everywhere they go is walking distance. What are they going to do, ride their bike two houses away? I don't want to put together a bike tonight. Not this late; it's almost time for dinner."

"Yeah, in a couple hours, mister. In fact, what are you barbecuing?" she says hopefully, pouring on the charm.

"Okay, I'll barbecue, but not a bike. Not tonight, okay? Some other time, but not after all that's going on with him now."

"Well, can I show you something downstairs in the basement?"

"Oh, I am afraid to look," he says, knowing this is a losing argument. "Lynn, what's in the basement?"

"Just come and look," she says, grabbing his hand to drag him down two flights.

After tugging on the pull chain that illuminates the darkened basement by a single bulb, Hank can see a corner addition of something hiding beneath a sheet. It's either a piano or a bicycle.

"Ta-dah," Lynn says excitedly, quickly swirling the sheet. She wanted to get a jump on the special occasion shopping this year, so this is where she stores early Christmas presents she finds in February, and special gifts for good little boys. "When I saw it, I had no idea he would be getting into the kind of trouble he has been having; but Hank, we could use this as incentive for him to stay on the right track. We've already pulled everything else away from him; he has nothing else to lose."

"So, you're suggesting emotional bribery?"

"Well, emotional, yes, but also attached to a bike. Look how cool this is. It's got the custom fatigue war paint on the entire frame and those fat tires almost look like a motorcycle's. He's gonna love it, Hank," she says excitedly.

"Oh, he's gonna love it, all right. I just want to be sure we're not sending a mixed message here."

"And the best part is, you don't even have to put it together. The store did it for me since it was a custom order. Pretty cool, right?" she says, standing back to marvel at her husband's smile as he strokes the paint job and keeps nodding his head.

"Yep, it's a pretty good bike, Lynn. How long have you had this down here?"

"A couple of months. I got some great deals after the holidays."

"What else is down here?"

"Nothing you need to know about unless you want Father's Day ruined."

"Looking at this thing, you know what I'm thinking it needs?" Hank says completely inspired.

"What are you thinking it needs?" She smiles at her clever husband.

"If he's getting a carpenter's box to cart around his tools, he needs a place to strap them. There's no way he's going to want a basket on that masculine bike—even if we painted it black. I'm going to make him something custom to go along with his wooden toolbox. I'll be back in an hour, and when I finish this project, then I'll barbecue whatever you've got in the fridge." He kisses her on the cheek and sprints up the basement stairs to find Slater dashing down the entryway staircase, almost colliding into one another.

"Hey, Dad," Slater says with renewed energy and wet hair.

"Hey, sport, where you headed?"

"Want to see what I did to the backyard?"

"I sure do. Your mom tells me you've been working really hard today at the White's and that you managed to get a paying gig out of it," he says, tousling his son's hair.

"Yeah, this girl from school came to play with Sibley and she said her mom wanted help clearing out their garage. Sibley didn't tell her the real reason I was there, so I just told her I help lots of neighbors."

"That's pretty enterprising of you, son. That's the way it begins. Think of a good idea no one else has thought of yet and figure out a way to charge for it. If you can do that the rest of your life, you'll always have money."

"And then, I even hoed the White's backyard. It's going to take me forever, though," he says as he and his dad scramble through the hall leading to the kitchen where they head out to the backyard.

"Grah-ham!" Slater screams with surprise, taking in the view of his once neatly raked piles which have now all been completely demolished by Graham and his little friend Jason. "What did you do to all of my leaves?"

"What do you mean *your* leaves? They're the yard's leaves and the tree's leaves and we made 'em *our* leaves 'cause nobody else was playing with 'em," Graham says logically while he and Jason continue sumo wrestling in their nest.

"Da-aaaad, look at what he did! I had about eleven piles out here that took me all day long to rake," Slater says, moved to tears now. "He's ruined everything just like he always does. Mom saw my work; she'll tell you I did it all, just like you asked."

"Slater, *you* ruin everything, not *me*. I didn't do anything wrong. How was I supposed to know these piles weren't for playing? You weren't out here guarding them. You didn't even put up a sign or anything," Graham says, huffing and puffing and holding his own without a single tear dropping from his eyes this time. "Mo-oom, Slater says I ruined everything; tell him he should have been more careful about his leaves," Graham complains when he sees Lynn coming out to see what all the commotion is about.

"Oh, for heaven's sake, what a mess!" She eyes Slater and Graham, sensing a stand-off. She looks to Hank and decides to handle this one quickly herself so he can leave and get back home again to work on his special birthday surprise. "Okay boys, here's what we're going to do. I'm setting a timer for fifteen minutes. Slater, you use the big rake, Graham and Jason—aren't you lucky you picked the right night to sleepover, Jason?—you two push the leaf piles as high as you can using your arms. I'll go to the neighbor's to get a few more rakes and I'll even help you myself. We'll get these back into your eleven piles just like you had in no time, Slater."

With these new plans in place, Hank runs his errand and she runs next door to retrieve multiple rakes. The boys are productive with the first three minutes it takes for them to determine who is in charge of which section of the yard before Lynn is home again.

"Ice cream for anyone who finishes the most number of piles by himself," she shouts like a cheerleader.

"Wow, your mom lets you eat ice cream before dinner? My mom never lets me do that," Jason Hamigachi says, amazed.

"Only sometimes, but I love it when it happens, so I'm gonna rake the most piles and then I'll share my ice cream with you. Halfsies, okay?" Graham says sweetly.

"Yeah, and then if I win, I'll share mine with you." A deal has been happily struck. Slater doesn't care. He already did this work once today, so this time around he moves slowly—very, very slowly.

Compared to the first four piles these fourth-graders have proudly organized, Slater is still only halfway into his second one. In fact, his mother doesn't even hound him about his sluggish pace because she knows this really should have been Graham's job since he and Jason made the mess.

But, since Slater neglected to say anything to Graham about keeping the yard preserved, this will teach him to communicate his expectations in the future. *People can't read minds*. It's what she always says. This is when Graham always takes it as his cue to crawl into her lap, placing his tiny fingertips on the sides of her eyes, saying right back to her while staring into her face, as if he is trying a new mind-warping trick of his own, "But what if they *could?*"

Dad finishes tinkering in his garage, finding tools to fill Slater's carpenter's box. He then builds a custom wood crate using the rich, dark brown, walnut-stained wood left over from the bookshelf he made for Lynn's closet to showcase her shoes. The tiger-striped grain pattern makes this bike look even more fierce than the army fatigue paint.

The black nail heads he uses look better than regular silver ones and the leather strap he weaves in between the wooden slats makes the frame especially sturdy for hauling. When he affixes the crate to the black metal rest behind the bicycle seat and above the rim, he stands back to admire his work. The whole thing looks like a million bucks.

The entire family is done with their piles when Hank is ready to start barbecuing. Once Jason shares his ice cream with Graham, the family eats shish kabobs skewered with steak, shrimp, chicken and enormous mushrooms and bell pepper chunks.

After an overly taxing day, nobody can stay awake while the movie plays to a clump of Hannigans, plus one little guest, who are all dozing, huddled together across the couch with legs and arms spilling onto the floor, blankets falling loosely around them.

At midnight, Lynn pulls herself from a deep sleep, waking only her husband, allowing the kids to stay just as they are before morning comes again too soon.

CHAPTER 10

Happy Birthday to Me

Sunday morning usually means waffles in the Hannigan household, something Jason Hamigachi is very happy about. Lynn brings out a platter full of two dozen and lays out deep bowls of homemade whipped cream, sliced strawberries, blueberries, sliced bananas and hot syrup.

When the family has been fed and Jason is equally satisfied, Lynn passes off Slater's morning chores to Graham. "But, why do I have to do it all? Slater's supposed to clean the bathroom; that's his job," Graham protests with all of his fourth-grade might.

"Well, today is when we are celebrating Slater's birthday, so he gets to skip chores, and good brothers help each other out for birthdays, remember?" Lynn says calmly in a chipper voice.

"Your birthday's *today?*"

"Nah, it's actually on Wednesday, but Mom said we're celebrating tonight because Dad's got a big meeting. Right, Dad?"

"Right-o, kiddo. So, Graham, help your brother out today and maybe Jason wants to chip in, too," he says, smiling over at the boys from behind his newspaper.

Jason looks at Graham, calculating if he should turn this into a trade transaction, or just be a nice guy and help for free. "Okay, Mr. Hannigan. Graham, I'll help you. It'll go fast. I know how to clean all the toilets in my house in under ten minutes. I'll show you," Jason says, ready to race upstairs.

"Graham, don't forget, you've still got your own kitchen duty. Load the dishwasher and wipe the table and counters. I'll do the pans since you have a guest," Lynn says bracing herself for some whining.

"Okay, Mom. Come on, Jason, let's race. You do all the counters and I'll load, then we'll do the toilets your way and I'll wipe the sinks and mirrors. My parents clean their own bathroom so we just do this little bathroom beneath the staircase and the main one upstairs."

"Okay, ready, set, let's go, dude!" Jason says energetically.

They stampede through the kitchen, working as fast as busboys ever have in a restaurant on a busy Saturday night. They bus all the dishes into the kitchen, spray them with hot water and avoid the temptation to use that sink hose on each other.

After nearly ten minutes goes by, they are ready to tackle both bathrooms with Jason on toilet duty downstairs first, while Graham does his part upstairs before they trade.

They never had so much fun cleaning by themselves. Before a half hour goes by, they are completely done with the chore that would still be taking Slater much of the morning to complete. He hates cleaning bathrooms, so his plan is to always go slowly, hoping his mother's impatience will take over and she will finish the job herself, putting him out of his misery. She never does.

With Jason and Graham off to play at Sugar Ridge Park around the corner, Lynn begins baking Slater's favorite birthday cake—chocolate fudge, with whipped cream in between the layers and all around the outside, and finally, chocolate covered strawberries in mounds over the top. She puts it in the freezer with enough time to be sure it will become cold enough to slice into with a butcher knife after dinner.

Today, Slater gets to do whatever he wants, and what he wants to do is see his friends. So, while he is off with Tobey Peterson, Macaroni Maroney, and Chicky Cicarrelli, his parents can enjoy a kid-free home for another hour before Graham is due back.

"Honey, I'm going to pick up the balloons, and I still need items for the lasagna," Lynn says to her husband, who sits at his desk, looking up at her briefly from behind his computer.

"I'll be right here," he says, rubbing his eyes after removing his glasses.

"What are you working on?"

"Doing some research about Chet and the work he's doing in D.C."

"You can tell me all about it when I get home. Hey, Graham's due back no later than one o'clock; will you be sure to get him started on whatever he plans to give Slater tonight?"

"Yep, I've got a few ideas, if he needs the help."

"I can't believe you guys got busted," Tobey says in awe to Slater and Chicky at their secret meeting inside their gazebo hideout at Sugar Ridge Park. This is the first chance they have had to get together since Friday's escapades to see Phil in Everly.

"Yeah, we got a huge lecture from my parents on the drive back and now we have to meet with the superintendent and everybody tomorrow. It's pretty bad," Slater says, not knowing what to expect.

"Man, I told you guys I had a bad feeling about that plan," Macaroni says powerfully, like his special abilities to predict the future should be taken more seriously by his friends.

"Dude, the plan could have worked, except for stupid Marilyn who ratted us out," Chicky says, sure this was their only downfall.

"Yeah, Marilyn," Slater says, echoing Chicky's tone.

"Who's Marilyn?" Macaroni asks.

"Oh, some girl at EMGATS who's just like Sibley, super know-it-all. She got put in charge of class that day because there was a lame sub. I saw her through the train window and she had the attendance clipboard, just staring back at me like, *oooh, I'm gonna tell.* I begged her not to, but now look at us. They all thought we were trying to run away or something. Totally got blown out of proportion," Chicky said.

"Uh, dude, you went on a train, like, two hours away. Of course they're gonna think you were running away. That's a long ways away from home," Macaroni says, surprised he and Slater still don't get it.

"Hey, how is Phil, anyway? You never told us—what'd you guys do?" Tobey jumps in.

"Oh, yeah, that was the best part. He is still same old Phil. The campus looks a lot like Esther Bookman with only about eleven wings, pretty small for a middle school. He says he's making friends, but we didn't meet any that day because, of course, we had to hide out with him." Slater fills them in on Mr. Moore's apartment and the ice cream they got after they got caught by the police.

"Yeah, I will admit, that was kind of scary. I was half-asleep when some shadow crossed my face and when I opened my eyes, there was, like, this big cop just standing there. *Which one of you is Slater and which one is Chicky?"* Chicky says, imitating the officer all formal sounding.

"Yeah, I was pretty scared, too. I did not expect that," Slater agrees.

"Mrs. Hannigan said she was going to split me and Slater up, no more friendship, no more study time, but then my gramps almost died in the hospital, and so now we get a second chance." Chicky brings them up to speed on the rest of it.

"*Second* chance? Are you sure that's all you're up to?" Tobey says, grinning.

"Yeah, my mom's real nervous that if I keep hanging out with you two, I'm going to end up a juvenile delinquent," Macaroni says, smiling broadly. "Hysterical."

"Well, if you're still allowed to hang with me by the time summer rolls around," Slater says, laughing to himself, "how would you guys like to come on the adventure of a lifetime? I'm going to this survival camp in the woods that my mom signed me up for. You gotta ask your folks if you can go, too. There's no way I want to do this thing alone. Where's the fun in that?" Slater says, hoping desperately to convince them.

"Survival camp? What are we surviving? Being eaten alive by bears? No thank you, I like my legs," Macaroni says, leaning back to look at the sky with his arms folded behind his head.

"Seriously, what are you surviving? Macaroni's got a good point. I don't want to be running from bears, either," Tobey says nervously.

"As if. You guys are ridiculous. Like my mom would really sign me up for a camp where I have to run for my life, or be eaten alive." Slater stops to think about this for a minute. "Yeah, I don't think there's any way a camp like that exists for parents as a way to punish their kids," he says, still thinking this through hoping he's not wrong.

"You never know about your mom; she's pretty clever. What if she just happened to find the perfect way to teach you a lesson, once and for all?" Macaroni says, sounding more like *his* mother.

"Very funny, Macaroni. My mom says there's this super long hike, like sixty miles, and you learn to eat berries from trees and stuff. You go with a whole lot of other kids from all around and it'd be so much cooler if you guys were there. Think of the things we could do to scare them and stuff," he continues, enticing his group until they all come up with their own pranks to play.

"Okay, I'll ask my mom," Tobey says, imagining the hijinks they could all have together.

"I will, too," Macaroni agrees.

"I gotta see what my grandma says with my gramps getting out of the hospital, but she will probably say okay," Chicky says hopefully.

"Hey, what's the name of this camp, anyway?" Tobey asks.

"Surviving Elmer Woods," Slater says slowly for dramatic effect.

While Graham blows through the front door just when he is expected, his dad whistles at him from inside his office. "Slow down, kiddo, and come see me for a minute."

"Hi, Dad, whatchya doing?" Graham says energetically.

"Just working on a few files for some big meetings I've got this week," Hank says, wrapping his arms around his youngest who is getting to be just a little too big to squeeze onto his father's lap the way he is wriggling himself now.

"Hey, Dad, am I supposed to get Slater a gift for tonight, or for

Wednesday, his real birthday?" he asks nonchalantly while putting his father's glasses on his own face, making his eyesight go all blurry. "Ouch, I'm blind," Graham says while poking around in his father's face with his eyes squinted shut.

"Oh, you're pretty funny, little man," his dad says, tickling him the way he hates until Graham is practically falling off Hank's lap.

"I give up, I give up," Graham says in his high-pitched squeal with his voice breaking between his words while he catches his breath from laughing so hard.

"Okay, there you go," Hank says, putting him onto the floor where he can collect himself. "As far as your brother's gift, do you have anything special in mind, or do you want some help from Dad?"

Finally able to breathe normally again, Graham says with a huge grin, "I know what he will really like from me is a coupon book to get out of doing his chores. But, what else do you have that's special?"

"Oh, you are right about that, he'd love to be getting out of all of his chores. That's a good idea, son. If you want a second gift to go with it, I have something right here in this drawer I wonder if you'd like to wrap for Slater."

Graham's eyes grow bigger as he shuffles on his knees, scurrying over to his dad's desk to see what is coming from its drawer contents. "Open it," Hank says, handing Graham a very small mahogany wooden box with its lid still closed.

Graham holds the object in the palm of his hand, easily prying the top of the lid open to reveal a compass that looks to be a hundred years old. "Dad," Graham gasps because it looks so ancient, like something Indiana Jones would use, "what does it do?"

"It's a compass, just like Lewis and Clark used in their exploration. It's got the same old-fashioned dial and face; it's even engraved with Slater's initials. This way, when he is camping or if he ever gets lost, he can find his way back," Hank says softly.

"This is way better than my coupon book, Dad. Maybe this should be *your* gift. He's gonna really like it," Graham says selflessly.

"Oh, bud, believe me, he's going to love your coupon book and we both know he'll use it. But, Mom and I already have a gift for him, so this compass can be from you. Will you wrap this and make a nice card for him? Maybe tell him a couple things you like about him?" Hank says, coaxing his sweet son to think about his brother differently than he usually does when Slater is going at him.

After second helpings of lasagna, and Caesar salad with his favorite homemade croutons, the family retreats to the living room where Slater awaits his gifts.

"Okay, who wants to go first? I'll take everything you've got," he says greedily, half-joking.

"Now, Slater, you remember that we weren't going to go overboard, right? It's been some year for you and I just hope we don't have another one like it—okay, mister?"

"Yeah, yeah, I know, Mom. Now where's my present? I know you got me one. Where'd you hide it?"

Even his parents can hardly stand the suspense any longer. "All right, but you have to close your eyes. Graham, will you please do the honors?"

"Okay, Mom, I know what to do," Graham says, happily leaping up from his place on the couch and going to stand behind Slater, wrapping his hands around Slater's head.

"Don't gouge out my eyes this time, Graham," Slater says, fake acting like he's annoyed, even though they can all feel the adrenaline in the air, anticipating Slater's first big gift.

"No peekies, Slater," Graham says, his sweaty little hands holding firm in place.

Dad quietly carries up the bicycle from the basement with the sheet still over it for Slater to whip off himself.

As soon as he sets it down in front of the fireplace, Mom yells, "Ta-dah!"

"Whoa! Is that what I think it is?"

Graham's grunts of equal excitement make it almost sound like this is *his* birthday, too. "Pull it off! I want to see!" he shouts repeatedly.

"Oh, what's it gonna be? Blue? Maybe red? No, I bet it's black, or chrome," Slater guesses as he walks slowly around the bike, feeling the frame beneath the sheet.

Frrrrrpppp! He rips the sheet away—and a gale of wind bursts from his lungs as he screams louder than he has in a long time.

"No way! It's awesome! How'd you get army fatigue color? Check it out!" Slater touches every part of his bike from the seat leather to the spokes in metallic green. "The crate is so awesome! Thanks, Dad! Thanks, Mom!" he says, not believing his good luck.

"Well, we know you've been wanting one for a while now," Lynn says first.

Hank chimes in, "And it seems like this might be the right time now that you are starting to get neighborhood jobs more than a few blocks away. Say, why don't you open up gift number two?"

"I don't know what could possibly be better than this, but I can't wait to find out!" He tears apart the army fatigue wrapping paper Lynn found to go along with the bike theme. "Wow! My very own tool set! I can tell I'm gonna be using these a lot real soon. Check out this box," he says, excitedly rubbing his hand across the wooden exterior. "Hey, no splinters."

"Son, that's what they call a carpenter's box. I made it for you and pulled together a starter set with some of the tools I bought when I first began doing fixer-upper projects for Grandpa when I was just a little older than you are now," Hank says with pride at Slater's reaction. "In fact, that is real pine wood stained in a dark walnut finish to match your hauling crate. I customized them so the toolbox could easily fit within the crate's frame. This way you don't have to worry about carting heavy tools around and walking wherever you need to go."

"It's the best!" He lunges toward his father, giving him a big hug and latching onto his mom to thank her for knowing what the best paint color would be.

"But, wait. There's more. You should see what your brother has for you. Graham, are you ready to present gift number three?"

"Yeah, Dad," Graham says, taking the lead from his father to ham it up a bit. "Here it is, the one you've been waiting for, not available in stores, never to be found again, the one and only *Graham Hannigan's Coupon Book for Doin' Stuff.*" He hands Slater a stapled packet of colored papers with some jagged edges since his safety scissors don't always cut the best on thick cardstock.

"Cool, brother," Slater says, carefully flipping through the pages, being sure to read each one so he doesn't miss a thing.

The first page is the dedication page that reads *To Slater Hannigan from Graham Hannigan, your brother. Happy birthday. You are the best big brother in the world, except for when you're being mean to me. But because it's your birthday, I forgive you. Ha, ha. Love, your brother forever, Graham Hannigan.*

"Hey, thanks, Graham," Slater says, looking over at Graham eagerly sitting on the couch with his chin propped up on his two fists, waiting to see Slater's expression when he reads all his coupons. "Now, let me see what I've got here. Hmmm, one for doing dishes—nice. I'll be using that when Mom makes her messiest meal. Mom, when are you making spaghetti again?" They all laugh easily at this one.

"Not this week, so you're saved, Graham," she smiles broadly.

"I've got a coupon for the bathroom, oh wait, *three* coupons for that chore, that's pretty good, Graham. And, I've got a coupon for staying out of my hair for two hours when your friends are over. I could've used that this weekend." He smiles at Graham. "And I've got two more coupons for making my bed, two for letting me have the remote, and one for being my servant for one whole day. Now *that* sounds familiar," Slater nudges his brother, remembering how Graham made Slater be his servant at his last birthday party in front of all Graham's friends. It was humiliating, but unavoidable. "Thanks, squirt. I like your gift a lot. And don't be mad when I start using it this week," Slater says, tossing a pillow across the room.

"Oh, I won't be mad, I promise. And, Slater, I have one more thing for you to open that's even better than my coupon book." Graham slides his brother the box wrapped in flowered paper with real flowers pasted on top. "Spring is for flowers and your birthday is in the spring, so I picked this paper for your gift," Graham says logically.

"Okay, well, I can't wait to see what's inside," Slater says, tugging at the tape and carefully removing the flowers.

"Hurry, hurry! You're gonna love it!" Graham says, eagerly encouraging his brother.

Slater holds the wooden box in his hands, propping up the lid. He has the same reaction to this gift that Graham did hours earlier. "Wow, a real compass! No way, Graham!"

"I know, it's just like the one Lewis and Clark used on their expedition," Graham says, practicing the words his dad coached him to say. "It has the original numeric etching on its dial face and comes with an aged bronzed needle," Graham finishes, proudly not forgetting any of the details.

"Hey, it's even got my name engraved, too! This is so totally cool! I bet I'll be able to use it a lot at my survival camp," Slater says nonchalantly, remaining completely transfixed on the needle, trying to manipulate it to move as he holds it up to the ceiling and shifts his positions.

His parents caught the remark but make no acknowledgement of Slater's agreeableness to the plan he was so angrily opposed to yesterday. "I think that'll work better if you hold it up to the sun, but you've got the right idea," Hank says happily.

"Who's ready for birthday cake?" Lynn says as she jumps from her seat and swirls about in the kitchen, placing twelve candles into the frozen layer of whipped cream. She returns with a lit cake that flickers when she walks. "Happy birthday to you, happy birthday to you," she begins alone until Hank and Graham join in.

"Now, make a wish, son," Hank says while his mother quickly reminds them about what has always been birthday tradition in the Hannigan household. "And don't forget, everybody else is going to make a wish for you, too. Ready everyone? On three. One, two, three." As Slater blows out his candles, he squeezes his eyes shut real tight thinking of a really good one this year, since last year's wish still hasn't come true.

I want to be famous.

His father concentrates on the very principle Slater still needs to master in order to become loyal and disciplined and successful.

Help him find his true north.

His mother shares her secret anxiety that keeps her up at night, even though she knows he is sleeping soundly in the next room.

Keep him out of harm's way.

His fourth-grade brother wishes the same thing every year.

Make him be nicer to me.

Once the night's excitement has worn down, and the boys have been tucked in bed without too much complaint, Lynn peeks in on Slater who should be fast asleep by now.

"I love you, sweet dreams," she whispers from the doorway astonished to hear a soft reply.

"Thanks for my birthday, Mom," he says sweetly.

She creeps in to sit at his bedside while he lets her pat his head this time. "Did you get everything you wanted, darling?"

"Almost," he says, dangling the one thing he has been waiting for even longer than a bike.

"What could a lucky little boy like you possibly still want?"

"My door put back on the hinges," he says, smiling.

CHAPTER 11

The Everly Way

The last words Slater's mother said to him before he walked out the door were, "Remember, change of plans. I am picking you up at EMGATS—we will walk together to the district office. See you at 3:30 p.m. Got it?"

Monday is uncomfortable for Chicky and Slater. Yes, the weather is sticky, and the spring winds have turned wild, whipping at their faces on their trudge to meet at EMGATS—but everyone knows, a real tornado can change its course in an instant, sparing the destruction of those once in its path. Marilyn Washington is not as forgiving.

She arrives at school early so she can sit on the curb to wait for Chicky to set one foot onto this campus. *Chicky and his stupid sidekick, Slaaaa-ter,* she thinks to herself. All weekend long, she has done nothing but brood. They made her look bad in front of Mr. Pastorino and, even worse, Chicky had the nerve to ask her to lie for him. *Who does he think he is?* She keeps on with the conversation that's been stirring in her mind for the past twenty minutes—*my* boyfriend, *or something? Well, I don't need no boyfriend like that, I'll sure tell you, Miss Mary-lynn.*

When she gets steaming mad, her brothers can always tell because she starts talking to herself, saying her name out loud, over-pronouncing syllables the same way her grandmother does. She has always prided herself on being a girl of strong character, so it hurts her heart to know that for one slow moment, she went weak for Chicky when he begged for her silence. *Maybe just this one time.* It was the only fleeting thought she had watching Chicky on that train.

Look where that got you, Miss Mary-lynn. The scolding she gives herself is quickly interrupted when the papers loosely deposited within her open bag are tugged by the wind, flying everywhere now. They dance along the curb and scale the building, adhering to the glass like dead bugs splayed against the car's windshield.

"Aaaack," Marilyn says, rushing from the curb to chase her important papers.

"Looking for these?" Chicky Cicarrelli says, holding the ones that blew across the street.

She can't help but smile at him. "Yeah, thanks." She extends her hand before he withdraws them from her reach.

"Tell me why I shouldn't just tear these up, Marilyn. You got me in so much trouble. You told, didn't you?"

"Chicky, give me back my papers," she says, grabbing for them before he can hide them behind his back.

"Why'd you do it? Why'd you have to go and rat on me?" He says it so harshly, like she's supposed to be intimidated. Boy, did he pick the wrong girl.

"Look, you've got some nerve, Chickeeeee. What made you think I should be the one doing any favors for you and that new kid, Slater? Huh?" Her words spew forth, her finger wagging and pointing in his face like she's conducting an orchestra. "What gives you the right? Expecting me to put myself on the line, ruining *my* reputation with the teacher for *you?*" She doesn't let up there and with every inch she moves forward, Chicky is taking a step backward. "Who are you to me, anyway? We're not ferrrr-ennnnnds. We don't eeeee-ven have lunch together. You don't do homework with me. It's not like you eeeee-ven know anything about me, Chick-eeee. So, go ahead and be mad, you big baby. You should be mad—at *yourself*—and your stupid friend."

With that tongue-lashing, Marilyn turns abruptly on her heels grateful she did not wear a skirt today, saving her the embarrassment from the wind blowing it up. She charges over to her bag, partially spilling along the curb, where she stuffs the rest of her papers inside.

Chicky stands there, flummoxed. He hasn't the slightest clue what just happened. She steamrolled him, and he didn't even see it coming.

"Hey, dude, what're you looking at?" Slater asks, coming upon Chicky after having caught only the last bit of their encounter on his approach from across the street.

"I have no idea," Chicky says, shaking his head.

"It's too bad we live in tornado country. If we were east, there'd be a name for the battering you just got. They'd call it Hurricane Marilyn," he says, slapping the back of Chicky's shoulders as they both chuckle.

"Whatever, man. Let's just go. We gotta deal with Mr. Pastorino. It's gonna be so awkward in class. What do you think? Should we just go see if he's in his room right now?"

"You mean to kind of get it over with before we go to that meeting this afternoon?" Slater has been wondering the same thing to himself. "Yeah, all right, I'll go. It's better than waiting out here for a branch to fall on me," Slater says, jokingly. He is on a roll today.

"Dude, you gotta be serious or else he's not gonna let us off the hook. We need, like, an advocate for us, you know?" Chicky has obviously had a very serious weekend talk about his future with his grandmother and gramps, now home from the hospital.

"An *advocate?* What are you even talking about?"

"It's like, you know, someone who will stick up for you and say *yeah, he messed up but he's really a good guy,*" Chicky explains.

"Dude, I don't even think Pastorino is gonna want to say that we're good guys when he's probably in so much trouble."

"Well, my grandma said I have to start making friends with my teachers, letting them know I'm serious about my future and asking for their help. I gotta do it," Chicky says, wiping his palms on the front of his jeans anxiously. "I promised."

Chicky's guilt is what's eating away at him. The thought of losing his gramps and then finding out he *wasn't* going to die has had a major impact. He hated hearing his grandma tell his gramps that he left a school field trip to take the train two hours away. His gramps could hardly believe it; he just kept shaking his head.

Chicky doesn't want to disappoint either one of them.

"Okay, I get it. Let's go, then," Slater says, suddenly serious.

Knock, knock. The soft rapping outside the wall of the opened door is a show of respect to Mr. Pastorino, whose concentration is deeply buried within his computer screen.

"Boys, this is a surprise. I thought you might be hiding behind your hoodies all day until our little meeting this afternoon," he says chidingly, taking a hot sip of coffee from his Number One Teacher mug.

"Hey, Mr. P., we wanted to say we're sorry about Friday's field trip," Chicky begins.

"Yeah, we just did it because we had a friend who moved away and we were worried about him and stuff," Slater continues.

"We weren't running away. And we didn't mean to make you look bad. I guess we didn't think about that part—of you getting in trouble because of us," Chicky says sincerely.

"We were wondering if you could be our advocate," Slater rushes, stealing Chicky's line.

"You want *me* to be *your* advocate? I think you've picked the wrong day to ask, boys. I am being reviewed this year and losing kids on a field trip does not look very good for a teacher. I'm hoping I don't lose my job over this smooth move of yours."

"Gee, Mr. P., I had no idea. We're gonna explain everything at the meeting, we swear," Chicky says, thinking of new ways to get his teacher out of hot water.

"Advocates are people willing to put their necks on the chopping block for someone else. *My* neck is *already* on the chopping block, so I don't think I'm in the strongest position to help you boys out. Sorry," he says, taking another long swig of coffee, not caring that his throat is burning. "I'm also sorry to tell you that I am referring you to the office, where you will spend class time reading and researching what you should have been learning at the Gods Exhibit. I've already filled out your detention forms, so I won't see you until this afternoon's meeting," he says, handing them each their own copy as he salutes them, signaling it's time for them to go.

"Detention?" Chicky says, the gravity of what the day will hold is quickly sinking in for them both.

"Uh, and, boys, don't even think about ditching today because the office already has your assignment and knows to expect you at the beginning of first period," he finishes flatly.

The boys turn away somberly. "Well, there goes that advocate. So much for my future," Chicky sneers out of earshot from Mr. Pastorino's room. "And anyway, Slater, *that* plan was my whole idea. You didn't have to just go and spill it like that. I shoulda been the one to introduce it," Chicky finishes, taking his anger out on his only friend.

"Yeah, I got a little carried away. It sounded like it'd be a sure thing. I just thought he'd say yes," Slater says quietly, his way of making an apology.

"Better go sit in the office and wait for the first bell, I suppose." Chicky starts walking while Slater keeps step with his strides.

On their way down the outdoor ramp, corridors are sandwiched between paths of bushes and trees. Leaves are stirring, engulfed in madly swirling circles spinning every which way without ever touching down. At once, Slater's ball cap is yanked from his head with a torrent of air that blows it straight into the rushing puddle of water overflowing from the boys' bathroom. "Man, this day sucks already."

This day is only going to go downhill from here.

Amanda Hiller is standing at the front desk awaiting their arrival after Mr. Pastorino's heads-up. There is no time for Slater and Chicky to take a seat in the lobby; Ms. Hiller sees to that. "Good morning, boys. I have your assignments waiting in study carrels," she says, escorting Chicky to one desk with three high-sided walls attached for privacy. She points to another at the opposite end of the Restitution Room for Slater.

Slater takes this as his cue to move along.

"Slater, before you get settled over there, let me start by saying to you both while we have this quiet minute alone that you have caused the EMGATS school a great deal of embarrassment. I want you to know that I understand middle school is for making mistakes, but your safety is our number one priority. Not only did you put yourselves in a high-risk situation, but you jeopardized our school's reputation, along with our district's reputation, and certainly the trust that every adult has placed in you to follow the Everly Way—up until now. So, this is what it's going to come down to: how sorry are you? I don't want to hear it in words. I hope to feel it from you this afternoon."

"We know we messed up," Chicky says, undoubtedly sincere.

"I know you don't want to hear the words, but I'm sorry. I just didn't think—" Slater attempts.

"No, you didn't think. What you did was really scary for us. We were worried sick about if we would find you, what kind of condition we would find you in—you have no idea the kind of horrible thoughts that race through an adult's mind when a child goes missing. There are strangers out there waiting for some foolish kid to walk right into their trap."

"Okay, I know, I said it, I'm sorry," Slater says, his bottom lip quivering awkwardly when he sees that Amanda Hiller has real tears welling in her eyes.

"Chicky, you're big. People are going to expect you to be a lot older than your age. This is going to mean one of two things: *act* like them or *think* like them. Don't put yourself in vulnerable positions where you can be taken advantage. Do you know what I mean?"

"Yeah, I know some kids who did some bad stuff at my old school.

They hung out with high school kids 'cause, like, they didn't have any family around, really."

"That's what I'm trying to say here; don't be a target. Don't put yourself where trouble is going to come looking for you because if you are in the wrong place at the wrong time, I promise you, trouble will always find you, Chicky. This goes for you, too, Slater. Stay on the right path," she finishes before dismissing Slater to his carrel. "Remember, you are here to work silently. The intercom is on. If you need anything, just ask. We're listening."

She steps away from the room knowing that both secretaries will keep one eye on them through the two-way mirror. Students are always forewarned this convenience allows for administrators and staff to check on students at any time without being a constant disruption to them—the *students,* not the administrators and staff.

Two hours pass by slowly. Marilyn and Mr. Pastorino carry on in class as though there is no tension between them, even though they both know he is in this pickle partially because she failed to immediately report to him what she already knew.

Before the recess bell rings, he stands at the door to say good-bye to his students and to wish them a wonderful Monday ahead until Marilyn approaches slowly. "Let's talk," he initiates somberly.

She is utterly devastated that her entire relationship with her mentor has been forever ruined and says as much in a flurry of words, followed by a rush of tears.

"I was wrong and I knew I was wrong. But as soon as I tried to make it right—well, you know the rest. I'm really sorry, Mr. Pastorino. You are the last person I thought might get into trouble. I can't figure out what to do to make any of this go away," Marilyn says, resigned to cry a bit more. "I just don't want you to think any less of me as your student."

"Go on, get it out. Sometimes, it feels worse if you try to lock it all inside," Mr. Pastorino says, reaching for the tissue box on the sink counter by the front door. As her sniveling subsides, she smiles uneasily as if to express her embarrassment.

"Feel better a little bit?" he asks genuinely. After she nods and dries her face with the wadded tissue in her hand, she takes a deep breath like her mother has always taught her to do.

"Marilyn, as disappointed as I was on Friday, it's not so much that I was angry with you; it's more about the situation. You're eleven. I don't expect you to be in charge of fixing things. Believe me, I thought about what else I could have done differently all weekend, too," he chuckles lightly, wishing he had something golden to offer.

He folds his arms and leans back against the sink.

"All I can say is, you don't have to feel guilty about anything; I know it's tempting when your friends want you to do something that goes against what you know to be right. It's called peer pressure. We all want to be liked, so I get that. I just don't want you to ever feel that I think any less of you."

Marilyn stands up taller now, a fuller smile beginning to surface. "Certainly, you have been one of my most promising students. You're one of the few who actually wants to know what I know, and I appreciate that a lot. So, believe me, I'm always going to be in Marilyn Washington's corner," he finishes as the warning bell signals that recess is coming to an end. "Looks like you better get going; have a great day," he says warmly.

"Mr. Pastorino, you're the best teacher I've ever had." She jumps in for a spontaneous bear hug and pulls away just as quickly so she won't be late to her next class.

Marilyn Washington knows how to get an advocate—a sincere approach always works.

Slater and Chicky fret their lunch away, commiserating over their awful start to the day and dreading its ending even more. "So, what do you think is the worst that's gonna happen to us?" Slater asks, knowing Chicky has had more experience in this area.

"Probably they're gonna suspend us. Gotta make sure no other kids get the same idea," Chicky says between bites of his turkey sandwich like it's no big deal.

"Like, for how long do you think?" Slater worries.

"Depends on how bad they think we are, I guess. Maybe they

even decide to kick us out of school. Or maybe they do something worse," Chicky says, not really having a clue.

As their nerves jangle all afternoon, so do the phones when the front office rings each classroom to call the boys down separately. Chicky is the first to be dismissed for his private meeting with Mr. Pastorino, *his* administrators—both of them—along with his grandparents, and the superintendent, Mrs. Delcia DeMarco-Bradley. Her office is even bigger than the principal's, even from when he was at Everly Middle Grade, and for sure bigger than anything he ever saw in elementary school. There are two leather sofas, the kind that have a lot of little buttons sewn into their seat back. They make a funny sound when the weight of a person squishes into them, like a crunching.

Mrs. DeMarco-Bradley says she doesn't like conference tables because they are too formal. "Let's sit here together, where we can be comfortable."

It looks like a fancy living room with lots of dining room chairs pulled up near the couches. She invites everyone to take a seat. She even offers sliced fruit on a platter and brownies cut into small squares.

"In case anybody's hungry, please help yourselves." After she shakes Carlo and Fiorella Cicarrelli's hands and thanks them for their time to come in today, she looks to Chicky. "How are you doing today, Chicky? I imagine you've been preoccupied about this meeting all weekend." She doesn't repeat the *actual* words from the conversation held with his grandmother earlier—she wants to create a compassionate environment.

"Um, I had an okay weekend, not that great, but my gramps got to come home from the hospital, so that was really good," Chicky says, rattling off some details she might not know.

"Yes, your grandmother shared that with me. I'm so happy for your whole family that everything is better now," she says, keeping her gaze intently on him.

He looks down at the top of his thumb, which he rubs nervously, hoping this will take his mind off what is about to come.

"Chicky, we're here to talk about what happened on Friday's field trip. For starters, I want to know from your point of view why you wanted to go to Pinehurst and how you planned to make that happen," she says calmly, never raising her voice, never taking her eyes off him.

"Well, me and my friend—" He is cut off directly.

"Chicky, I'm going to ask that you look me in the eyes when you speak. Can you do that? I just want to know your version and I want you to tell me to my face what happened, okay?"

"Yes, ma'am. Well, like I was saying, we were all excited to go to the Gods Exhibit but when we found out the train taking us there ended in Pinehurst, well, we got even more excited thinking about an old friend who moved there over the winter break and we just thought, like, maybe we should go see him. Maybe nobody would miss us and then we'd come straight back before school ended. Swear," he says, keeping his eyes locked with hers.

"Have you ever been on a long train ride before?"

"Sometimes, when I was littler, with my grandma."

"So, you knew that someone would expect you to have a ticket?"

"Uh, yeah, I told my friend he better buy them and that I'd pay him back for my share as soon as I could 'cause, like, I didn't have my money together," Chicky says, his eyes darting toward his hands again.

"Do you understand why the school and your grandparents were so afraid when we found out you were missing? What do you think we were all worried about most?" She applies pressure, gently.

"Uh, I guess, you thought, like, maybe we were running away, or, like, someone was gonna steal us off the train, but I thought we were pretty safe. I knew we weren't gonna be hanging out in town where we could get lost, and I knew Phil's school was real close, so I knew we probably wouldn't get hit by a car or anything just crossing the street."

"Okay, so you have a pretty good understanding of everything we feared, except you forgot to add that sometimes trains get in accidents, too. Then how would we know where you were, or if you were okay? You knew right from wrong and chose to do wrong anyway. You planned this in advance, so it was not spur of the moment, and you put the reputation of our school's good name in jeopardy, not to mention the reputation of these fine folks. Chicky, do you have anything to say to your teacher and to your administrators here?"

"Yeah, I feel pretty bad today, Mr. P. I'm sorry I lost your trust and that I made you look bad at the school. I swear I wasn't thinking that this would come back on you. And I'm sorry, Ms. Hiller and Ms. Templeton. I didn't mean to make you worry or get in any trouble for my actions. I'm sure you're gonna punish me and I won't give you any more trouble," he says, practicing an awkward stare, looking into their faces for as long as he can stand it before he has to look away.

"And what do you have to say to your grandparents?"

"Nonna, Gramps," he says, choking on his last word, breaking his composure with sobs he cannot stifle, hard as he may try.

His grandfather leans in, wrapping his weathered hand around Chicky's shoulder. "Chicky, we don't know why you don't want to be a nice boy. You can't keep a doin' the things that you been doin'. You've got to be a man now, Chicky. You've got to be the man for your Nonna if anything ever happens to me. Right? You understand now, Chicky?"

Chicky keeps silently nodding his head while hiding his face with his arm.

There is not a single dry eye in the room.

After two more long minutes of Chicky saying his apologies to his Nonna, it's over. Nearly.

"Chicky, the Everly Way is not for me to assign your punishment but for you to discover the reasons why your behavior was so hurtful to others and possibly to yourself. If you are in agreement, we have a Peer Review set up for you tomorrow morning when you will meet with a panel of eighth graders who are seen as leaders at Everly Middle Grade. It is between you and them to determine your punishment. Some of them have experienced trouble in their own histories and might feel open to sharing some personal insight with you. At the end, they are going to pledge to be your mentors. How does that sound?"

"What, like they're gonna be my new friends?"

"In a way. But they will be more than a friend because they are going to advocate for you. Their goal is to find ways to involve you in positive school experiences. Sometimes, friends have fights that ruin a friendship. These leaders have been trained to strategize with you so that you can have some real opportunities when you leave middle school. Are you agreeable to this arrangement?"

"Sounds okay to me," Chicky says, looking over at his grandparents who are both eagerly nodding their heads.

"Thank you, you're a kind lady," Fiorella Cicarrelli says to Mrs. Delcia DeMarco-Bradley before turning to the rest of the adults. "Thank you to all of Chicky's leaders; you're such a nice people." She reaches for Mr. Pastorino's hand and holds it up to her cheek as her signature way of thanking him for being Chicky's teacher. "I'm sorry he caused so much a trouble for you."

"Well, thank goodness everybody is *safe*," Mr. Pastorino says, eyeing his administrators and superintendent, hoping that his job will be too.

Once Chicky says good-bye to his grandparents, he is returned to his tutorial session in progress, while the secretaries prepare for the Hannigans to arrive.

CHAPTER 12

Father Warrior

"Mrs. DeMarco-Bradley, do you want me to sit in on the meeting to take notes?"

"I do. We will be forwarding them to our legal department in the morning, so be sure that they are ready and accurate."

Helena Price is always accurate. Her previous work experience as a court reporter has served her well in her role as administrative assistant to the superintendent. She often finds herself asked to sit in on sensitive meetings just so all in attendance have a record of what exactly occurred, therefore nobody can argue from faulty memory. Mrs. Price still applies the two rules of practice she learned from her years in the courtroom: *one*, never breathe a word of what is said during the trial; *two*, don't let fingernails grow so long their sound makes a distracting clickety-clack across the keyboards. Her professionalism and quiet nature are part of why the superintendent personally handpicked Helena Price to be her administrative assistant.

There is hardly any time to discuss the impressions from Chicky's meeting ending a few minutes earlier because a loud baritone voice can be heard from the front lobby. "Hank Hannigan, and this is my wife, Lynn. We're the parents of Slater Hannigan in for a meeting with Mrs. DeMarco-Bradley." He states it so assuredly, looking every bit the part in his formal legal suit of dark navy blue pinstripe.

Even the other secretary stirs more awake now, her nerves on edge, a bit rattled by his volume. "Sir," Marion Weatherbee says in a very low voice, trying to model for her guest the comfortable speaking tone expected in the district office, "you and your wife may have a seat over there and we will bring you back shortly."

"Are they running late today?" He continues in his commanding boom, deliberately not taking her hint.

"I'm sorry, if I could just ask you to lower your voice a little—"

"You want me to use my library voice?" he asks conspiratorially, giving her a little smile. "I'm much more comfortable with my courtroom voice."

She is confused. *Was that a smirk?*

Fortunately, Helena Price whisks them away. "Mr. Hannigan, Mrs. Hannigan, thank you for waiting," she says formally, escorting the guests to the back office where Chicky's family slipped away from through a separate visitor's door minutes ago.

"Mrs. De-Marco-Bradley, the Hannigans are here to see you,"

Helena Price says, before quietly taking her seat where she will type copious notes about every word uttered from this point forward.

The superintendent reaches her hand out to greet Lynn Hannigan first. "Happy to meet you," before turning to the husband, "thanks for coming in today—"

"Where else *should* I be?" Mr. Hannigan asks seriously, as if he needs to make clear that his obligation is to protect his child, even if that means he needs to miss work.

The atmosphere in the air has turned frosty. How this will be conveyed in Ms. Price's report is still unclear since she is only to write what is *spoken*, not create impressions about the mood between parties attending this meeting.

"Let's get started, shall we? We'll be inviting Slater to join us in just a few moments, but I'd like for us to talk privately first. Are there any concerns you have that you want to share now?" Mrs. DeMarco-Bradley is seated in her wingback chair with her legs crossed and her hands collected at her side. She is patient. She is laser sharp in reading the room and preparing for some tension. The EMGATS team of administrators is seated on one couch with Mr. Pastorino, while they face the Hannigans across from them on the second leather sofa.

"First of all, I want to know how soon you can change Slater's schedule to move him away from classes he has together with Chicky. Then, I want to know why the teachers took far too long to figure out that my child was missing. Finally, I want an apology to my son for overlooking him. How do you think that makes a young boy feel when he is not noticed by *anyone* for hours?" Lynn has begun to throw darts, aiming for her target—the preservation of the Hannigan family reputation.

Mr. Pastorino's is the first jaw to drop. He can hardly believe what he is hearing. *Slater sneaks off and I am made to apologize?*

"Why don't we establish what we know?" The Superintendent speaks calmly, her voice as buttery as a Disney villain, before her poison apple is refused, unleashing a terror within. "Slater pre-purchased two round-trip tickets on Thursday to Pinehurst from Clifton. We know Slater initiated the calls to Phillip Moore in Pinehurst because Mr. Moore was kind enough to share the message thread. He wants to be of help," she adds, hoping this does not raise either one of the Hannigan's tempers. "Do you agree to these facts?"

"Oh, we are very aware," Mr. Hannigan speaks firmly. "May I ask what the school's policy is toward reprimanding teachers who are not equipped to be chaperoning minor children?"

He and Lynn switch off playing offense for their Hannigan team.

"Mr. Hannigan, one of the teachers was absent on the day of the field trip, so we had a substitute filling in. We met our legal obligation to keep children safe by providing one credentialed teacher to each class. I don't think anyone expected the events to unfold as they did, and speaking as a parent myself, I can only imagine the worry you both felt. You are right to have concerns over supervision. I think we would be willing to *review* our student-to-teacher ratio on field trips to prevent something like this from happening in the future. Perhaps if we had more involved parents like you, we could count on more volunteer chaperones," she says. Her sentiment is full of the right words, but something about her sickly sweet manner seems insincere.

"Let's talk about our approach for Slater. He will be made accountable in a peer review panel tomorrow morning. This is the Everly way," Assistant Vice-Principal Amanda Hiller says as warmly as she can, knowing full well this meeting is going to run long. "We like to assign students on the cusp to peer mentors who act as guides for the rest of their time in the Everly District. It's a way to keep Slater focused on positive school experiences. We want for him to feel better prepared when he goes to high school and *not* feel that he is invisible," referencing Lynn Hannigan's earlier comment.

"Then what?" Hank asks.

"The entire peer review is private and offers students a chance to bond with each other through this very personal time of discovering how one's actions impacts others. Together, they will agree upon an appropriate discipline outcome, and I imagine a one-day suspension in-house will be a logical conclusion."

"Mr. Pastorino, how did you not know Slater was missing?" Lynn asks, clutching the seat of her leather couch cushion beneath her, as if she might spring from it in a cougar-style lunge.

"Ma'am, I wish I had a better answer for you. As I sit here, I know how awful this is going to sound. I had to make a decision to switch with the substitute who took over a difficult class. In my judgment, I needed to step in to manage some behaviors with kids I happened to already know pretty well. I knew I could count on my class to be in line with my expectations and not give her any trouble, so I offered a trade. Unfortunately, the buddy system back-fired on me because we didn't have straggling kids; the two buddies up and left with *each other.* There were a hundred kids out there. I know we probably missed a few steps in hindsight, but I am so glad the boys were found to be safe."

"Incompetence. That's what it sounds like to me, Mr. Pastorino," Hank barrels in. "You're telling me no one thought to take roll as soon as you deplaned the train at the platform in Clifton? I'm not a teacher, but that seems like the first bit of common sense in managing kids. Where am I wrong in this?" he says, eyes fixating on Mr. Pastorino.

"Look, you're right. Things could have been done differently. There are a thousand things we could have done better. We do a lot of field trips at this school. We're known for the hands-on experience offering, which is what helps kids learn. So, kids are usually pretty excited to attend these venues, and we have never had this kind of a situation in the past," Mr. Pastorino says, gesturing with his open palms as his hands are thrown open several times during his remarks. "I suppose you can fire me. I've been a pretty effective teacher helping students to learn what they haven't been able to learn before, but you can just throw that out the door if you want to make a federal case out of this incident."

"Funny that you mention federal case, Mr. Pastorino. You do

realize I prosecute cases all day long for the state?" Hank says, trying to intimidate the school this time.

"Yes, sir, I do know," Mr. Pastorino sighs.

"Mr. Hannigan, is it your intention to raise an issue about Mr. Pastorino's employment within our district over this matter?" Mrs. DeMarco-Bradley asks squarely.

"I intend to exercise all the rights available to me as a parent."

"I want to share with you a copy of the permission slip your wife signed," Mrs. DeMarco-Bradley says evenly, handing over the paper where the bottom paragraph has been highlighted in yellow, with a big circle drawn around Mrs. Hannigan's signature. "Clearly, your rights have been waived in this matter. Field trip permission slips are standard. While we do our level best to provide safety and security for all children in attendance, the risk your child put to his own self is not the responsibility of the teacher."

Hank Hannigan recognizes a protection clause in a legal agreement when he sees one. All he can do is look to his wife, as if this is somehow her doing, even though they both know he could have easily have been the one to blindly sign this form just like they've done a hundred times before.

"Look, I think what's best for Slater is that we move him out of joint classes with Chicky, then transfer him back to Everly Middle Grade in the fall. In fact, the more I think about it, there are some deep flaws in the system that is going to protect your teacher over my missing child, so I would prefer to part ways at this point and

get Slater back to his old school as fast as possible." Hank looks
at his wife Lynn who is nodding in agreement before she speaks.

"I would also like to hear Mr. Pastorino apologize to Slater before
our meeting today finishes. This has been a horrible experience
for Slater. Yes, we realize he made some poor choices, but he's
a little boy still, and he has a lot to learn about life. But I am
more concerned about the message that says *No one is paying any
attention to you because you are invisible.* That is the message
that Slater will be taking away in all this. If you had done your
job, if you had filed those kids off the train with their buddies, you
wouldn't have had such a cluster fumble at the platform," she says,
forgetting to breathe as her emotional outburst erupts.

"Mrs. Hannigan, we all appreciate how worrisome this situation
was for everyone involved. We have acknowledged that there are
better systems we will be putting into place in the future. We have
acknowledged the worry and undue stress we have caused while
Slater was in our care. We are willing to look into a transfer back to
Everly Middle Grade as soon as we can verify that Slater's grades
are passing." The superintendent pauses to ask EMGATS Assistant
Principal Amanda Hiller to pull up his schedule and current grades,
"but unless he is meeting our minimum requirements, we will not
be sending him back; it's not the Everly way."

"Look, I understand the rules are supposed to benefit Slater, but
I am not sure he is going to recover intact from this excursion on
Friday—" Hank says before being interrupted by his wife.

"What we mean is, Slater is going to earn a reputation over here, and we don't want that. We want him to have a fresh start again, and now that he has been gone from Everly for a couple of months, I think he can finish the term over there and not have to extend into his summer with the EMGATS schedule. We have plans for him this summer that include a discipline camp," Lynn says, willing to admit out loud that she is aware of her son's shortcomings.

"So, you *are* taking proactive measures to teach him accountability?" Mrs. DeMarco-Bradley asks, sounding impressed.

"Of course," Hank chimes in. "We have always taught accountability in our home; it's just going to take a few more reminders before Slater fully understands what this means," he says more calmly now.

"Slater needs a special environment where he can thrive and not feel as though he is being picked on or made to feel like he is the example. We keep hoping for the right kind of teacher who can reach him in this way, not to say anything negative about Everly District teachers, but we still need a little something extra that we have not yet found," Lynn ends it here even though her sour note hangs in the air during the second part of their meeting.

"Let's bring in Slater for this next part. We want to explain the discipline process so he feels—"

"What is your discipline process?" Hank asks abruptly.

After the superintendent explains to the Hannigans what she has already explained to Chicky's family, both Mr. and Mrs. Hannigan have deep reservations about Slater being put on the spot.

"I am not sure minors can be trusted to keep such confidential information to themselves," Hank says, doubting the process of sworn secrecy for panel members on the student review disciplinary board. "We have put forth some restrictive measures of our own at home. If you want to suspend him for one day of school, that's fine, but I do not give my permission for him to go before a review panel of his peers. Sorry, I'm not comfortable with that," Hank states firmly, locking eyes with the superintendent.

"Well, then," Mrs. DeMarco-Bradley says in a cool voice, "I believe there is nothing further we can offer you as a way of support to Slater. Our entire goal is to be sure the child who is on the cusp is set to receive exponential mentoring from student leaders and invitations to become more involved in positive school experiences, but if you are not interested in this for your son, then that is, of course, your choice. But, I need to make clear, that this is not what we recommend for Slater. Our peer mentor program has made an impact on many at-risk students and prepared them better for high school—"

"So, you're saying you won't be able to better prepare him for high school unless he goes through this peer review?" Mrs. Hannigan asks, adding a sting.

"That's not what I'm saying. All our students are well-prepared for high school, but those students who have a history of academically underperforming, or require behavioral outreach, are usually in need of social outreach too. You are his parents. If you do not wish to take advantage of the services we offer, the choice is yours. Are we ready to invite Slater to join us?"

The superintendent nods to Amanda Hiller, taking this as her cue to jump from her seat, leaving the room filled with tension and awkward silence to bring in Slater from the lobby.

"Come here, son," his dad says, patting the seat next to Slater's mother on the couch.

"Slater, I'm Mrs. DeMarco-Bradley, we haven't met. Hello," she says warmly. "We've been speaking with your parents about what happens next." She runs down the details of what all adults in the room already know to be true about Friday's events. She invites Mr. Pastorino to say a few words, which is his cue to apologize, satisfying Mrs. Hannigan's third demand.

Slater, I must say, after all my years in teaching, I have never met a kid who wanted to get out of learning about the Greek gods as badly as you.

Mr. Pastorino silences his inner thoughts to put forth a most sincere-sounding apology. "Slater, I am so relieved that you were found safe in Pinehurst. Not because I'm worried about my job if something happened to you, but because you matter to me. You matter to our class. Even though you've only been with us a short couple of months, you have a fun sense of humor and I've enjoyed getting to know you," he says, trying to look at Slater directly. "It was a crazy day on Friday and I am so sorry I didn't figure out until the train had already pulled away that you were still on it. I'm sorry if you thought I might have overlooked you because you were *invisible* to me. Nothing could be further from the truth."

He said it. His administrators are all gently nodding their heads.

He said it and he said it the right way. Now on to the other two demands Mrs. Hannigan laid out.

Slater just looks at Mr. Pastorino, completely confused. Only this morning, his teacher told him he wouldn't be able to be his advocate. So why the apology now?

"Your parents tell us that you have had some restrictions placed on you at home for your actions on Friday. We, too, have accountability measures that must be taken so you understand the gravity—the seriousness—of your poor choices. We usually offer a peer review board made up of student leaders to help you recognize why what you did had such an impact on so many people beside yourself. They would serve as your mentors to help introduce more positive school experiences, but your parents are requesting that you take a one-day suspension and that you be transferred back to Everly Middle Grade immediately. How do you feel about this?" Mrs. DeMarco-Bradley leans in, waiting to hear what will most certainly be complaining about being separated from Chicky before the year is over.

"Whatever," Slater says, resigned to following his parents' will.

The superintendent turns toward Amanda Hiller, who has her computer open in front of her. They communicate with their eyes and seem to be in agreement that they understand what the other needs. "Ms. Hiller says you are doing well in your EMGATS courses," she nods toward the assistant vice-principal.

"Yes, Slater," Amanda Hiller scrolls through her screen, "it looks like you have solid Bs and Cs right now. That's a nice improvement.

We will release your grades to Everly Middle Grade where you will be returning the day after tomorrow, since I believe your suspension will be served at home now that you will no longer be part of our campus. Is that right, Mrs. DeMarco-Bradley?"

"I think that's most appropriate," she agrees, looking toward the Hannigans now to question, "Can arrangements be made to supervise Slater?"

"I'll be home with him," Lynn says, brushing the hair out of his eyes as he jerks away.

"All right, then, I think today's meeting is adjourned." The superintendent says farewell, while the other administrators tell Slater they are sorry to see him go.

"If you ever do want to return, for more support down the road, we are always here for you, Slater," Amanda Hiller says, patting him on the shoulder while he walks by.

The next day, while Chicky is sitting through his first peer review, meeting mentors who will become some of his closest friends in the months to come, Slater is at home.

"Well, how would you like to go shopping with me for some clothes that are *not* for your birthday since we promised to keep it simple this year? Then we can go to lunch at Panorama and maybe see a movie. How does that sound?" Lynn is the best mom in the whole world. At least this is what Slater keeps telling her over and over again.

She knew she had him when his eyes lit up at the sound of Panorama, the new 3-D restaurant that rotates views of the world on their mural walls while the restaurant stands still. Cut outs of tourists in silhouettes are seen looking on at the depths of the Grand Canyon, the soaring heights of the Egyptian pyramids, the Great Wall of China, the ferocity of the Safari wild cats and charging rhinos. Slater hardly remembers to eat his pasta with the exhilarating life-size slide show playing out in front of his eyes.

Home again, Slater and Lynn Hannigan have the house to themselves. "Mom, thanks for today."

"You're welcome, my sweetheart. But, let's be clear, this is only because I am so relieved and grateful nothing awful happened to you last week, *not* because you attempted something incredibly stupid."

"I get it."

"Tomorrow is a fresh start—again. Make it count, okay? You only have about six weeks before school lets out."

"I promise, Mom. I won't get into any more trouble."

He meant it when he said it. He just didn't know that the future would hold different plans for Slater Hannigan.

CHAPTER 13

Making the Grade

While Slater enjoys his shopping spree, Chicky spends the morning getting grilled by his peer review panel. It is not as horrible as he expected, but it is exactly as the superintendent and his assistant principals laid out for him. When his morning session ends, there are exactly three people who have already extended him invitations. Selena Martinez asks him to help her run the school bake sale during the Everly Middle Grade play Friday night. "I know lots of people I can introduce you to in case you ever want to come back to Everly and be in the next play, or even work stage crew. And even if you don't come back, these guys are always going to movies on the weekends and there's always room for one more, Chicky," she says, bubbling over with enthusiasm.

Will Potter has an extra ticket to Saturday night's college

basketball game to see Aaron McMann set another record for scoring the most three-pointers of his season. "Every time he plays, he outdoes his last performance. This weekend should be memorable because the pro scouts will be in the stadium. I know because my dad has connections," Will says, slapping Chicky on the back as they meet at eye level. Will is one of the Everly kids who will most likely play varsity basketball as a freshman in high school next year. He's that good.

"Hey, you want to come over to my family's house for lunch on Sunday? We always have a big meal and we kids invite someone from the neighborhood every week. My mom and my sister put on this huge spread when we get home from church and I'm telling you, they know how to cook," the third invitation begins.

"Um, well, I gotta check with my grandma and gramps because there might be something going on," Chicky says, unsure of how to turn down his invitation.

"Hey, Chicky, it's not like you have to come to church—unless, of course, you *want* to—it's just a lot of singing and preaching, but I'm telling you, the food—well, it's something you gotta experience. They make all sorts of pies for dessert too. You like southern pecan pie?"

"The kind with those big nuts and that gooey stuff? Yeah, that's a good pie," Chicky says, more interested now.

"Well, my sister, she likes to play around with recipes and she makes it, so there's some chocolate at the bottom of that pie. You've never tasted anything like it. All I'm saying, man, is you're welcome to eat at my house and it's cool if you want to bring your grandparents. My mom says anybody's welcome. We're always having people," he says persuasively.

Chicky is not sure what to make of Reginald. When he first met him, Reginald was intimidating—his tall stature could easily match Chicky's if they were standing back to back. He was imposing, in a quiet way. The fact that he was the last to speak in the review panel seemed like he had more importance than the other leaders, especially since they all waited for Reginald to give the final disciplinary speech.

"Chicky," Reginald began earlier this morning, "some of us know the world you come from. Some of us have never known it but hear plenty from our friends. The only difference between us and you is that we accepted the help when somebody offered to get us out of a bad situation. We *accepted* it. There is an exchange made when you take the thing somebody offers you. Gratitude is the first piece of what you give in exchange. If you truly want the help, and somebody's there to give it to you, appreciate what they have done for you. This means don't make that mistake again, don't be a fool and ruin the trust that person put in you, hoping you'll be doing better next time around.

"We're making this exchange with you here today. You blew it, Chicky. You put the teachers in a bad light at EMGATS, and you put yourself in jeopardy going so far away on a train. But, you seem really sorry about it, so the panel wants you to have only one full day of in-house suspension in the restitution room on campus tomorrow. We're gonna come eat lunch with you, but in the morning and in the afternoon, you gotta be on your own to do some schoolwork from your teachers, and then you gotta do a report for us. It's the LePo report that we give to every candidate," Reginald says.

"So, I gotta read a book and write a book report, or something?" Chicky asks.

"No, not even. You gotta answer some questions—honestly—about *you*. It's your Leadership Potential report. We give it to every candidate who faces peer review—"

"You mean *bad* kids, like me," Chicky says as more of a statement, not a question.

"No, Chicky, you're not a *bad* kid. You made a really bad choice, but you're still just a kid. We've all done dumb things, and we told you about some of them this morning. But, we *learned* from our mistakes, and when somebody thought maybe we could become something more, that's how we got into Student Council and leadership. Not saying it's for you, or that you'd even be interested; that's for you to show us. But, every candidate has to evaluate his or her self and the kind of life they want. So we created the LePo report, written by kids for kids, and graded by kids. Man, you said this morning that being in trouble at school makes your grandma and gramps real sad, and you didn't want to disappoint them. What if your life was gonna turn out differently? What if you had some control over it? What if your LePo report showed you had a high potential for something you never considered? Never even knew existed? School is for learning lots of stuff, not just from books."

When Reginald finished his speech, Chicky felt a rush inside him. He got real warm and kind of excited wondering what *his* report would say about him. What if it said he wouldn't be good at anything? He looked at Reginald whose big dark eyes were burrowing into Chicky as he stood there, leaning against the desk with his arms folded across his chest, patiently waiting for Chicky to show a sign of willingness.

"Like, what kind of questions? About math, or reading, or stuff?" Chicky asks, unsure of wanting to take one more test like in all his other classes.

"No, man. Like questions about how would you react in certain situations. We give you these dilemmas of people in trouble and you have to explain how you would react. The questions show how your brain and heart respond to emergencies, basically. Before we wrote the survey, we had to read all these business books to see what leaders do to motivate their people and what they look for when they hire people and how money isn't the only thing that people want from a job. They want respect, they want some power, and they want to create and get some recognition. We just started thinking about what *we* wanted from school besides an education. This is how we lead. The school can't be good for everybody if everybody isn't feeling a part of things. So we get candidates more *involved*. But we need to know what your potential is for certain situations." Reginald sits back, watching Chicky run it all through his mind.

"Sure, I'll do it," Chicky says, agreeing to the LePo report.

It isn't until later this morning that Chicky learns Reginald is the eighth grade Student Body President at Everly Middle Grade. Despite his athleticism—he knows football is only his free ticket to college—he doesn't want to go pro like his coach and his friends hope. He prefers to focus on leadership classes when he gets to high school so that when he graduates from college, he can be in charge of *something* someday.

Chicky has the same look on his face as he did earlier when Reginald was waiting on his answer about participating in the LePo report. "Well, man, you want to come to lunch? Bring your grandparents with you. It's cool. You don't have to worry. In fact, my sister might even be in one of your classes. She goes to EMGATS now."

"Who's your sister?"

"Marilyn—our last name's Washington. Know her?"

Chicky did not see that coming.

The outer corner of his mouth turns up. "We've got a class together." Then his eyes squint with a little gleam, his cheeks smiling more fully now, "So, what time is lunch?"

Between the invitations and the high ranking on Chicky's LePo report, he heads into the Washington household with a lot of confidence. His grandmother is happy to help in the kitchen as Marilyn and Mrs. Washington prepare their traditional Sunday meal. Everything fried is popping and spitting on the stove. Hot grease droplets are slapping against bare arms that should know better by now. Chicken drumsticks, breaded zucchini, and onions sautéed with green beans all fill baskets and bowls, before being set on the table next to yellow cakes of cornbread that have just come out of the oven. Chicky watches from the table as Marilyn whips dollops of honey together with sticks of butter using her electric hand mixer. She ignores him completely.

While the families get to know one another better, passing servings of mashed potatoes and grits around the table, conversation bounces between sports, school and summer plans. There is never any mention from Reginald or Marilyn about the EMGATS field trip event and the Cicarrellis are so happy to be included in another family's home. Mrs. Washington talks about her jobs and Reginald keeps an eye on the four younger brothers who are doing their best not to disrupt the table with their high-spirited behavior.

"Are you planning to stay at EMGATS in the fall, or will you be returning to Everly Middle Grade, Chicky?" Mrs. Washington asks innocently, clearing plates while her daughter hoists pecan pies onto cake stands for everyone to admire at the table before she carves them into slices.

"I like Everly," he says wistfully because he misses his true friends, "but I like EMGATS, *too*," he emphasizes, hoping Marilyn will look up so she can see that he means *her*. She doesn't.

"Yes, I think the district has done a fine job offering two different programs to our students. I liked it as soon as I heard about it. If Reginald didn't have his sports priority, I would have gladly signed him up for EMGATS," she says, smiling at her boy, beaming with pride. "But you are just too good at football, Reggie."

"I know, Mom, it's a gift," he says, repeating the words she often says to him after every winning touchdown.

"Someday, those scouts are going to see you play in high school and then, well then, your whole future is going to open up, baby," she says, beaming.

"Well, first I've got to get out of middle school, Mom," he says humbly.

"Who wants some pie?" Marilyn asks coyly, holding a butcher knife in one hand and ten paper plates in the other.

"Yes, please," Chicky shouts first. He looks at her steady hand as she cuts through the thick crust she pinched herself to create a wavy look around the edges. Her mother lines up plate after plate while Marilyn quickly scoops slices out with the fat blade turned sideways.

After all the brothers have been served, and the guests have had their Sanka—the cheap brand of decaffeinated coffee that even Marilyn drinks—Fiorella insists on offering up Chicky's help in the kitchen.

"My Chicky knows how to dry dishes real good. You let him help you, Miss Marilyn, yes? That would be so nice. He needs to work a little to show his appreciation; it's what we try to teach them, right?"

"Oh, I understand what you mean. My boys know there is no such thing as girls' work or boys' work—it's *all* work that anyone with a free pair of hands can do. Even my littlest ones started cleaning toilets when they turned five years old. I'm not working two jobs and coming home to a dirty house, not when I've got six kids. We never bought those video games and I try to limit their television viewing; it's just a whole lot of noise and nonsense these days anyway. Am I right?" Mrs. Washington is about to get to preaching when Fiorella Cicarrelli has a thing or two to add.

"I don't like all the computers. We don't own any because life is a good when it's a simpler. That's how we were raised and that's how I want my Chicky to know his home. It's not a bad life, is it, Chicky?" she says, holding his hand and squeezing her eyes shut tight as she smiles up at him.

"It's a pretty good life, Nonna," Chicky says, feeling relaxed and happy for the first time in months.

When Marilyn starts running hot water into the sink, filling the dish tub with suds, Chicky and Reginald head to the kitchen to scrape from the plates what little food is left and prepare to dry and put away the good dishes used for guests—mismatched pieces of china, but all in the same lemon color. Mrs. Washington believes food always looks better on a cheery plate. She is right. The greens look greener, and only the cornbread blends in almost so it disappears. While Marilyn washes, handing Chicky the dishes to dry, and Reginald puts things back into the cupboard, he asks the obvious question.

"So, what class do you guys have together?"

"Mr. Pastorino's social studies," Marilyn answers succinctly.

"What are you guys learning now?"

"Um, all about the Greek gods and stuff," Chicky says quickly, hoping to avoid this line of questioning. "Hey, when's your next game? What position do you play? I could come watch, maybe," Chicky offers.

"That'd be cool. I'm quarterbacking this year. My favorite thing is to run with the ball, so I try to sneak in some of those plays when the other team least expects it," he says, watching his sister fake like she's not hanging on every word Chicky says.

Reginald watches as she stirs the suds, feeling for another dish to wash. She gracefully scrubs the plate in twenty circles with the brush, then runs her fingers over it on both sides to be sure every ounce of mashed potato has been removed. *What is she doing taking her sweet time?* he wonders. While Chicky takes the plate from her, he dries so urgently until the dish is warmed again by the friction of his towel whipping across it as quickly as a shoe-shine boy. That china has never been so finely scoured.

"Hello and good-bye, Everly," Slater reels off, high-fiving Tobey Peterson and Macaroni Maroney. His old buds are happy to finally have him back for the final weeks before sixth grade lets out for summer. Poor Chicky will miss out on all the plans these three have made without him since he'll be stuck at EMGATS through early August.

It is no big deal for Slater to fit right in with the group he left behind before he went over to EMGATS for a few months. It is, however, a bigger deal for the teachers who must figure out what kind of grades to give a kid who has only been newly placed in their classes for the final weeks of the school year. As long-term projects and final exams are coming due for the students who have been at Everly all year, Lynn has to protest.

"It's not good for my son to come into a stressful situation like any other new transfer student would and suddenly be faced with test after test for days on end," she says logically to the principal who last sat across from Mrs. Hannigan before winter break when she had Slater transferred to EMGATS for plagiarism so many months ago. "It takes preparation to study for an exam and how is Slater expected to feel successful when he is slammed with multiple tests from all his teachers at once?"

"Oh my, Mrs. Hannigan," she says, faking a sympathetic tone, "it is unfortunate that Slater did not wish to finish out his term at EMGATS. This is a real conundrum. Our schools operate separately, so even though we have received his marks from EMGATS, there is no *transference* of grades. We only count EMGATS as fifty-percent of his report card—Slater must earn his final scores for the year, just like our other Everly students." Principal Miriam Horowitz lets the words slither from her mouth.

Lynn lets out a sigh, louder than she intends. She can see the trap she has fallen into here. "There must be another way for Slater to get passing grades without having to take a million exams." She smooths the wrinkles from her skirt, giving her time to pause so she doesn't say something she will regret. "Is there a chance Slater might do some kind of class presentation instead to demonstrate his knowledge?"

It is not an unusual request and Miriam Horowitz says as much. "I will certainly speak to Slater's new teachers to see what kind of creative alternatives to testing they might accept from him before the grading period closes. You should have a new assignment before the end of the week from each of his teachers."

Feeling satisfied that she has gotten what she wants for her son, she stands now to shake Miriam Horowitz's hand. "Thank you for your time and for understanding my position."

"I truly hope that Slater *will* find a way to pass these courses so he might remain with us for seventh grade in the fall." The words are right, but the feeling is missing. She does not smile. She is not warm. She will be the first one to probably say *I told you so* when Lynn's plan fails and Slater gets transferred to EMGATS again.

For two weeks, Slater prepares for the final projects each of his teachers have challenged him to complete for his trimester grade.

He has one shot to prove he has learned anything this trimester at EMGATS to teachers he has never met—since the principal believed it would be a poor idea to return Slater to Mr. Blackwell's class after Sibley White and the whole plagiarism debacle got Slater transferred out of Everly in the first place.

His English teacher, Mrs. Baldwin, allows Slater to do an oral presentation demonstrating his knowledge about the six topics they discussed deeply, including the Tom Sawyer novel they read. If he cannot complete this task with a satisfactory grade, then he must take the two exams instead, plus write an on-demand essay in class.

His science teacher, Mr. Falcon, is happy to assign five virtual lab tours for Slater to participate in through his computer. Once he has completed the online experiments, a printout will notify Mr. Falcon of Slater's results. If Slater does not manage to pass all five labs, he must create a fifty-question test for each lab he fails. Slater's not really worried—he has spent two hours a day in science labs at EMGATS for the past four months. He's got this.

His social studies teacher, Mr. Reese, has different plans. Slater must write a compare and contrast report about what modern-day leaders have learned from heroes like Alexander the Great or Julius Caesar compared to any of our presidents, analyzing strategies still used today that were originally designed during the Ancient Greece or Roman Empires.

For any other kid, this might be too difficult. But, fortunately, having a father who has shared his interest in politics with Slater his entire life, he has been brought up with current events and knows how to read a newspaper and discuss modern politics.

His math teacher, Miss Perlance, insists the only way to measure a child's knowledge of mathematics is to give him some problems to work out. So, Slater will take a standardized test, hoping to show the same skills for math that have always made this the one subject that comes easily for him.

By the time Slater has pulled off a solid B on his labs in science, earned the A he fully expected on his fifty-question math test, and squeaked by with a C+ on his social studies essay—okay, he knows how to *read* a newspaper, but he hates writing about what he's read—Slater is left with his oral presentation for Mrs. Baldwin.

The day is here and all eyes are on him now. He is the new kid to many of these students—many of them came to Everly Middle Grade from other elementary schools outside of Esther Bookman, his old school. They watch him rustle from his seat as he takes the slow walk to the front of the room. Without one familiar face—Chicky Cicarrelli, or Tobey Peterson, or Macaroni Maroney, or even Sibley White—to cheer for him as a show of support, he steps over backpacks in the aisle, hoping he does not lose his nerve.

He stands at the front of the room, looking to Mrs. Baldwin for her signal to begin. The students wear a bored expression, defying him to dazzle them. For the first time, Slater is nervous. Suddenly, he sees sixty eyeballs staring straight at him and he freezes. He has completely forgotten his first line. His paper is in his backpack beneath his desk. He didn't think he needed it because he nailed this last night rehearsing for his family.

"Uh, I forgot something at my desk, can I go get it?" he says, throwing a desperate look to Mrs. Baldwin.

"Quickly, Slater," she says, rushing him now, wondering if this is going to be a mistake when all the other students have spent the year delivering finely-tuned oral presentations for the duration of five minutes.

He races back to his desk, swiftly grabbing his notes, and moves clumsily up the aisle, dodging the newly-placed backpacks that have been put in his way on purpose.

The pressure is mounting. He can feel his throat closing up. His neck feels hot and time seems to be moving very slowly. He stares into the audience, steadying himself to throw out his first line when suddenly someone coughs loudly, shouting beneath their breath, "Loser." The rest of the class starts giggling until Mrs. Baldwin settles them down again.

"Class, let's allow Slater a moment to collect himself. You remember *your* first time being on stage? Well then, I expect the same kind of respect and attention," she says sharply.

He puts his notes on the floor just in case he needs to reach for them, and then he says to Mrs. Baldwin, "Hit it."

She depresses the button on her computer to display his slideshow with background music of a mash-up of his two favorite rap artists, while he sings his own version of lyrics about Tom Sawyer and the rest of what he knows.

He struts around while the beat goes boom-boom-boom ba-da-da-da-boom-boom. He dashes off the lights during the slides that feature the murder in the graveyard Tom Sawyer witnesses, roping in the entire audience who already know their favorite music so well.

Kids move to the rhythm in their chairs, smiling widely and doing the hand motions from the video they have seen more than a hundred times before while Slater takes his performance to the next level. He slides across the stage floor, pretending to play an invisible DJ turntable for the finale. It comes at the best part of the song where he lets loose, rapping about the picnic, the cave and Injun Joe getting sealed inside to meet his certain death. The whole class is applauding enthusiastically anticipating the final scene, when Widow Douglas adopts Tom who has found the long-lost treasure. Slater throws his hands in the air, and all the kids stand on their chairs, mimicking him as if they are at the same concert. Even Mrs. Baldwin looks to be enjoying this lively show.

There has never been such a ruckus inside a classroom when learning was taking place. Slater nails his oral presentation, receiving an A for English. Even better than the grade are the scores of new friends Slater makes who think he is the coolest, most original kid they have ever met.

Knowing they will all be looking forward to his return as a seventh grader makes the summer go by even faster. He has tons of new party invitations that he attends happily, even if Macaroni and Tobey aren't included. It won't matter; nothing can replace the friendship he has with his lifelong buddies—and the week-long adventure they have together at survival camp will never separate them again.

CHAPTER 14

Summer Comes at Last

"It's as if he's turned a corner, Hank," Lynn Hannigan says to her husband about the lack of drama in their household since school let out four weeks earlier.

"I told you he would come around," he says agreeably, watching her fold Slater's clothes into little pocket squares before delicately placing them into his survival pack.

"Seriously, do you think it's because he's been hanging out more with Macaroni and Tobey since Chicky's still in school?" she wonders, ironing the rest of his tees and underpants.

"Lynn, the kid is not going away to prep school," Hank says in jest, ripping apart the forty-pound backpack recommended by the camp directors. "He is maturing; it was bound to happen sooner or later," he says, layering the base with the sleeping bag,

201

then rolling the bare minimum of clothes allowed: two sets of underwear and tee shirts, two long sleeve shirts, a change of long pants, socks for each day, and a down parka that collapses into a pocket pouch—plus, the dry food packets, poked to let out the air, then taped to seal their freshness.

"Honey, that's not even enough for three days," she says, bringing the clothes from the ironing board to the bed where they have been sorting and packing for Slater who is painting shutters at Sibley White's.

"Dear, it's not a fashion show," Hank says, tossing half of her suggestions into the pile on the floor along with the other items that did not make the cut: his neck pillow, two books so he can stay ahead on his summer reading, his flannel pajamas in case he gets cold, the scarf she knit him four Christmases ago, the hat that matches—again, in case he gets cold—and the bathing suits in case they find a spring to go swimming.

"Hank," she says, eyeing the growing pile, "I still don't understand how he is going to swim without a suit, or what he's supposed to do if he's freezing to death at night."

"They're boys, Lynn. They'll rough it and swim in the buff, and he'll do jumping jacks if he's cold before he goes to bed," Hank says with a chuckle. "They are going to learn how to survive the elements with as little as possible to assist them. It's going to be awesome. Wish I could go," he says, only half kidding.

While he finishes layering the pack with the heaviest items at the top, tucking in the mess kit beneath the bed roll so Slater's head will have a cushion as he walks, she jabbers away about the transformation of the White's house.

"It's really quite amazing to see what he did to that place in just a month."

"He's a hard worker, that's for sure. At least, when he wants to be," Hank grunts, wrestling to zip closed the snack pouch. "Lynn, put this on so I can adjust the straps to fit Slater."

While his wife accommodates his tugging and jostling to test out the weight distribution, she worries that Slater is going to be without any communication for a whole week. "What if something goes wrong? What if we don't hear about an accident for days? What if—"

"Lynn, we talked about this already. We have to trust that this place knows what it's doing," he says, stuffing Slater's birthday compass into the hip pocket before zipping it securely closed. "He needs this experience and you never know what kind of kids he'll meet. Maybe he'll make some new friends who can teach him a thing or two. It's healthy for him to get away from us for a while."

"Maybe he'll appreciate us more if he misses us a little bit," she says, slipping an envelope into the front pocket of his pack.

"What's that? You can't send him to survival camp with a lunch note, Lynn," Hank says, pulling it out of the pouch. "The other kids will pounce on him. He'll never hear the end of it. Just give it to him before we leave."

She holds the sealed letter in her hands, looking sheepishly at the cursive spelling of Slater's name with a little flower drawn beneath, her signature design on every card. She has a haunting feeling that Hank might be right. Slater might be getting too big for love notes from his momma.

"My mom wants to know if you want lemonade?" Sibley White asks, holding a tray with a pitcher and two frosted glasses, including one for her.

"Sure," Slater says, holding a stiff brush to the shutter he is painting black. It's the first one he's given a second coat to; the others are waiting their turn. "Just put it down. I can't get to it yet or my brush'll dry up and then I won't be able to paint the rest of these today like I want," he says so officially, like he is a member of the paint police now.

"You can't even stop for a *minute*?" She is more disappointed that he hasn't even turned her way to notice the new pink gingham checkered romper her mom just bought her for summer. "But, the lemonade's cold *now* and I've got glasses that I frosted in the freezer—I mean, my *mom*, frosted—so it would be just perfect for you," Sibley says awkwardly. "Well, that is, if you're thirsty."

"All right, thanks, Sibley," he says, looking over his shoulder after painting a nice even panel of glossy black down the last part of the shutter. "Just give me a minute." He taps his paintbrush into the can, resting it across the top before reaching for a glass.

Sibley pours from the pitcher, sloshing some over the side, its contents heavier than she expects. "Oh gosh, sorry about that," she says, worrying about his shoes.

"It's nothing, these are just my work shoes, meant for getting dirty," he smiles, gulping quickly when Sibley offers him a second glass. "Sure, it's really good. You guys have lemons in your backyard, right?"

"Yeah, I squeeze them myself then add a little sugar, water, some lime and mint. It's the best combination," she says, filling his glass again, pouring more carefully this time. Slater has no idea that Sibley had to squeeze a big sack of lemons for a half hour to make just this one pitcher.

"If you're hungry, my mom's making sandwiches. Maybe you can stay for lunch, seeing as how this is your last day working," Sibley says, hoping he will.

"Gosh, Sibley, I've still got five more shutters to paint; I think I'm gonna be a while. But, maybe you can come eat out here while I'm working. I won't mind."

That's good enough for her. In another half hour, Sibley returns with big sandwiches cut into triangles, just in case Slater wants to take a few bites. There's roast beef and tomato with cheese or turkey with Swiss and extra pickles, both favorites in her household.

They talk about their school years and Slater's final tasks at Everly, and what it was *really* like attending EMGATS, and is he happy to be coming back for seventh grade, when Mrs. White pokes her head out to check on Slater's progress.

"Slater, my husband and I are both so pleased with what you have done to our front yard, and especially the backyard. I know I'm not supposed to pay you for this work, but I wanted to do *something*, so these are for you."

Slater Hannigan, Curb Appeal Services. Specializing in front and back yards. Give me your worst, I'll give you my best. 635-575-1524

"Wow! Nice," he says excitedly, rubbing his finger over the embossed lettering of his name in a bright navy blue. "My very own business cards." He even loves the logo Mrs. White included of an illustrated boy in a baseball cap pushing a lawn mower.

"Believe me, after the transformation of our home, I am sure the neighbors are wondering who did all the work. This will be a great chance for you to boast a little, Slater. Maybe you should make a flyer and include a before and after picture of our house. I'm sure you will get lots of paying customers," she finishes, smiling at how mesmerized he is by his box of fifty cards.

"Yeah, my dad got me this cool toolbox to fit on my new bike. I can go anywhere now that I've got my own wheels," Slater says appreciatively. "Thanks, it's real nice of you, Mrs. White."

When Slater finishes painting the last shutter, he stands back to admire his work, realizing the only thing left to do is sweep the great big porch. The bright yellow marigolds he planted alongside the lawn bordering the driveway look alert and cheerful, standing at attention in their row. The hedges that had become overgrown, with twigs poking out from every direction, have been clipped into a square shape, their tops now in line with the porch railing, instead of the brambling bushes that made them look to be pushing their way in through the front living room window. The most notable improvement is the grass that is now coming in green and lush after Slater pulled weeds for hours.

He painted the porch railing in white trim to give it a face-lift, and he fixed the crooked shutters dangling in places before returning them to their original glossy black. The old wicker furniture that sat for years untouched on the front porch had amassed cobwebs that were in bad need of hosing off. A few spray cans of navy blue paint turned the oversized chairs into comfortable seats. When Slater's mom told him he could reclaim some of the old pillows she kept in the basement after a hotel project she no longer needed them for, he chose the pair he liked best for Sibley's house. Their stripes of bright sea blue and turquoise added a nice touch.

The entire backyard alone took him half of his work hours to complete. He hoed and pulled and wrestled with weeds as tall as he. Most of them came out of the ground easily, but after growing for years, just clearing the field made the yard look huge again and then, nothing else really needed to be done. He planted a row of marigolds out back to match the front driveway, and left it alone. *Clean and simple*, which is his mother's motto for design.

It will be a little weird for Slater to not show up at Sibley's house anymore to work these long Saturday mornings. She has been cool to talk to and she didn't get in his way too much when he was working.

At least she doesn't seem to be mad at me anymore.

"Dudes, Elmer Woods, here we come!" Slater shouts across the neighbors' lawns to Tobey already standing in his driveway, getting ready to load his sleeping bag, tent, and backpack.

"Let's see what this whole survival thing is about. Probably not half as scary as if we were gonna be in charge. You know what we'd do to all those first years? Oh, it'd be so much fun making them cry by creeping up on them outside their tents and making scary noises."

"Oh, I hope they try and do that to us. We'll be ready for them. We should set some booby traps—"

"Oh, hi, Mom," Tobey says quickly, acting innocent while Slater chimes in right away.

"Beautiful day, isn't it, Mrs. Peterson? Thanks for the ride—"

"Hey, Macaroni," Slater has turned his attention to their other pal who is dragging his overly stuffed pillowcase behind him while he wobbles beneath the weight of his pack.

"My noodle, slow down so Momma can readjust your straps," Mrs. Maroney speed walks from around the corner to catch up to Macaroni who seems to be ignoring her chase.

"He's already sweating; how's he gonna survive the whole week? Man, check him out," Tobey says, chuckling louder as Macaroni clangs when his canteen bangs against his mess kit, both tied to his side belts. He looks like a pack mule.

"I made it. She still following me?" he says with a smirk on his face as if he has been intentionally trying to ditch his mom ever since she started squawking at him in his driveway.

"Macaroni, be nice to your mother. She's the only one you've got," Mrs. Peterson says in a kind reprimanding voice.

"I know, Mrs. Peterson. She just wants me to pack more stuff she thinks I need and I can't carry anything else. I don't have any more room for a family-size bottle of sunscreen," Macaroni says, finally catching his breath.

"Well, if you do find yourself in need, I am sure Tobey can lend you something, or the camp director will surely have extra supplies. They will be protecting you in all ways possible," her voice trails off as she listens to the phone ringing from inside her house.

"Man, you are never gonna make it on that sixty-mile hike; you can barely walk around the corner from your house," Slater says, laughing out loud now before Mrs. Maroney approaches.

"My darling, you were hard to catch up to; I didn't know if you could hear me calling you," she says, panting, while wearing a scarf, hiding the rollers still in her hair. "You forgot to take these with you." She holds out a few comic magazines, a tin of chocolate chip cookies she just baked this morning, a vest in case it gets chilly, a bigger flashlight in case Macaroni needs to do his business in the middle of the night, and, of course, the family-sized bottle of sunscreen with one hundred twenty-five SPF protection.

"Geez, Mom, it's never gonna fit—"

"Oh, we can help him, Mrs. Maroney," Slater says, reaching for the cookie tin first while Tobey jumps in to grab the comic books and flashlight for the bear hunting they plan to do after everyone has gone to sleep.

"Oh, you boys are so sweet. You see, Macaroni? You are going to have a wonderful time with your friends. Boys," she says seriously with her little mouth, complete with peach frosted lipstick, "we are all counting on you to stay away from matches or anything else that might burn down the forest." Somehow, the way Mrs. Maroney says it doesn't sound as bad as the thousand other times they still hear this from their fathers.

"We know, Mrs. Maroney," Slater offers agreeably.

"We won't, you don't have to worry about that," Tobey complies.

"Mo-om, sheesh, we're not gonna get in any trouble," Macaroni says, unbuckling his pack and dropping everything at once behind him on the grass. "Okay, we're going now. I'll see you in a week," he says, standing there for the inevitable teary good-bye.

"Oh, my noodle, your father and I will miss you. We're so proud of you going on your big adventure," she says, sloppily giving him a hundred little kisses from ear to ear, all around his head and both cheeks.

"Yuck, Mom, now I smell like perfume," he says, wiping at his hair with some clumps of grass to get the scent out.

"Oh, my noodle, Mommy loves you." She starts walking away, slowly.

"Mom, it's going to be fine. At least I'm with Slater and Tobey;

don't worry so much," he says, content with the dirt newly ground into his fingernails from the crumbled soil still in his hands.

The boys pile into Tobey Peterson's SUV after they load the last of their belongings. "Anybody have to use the potty one more time before we hit the road? It's a good hour drive and we're not pulling over."

They look at each other and decide everyone needs to get out of the car again. Once they have finally piled back in, Mrs. Peterson plays her book on tape so she can drown out the noise of three excited boys all huddled in both of the backseat benches.

They attack Mrs. Maroney's chocolate chip cookies before they even cross Sugar Ridge Drive, then they get back to planning the destruction they have in mind for their night crawling.

"Hey, you guys wanna see the compass Graham gave me?" Slater asks, digging into the front pocket of his pack.

When he opens the box to show his engraved name, both boys are super impressed. "That's really nice," Tobey says, before asking to hold it.

They eagerly watch the needle nervously shake before landing on due north, matching Mrs. Peterson's navigation system. "See, it always knows," Slater says, even more amazed at its accuracy, despite it never being wrong in any of the last million tests he conducted already.

"Hey, hold it out the window, and see if it changes when your mom turns the corner," Macaroni suggests before Slater grabs it out of Tobey's hands.

"No way, dude; I don't want it getting lost on the freeway. I'm keeping it with me," he says, petting it before sticking it back in the assigned backpack pouch where it belongs.

"Too bad Chicky can't come," Macaroni says, still holding the cookie tin in his lap.

"That would have been so fun," Slater says enthusiastically, "but he's got like five more weeks of school."

"Such a bummer," Tobey pipes up. "Hey, how did you manage to get out of EMGATS early, anyway?"

"Oh, my dad didn't like how things were turning out over there and wanted me transferred, that's all," Slater says, keeping the information to a minimum, abiding by his parents' rule.

"Well, we wished you had come back to Mr. Blackwell's class, but maybe we'll be lucky enough next year to get the same schedule again," Tobey says, looking out the window at freeway billboards for Elmer Woods. "Hey, check out that sign. Did you see it?"

"No, what?" Macaroni asks.

"Dude, they had a big picture of a kid running away from a scary looking forest. You should have seen the look on his face. What kind of advertising is that, anyway?" Tobey says sounding a bit alarmed.

"They probably think it's really funny, like a joke. I'm sure our parents wouldn't be sending us unless they checked it out, right, Mrs. Peterson?" Slater says politely.

"What's that, dear?" she asks, pausing her book, which is just at the good part.

"Mom, did you see that scary looking billboard for Elmer Woods?"

"Yeah, they have those all over the website, too. Why?"

"That kid running away from the forest doesn't *concern* you?"

"Oh, honey, what do you think is in the forest? Maybe your mind is making it scarier than it really is. All I know is they wouldn't call it survival camp if you were just sitting around counting butterflies on poppies all day, right?" she says, looking in the rearview mirror at their puzzled reactions. "Where's your sense of adventure? I think you are going to have an unforgettable time, guys."

If the adults only knew that the billboard campaign is nothing compared to the real adventure lurking among the trees. These boys are about to get the scare of their little lives—and not the one their parents agreed to pay for after reading the brochures.

CHAPTER 15

Surviving Elmer Woods

The brochures entice parents into believing the safety and security of all children is the top priority. "Preparation prevents poor performance. This will be a life test." The skills gained in leadership, problem-solving and competition aptly transfer to school academics and athletics, and will be forever used in the adult world.

When Lynn explained it to Marcy Maroney and Brenda Peterson, they immediately recognized the benefits of sending Macaroni and Tobey along. "This is exactly what Jim and I have been thinking about for Tobey," Brenda leans in. "One day, Jim hopes Tobey can take over the pizzeria instead of going to college. The only thing Tobey needs is some accounting courses and then he can run the business while we travel." She looks around, wondering if she has said the wrong thing.

"No college? Brenda, you can't be serious," Lynn says.

"Business is good. Why should he have to go to school to learn how to run the business when Jim has been tutoring Tobey since he was eight years old about taking care of the store and handling customers—the life bread of any operation. Are they teaching customer service at Harvard?"

The ladies all chuckle. "Well, I know my Macaroni has got to go away to school in order to learn a little independence, and we can't teach him how to be a doctor by carving prime rib or turkey at the holidays," she laughs.

"Well, no matter where these boys end up, doesn't this camp sound like a dream experience? They will work harder than they ever have, teaming with strangers to perform challenge tasks—they can't just rely on each other for the rest of their lives," Lynn says convincingly. The other moms all nod their heads vigorously, agreeing this camp will be worth every penny of the eleven-hundred-dollar fee.

At the drop-off circle, parents are asked to stay in the parking lot for their swift good-bye. Police academy cadets check in each boy, after which, he is expected to haul his own pack into the lodge where he will await the camp director's instructions.

Mrs. Peterson can hardly contain herself at the curb. She watches the inefficiency of Macaroni's luggage compared to the other experienced-looking campers, now belting their backpacks with a single waist strap and heading forward at an urgent pace. "Sweetie, let me carry some of this in for you; maybe someone inside can help you rearrange yourself," Brenda Peterson offers kindly.

She starts to move away from her car, intending to escort Tobey, Macaroni and Slater into the lodge, before she is abruptly stopped. A cadet dressed in fatigues holding a clipboard stands in her path. "Ma'am, we ask that families say good-bye in the parking lot before boys are allowed inside. Independence training begins now," he says seriously through dark shades beneath his uniform cap.

"But, this one can barely carry all his stuff. I just need to help him get inside and then I'll be on my way. I promise, I am not planning to stick around," Brenda Peterson says reassuringly.

"Viper, we need a tag in the lot. Over," he says succinctly into his earpiece without any emotion.

"Ma'am, we'd like to thank you for dropping off your children. They will be safe in our hands for the week, no worries about that," a taller version of the first cadet emerges. This one wears a label above his pocket reading Viper. His cadet companion wearing a similar bar embroidered with the name Coyote hangs bright yellow tags on all of Macaroni's loose bags and possessions that were supposed to fit into his backpack. He tells Macaroni to load them onto the cart that looks just like a red wagon spray-painted in war fatigue and to move it inside.

Slater and Tobey are glad they were able to fit their stuff inside their packs, so they don't have to suffer the embarrassment poor

Macaroni is experiencing now. Mrs. Peterson takes the tin of mostly eaten chocolate chip cookies away from Macaroni, who is looking helpless like he wants to come with her.

"You guys are going to have a really good time," she says with a crooked smile, looking over to Viper standing there as if he wants to be sure she is leaving soon. "You get to be together and meet some new friends." She leans in to give Tobey a hug first then says good-bye to each of them. "Don't worry, Macaroni, I'm sure they're going to help you re-pack. They're just teaching you guys some organizational skills. It'll be fine once you get inside," she says feeling a swell of anxiety move through her tummy. "Slater, watch out for everybody. You guys be safe and stay out of trouble, okay?"

"We will, don't worry," he says without the slightest hesitation. He knows all the things adults want to hear and has become the master of well-rehearsed answers he reels off easily. His most frequently used responses are *love you too, okay, Mom* and *not a problem*. That last one he picked up from his dad, listening to how he speaks on the phone.

As Brenda Peterson waves again from behind her steering wheel, she pulls away slowly, wishing the end of the week was already here.

There are about a hundred kids finding seats on carved out logs used for benches inside the lodge. The windows that run floor-to-ceiling alongside the forest wall give the impression that this is some kind of wooded hotel. Nothing could be further from the truth. *This* is the *only* building—the rest of the woods are littered with army tents that will serve as base checkpoints.

"This place is kind of cool," Slater says, taking in his surroundings. There are ten cadets in fatigues positioned around the room. They all wear the same serious expression beneath dark glasses. Each of them has a nametag sewn above their breast pocket—each of them strong and confident.

"I don't know, these guys look pretty mean," Macaroni says nervously.

It is hard to imagine that these cadets are only ten years older than Slater, Macaroni, and Tobey because they look like they have been doing this for a lifetime. It's the training they have already had at the police academy, which has prepared them well for many real-life situations. Part of their service to the community is to volunteer at booster camps designed for creating effectiveness and power. The only way to be sure kids don't go into a life of crime is to give them a head start so they can develop leadership skills and become a success at doing something for *good*.

"Hey, that big guy's gonna talk," Tobey whispers now.

"Surviving Elmer Woods," his booming voice echoes through the room, "has been designed by some of the toughest recruits to ever graduate from the police academy. We promised your parents that we would teach you life skills that transfer well beyond your school academics and athletics. You don't need to become a police officer, but we're going to teach you how to think like one. Whenever you are faced with a problem—it can be any kind of problem—can you find a solution? We are going to teach you that skill. Competition, team-building, and independence—these are the three components you will need to survive this week."

"Dude, this is no joke," Slater says to Tobey and Macaroni.

"I really want to go home now," Macaroni says, looking around at all the other boys appearing to be his age or a couple years older. "This is not for me. I don't want to stay," he says, rubbing his hands back and forth over his thighs, hoping the sweat building up on his palms will dry soon.

"The only way out is through. Some of you may feel like the challenge tasks we set up are too hard for your ability. There is no going back. There is no going around. There is no going under or over—the only way to finish is to go *through it*. Campers, do you understand me?"

"Yes, sir," can be heard from most of the boys who shout enthusiastically. Macaroni is not one of them. Even Tobey and Slater are feeling a bit apprehensive.

"Good. Now on to the rules. Rules are to be abided at all times. Rules broken will result in points taken away from your team and will likely result in a group punishment for your entire team. There is no individual achievement here, only team rewards," Viper continues, eyeing the rows and rows of sloppy-looking boys squirming in their seats.

"One of the rules we sent home was about your backpack requirements," he shouts so everybody in the back of the room can hear him loud and clear. There should be no worry about that since the vaulted ceilings and wooden beams help to carry the decibel-level of his voice beyond the walls of this lodge.

"Uh-oh, I have a bad feeling he's talking about me," Macaroni says, sitting right in front of his wagon cart.

"Because I am in a good mood today, I am going to go easy on those of you who have already broken the first rule of packing. Instead of bringing you up here on stage so I can berate you in front of the others to make a spectacle out of you, I'm going to give you a second chance to get it right. But, this is going to be points for your team. Believe me, you need the points. You might be able to exchange them for hot meals for your team, or firewood—and let me tell you, it gets cold out here at night.

"So, here's what I need to see. There are several carts planted around the room full of items careless campers could not fit inside their forty-pound packs. We are going to put you in teams of ten. You will be given a five-minute time limit to determine if each of your group members has all his items within his pack, or secured to his military issue camping belt. *Anything* that does not fit gets left behind on your wagon. Each team starts with one thousand points, and for each boy who does not pass this test, a hundred points will be subtracted from your group. Are we clear?"

"Yes, sir," a thunderous roar can be heard from the throng.

Two whistles are heard in quick succession. Viper has signaled to the surrounding cadets to fall in at the head of each log—a row long enough to hold just ten campers. Each cadet uses hand motions to communicate non-verbally that the entire line of boys seated in front of him are now under his charge—his unit.

"I'm Bear, your base instructor. Follow my lead, I'll help you to be safe and smart. In all we do, remember that—be safe, be smart. In another thirty seconds, Viper's whistle is going to blow hard. That's when our five minutes begins. All ten of you, I want to see you in a line in front of me with your belongings on the count of three. Alley-oop." He watches them scramble, the six older boys understanding his command to get moving. Macaroni is a little clumsy, tripping over some of the other boys who have whisked by him in their fury to get in line. Finally, he stands behind his wagon, relieved to see that there is one other boy in the same predicament. "One, two—" Bear screams in quick beats, "three." The last of the group is in place ready to be inspected by Bear.

Thrrrummmm, the long whistle blares. Bear watches his team struggle to figure out their first steps. At first, they begin to chastise Macaroni and the other kid for neglecting to follow the packing rules. "Now we're gonna lose points and if we have to sit out in the cold, it's gonna be your guys' fault," Drake whines.

"Guys, we're supposed to be *helping* each other," Slater says, taking charge. "Dude, you five work on that kid's pack, and we'll work on Macaroni's," he says to the biggest kid at the end of the line who looks like he might know what to do. "Rip it open, take everything out, keep one of everything, no duplicates." Slater speaks efficiently, using very few words so they can hurry through this.

"Four minutes, guys, work together. Each person, take a different section of the pack. Light bottom, heavy top, necessities on sides, snacks up front." Bear gives them guidance in clipped phrases. Slater understands and puts Tobey in charge of sorting the contents they pull out into essential and non-essential piles while the other two strangers work at rolling the items that will be going back inside.

"Campers, you've got two minutes. Who's gonna get to eat a hot meal tonight? Which of you will be making s'mores over a nice warm fire with wood from points you earned today?" Viper taunts relentlessly.

"Macaroni, how many sets of pajamas did you bring?" Tobey ribs his pal, tossing three flannel pants and matching tops into the wagon.

"I don't like to be cold and who knows how dirty we're gonna get. I like to have a backup," Macaroni says sheepishly, standing by while the others perform surgery, cutting his contents in half and manipulating the space folds to hold more by stuffing socks into crevices.

"Final minutes, cadets. Get ready to account for your team's points," Viper bellows.

"Guys, you're nearly done," Bear says encouragingly, walking down the line to review the other wagon cart being loaded with the same kind of extraneous items.

Thrrrrrummmmm. The final whistle blows, indicating it is time for teams to stop what they are doing and step aside. The cadets walk their lines, clipboards in hand, checking off the number of teammates whose packs meet the forty-pound guidelines. They tug on the waistlines, making sure the items dangling from the belts are secured in place. They ask each camper to take a few steps forward, estimating how easily he can walk while lugging the weight of the pack on his back. So far, Bear's line looks to be in good enough shape.

"What's your name, camper?"

"Macaroni Maroney," he says proudly, happy to be lightened of his load.

"I like it, Mac-a-ro-ni," Bear says pulling on the pack ties to test their strength. "Good knots. You seem to be in order, so I give you your full one hundred points, Mac." Bear continues down the row, giving the same amount of points to Tobey, Slater, and James, before stopping for a careful review of the other camper who also over-packed. "What is your name, camper?"

"Keller," he says quietly.

"Well, Keller, you see all these bulges coming from your pouches? Can't zip these closed. So, are you gonna make the decision of what is coming out, or am I?" Bear looks at the other boys who helped him remove more than Keller wanted to already.

"But, I sort of need all of this stuff—"

"That's my cue." Bear starts pulling at the top items squished beyond their capacity to determine what stays and what goes. He tosses a hooded sweatshirt and keeps the down vest, which balls up into the size of a paper wad. He throws the cooking pot onto the wagon and keeps the mess kit. "Your plate can double as a frying pan," Bear reasons. He pulls a pair of jeans from the pack and tosses them behind him. "The ones you have on are enough." Soon, Keller's pack meets the standard forty-pounds, with every compartment able to be zipped, and every essential item in its proper place.

"Yeah, feels a lot better," Keller says, bouncing his knees to test how much lighter his pack feels.

"Keller, you cost the team one hundred points today. You gotta be ready when we say go, and you gotta get things done right the first time around," Bear says flatly. "Team, you're at nine hundred points; not bad for day one. Let's hope you don't lose any more tonight."

Keller's friends are swarming around him, telling him not to worry, while Slater and the guys decide now is the best time for introductions. "Hey, it's okay, we only had the five minutes; it was a hard task. Now that we know what they're looking for, we can do better on the next ones. It's okay, Keller, we don't hold it against you," Slater says evenly. "This is Tobey, Macaroni, and I'm Slater."

"Who are you, our leader or something? Look at this guy, acting like he's in charge of us," James says to the others, but to no one in particular.

"Just wanted to say hey," Slater says, not knowing what this kid's deal is.

"Well, I'm James, and me and Keller and Drake here are gonna be in charge of this little team, isn't that right, Drake?"

Drake looks at Keller and Keller looks at the ground. "That's right," Drake says, a man of few words.

Just as Slater is about to say something back, Bear steps in, sensing a stand-off between the new neighbors. "Getting along real nice down here?" he says, pushing his index finger into James's shoulder. "There's going to be plenty of teams trying to tear you apart and find your weaknesses so they can steal your points. The teams with the advantage are the ones who figure out how to work *together.*"

Thrrummmmm sounds the whistle again. "Cadets, fall in," Viper commands. "The ten trails you know well will have trackers a day behind you. So, in case you are running into any trouble out there, back-up will be along within twelve to twenty-four hours. You know the drill: lock up their technology in the lodge before you leave. First team to make it to the daily checkpoint will get an extra thousand points. Teams who are late will lose one hundred points for every hour they are delayed. Have a good run, cadets," Viper finishes encouragingly. After he gives his first set of instructions to the team leaders, they get set to move out.

While each captain takes the map for the section of the forest he will be hiking, the campers look on with high anticipation.

Bear gives orders to his ranks, "Campers, we are hiking out our first five miles to the starting point of our trail—White Feather Falls. There are ten of you, so buddy up, walk side by side, follow my footprints, step where I step. I know this trail and I know the nine other trails the other teams have been assigned. These are all challenging in the middle. By day five, you are going to be hurting, hungry, tired, and wishing you were already home. In two days after that, you will be home—unless you go against everything I teach you out here. Understand me?"

"Yes, sir," they all say weakly in unison.

"I need a little more commitment from you."

"Yes, sir," they shout a little louder this time. They hear the other teams sound just as robust. They must be getting the same kind of speech.

"The next hour and a half should be an adjustment period for you to get to know your pack and how to balance it. There is a lot of flat ground ahead of us, but by the time we get to the slope, you won't want to be wrestling with the girth on your pack, or it could tip you over—drag you down a hill, while we watch your buddy struggling to pull you up from that ravine. Don't worry, we're going to teach you about ropes and knots and how to spot limbs you can use as support to rappel, even with a weighty pack. Give me ten hours and you're going to be feeling pretty comfortable with some good basic skills." He smiles for his first time.

After, he asks them all to straighten their socks, re-lace their boots, relieve themselves behind the trees, and pull out their compasses. Only one kid remembered to bring his.

"Your packing list required each of you to bring a compass. I see—what's your name, dude?—Slater here is the only one who read the list. Minus one hundred points each for the other nine of you. Being out here in Mother Nature means you have to be prepared. You can get lost easily unless you know where you are going. If you can find North, you can read a map. If you don't have a map, you can learn to spot markings in the land. You might find a bear den, flattened bushes, remnants of prey scattered around. Pay attention so you don't get turned around and end up there again. Look for water sources—falls lead to rivers, which travel downstream, leading away from the mountains, usually to a populated place. If you noticed, the lodge is settled close to the river. You can always make it back here if you follow its current south. Between now and the end of our first five miles, I want you to think of a new animal or bird name we can call you this week—something that reflects your personality, your new identity, so to speak. Ready to move?" They certainly are.

Slater and Tobey partner up together, while Macaroni and Keller naturally gravitate toward one another after their shared packing debacle. "Sorry about costing the team some points," Keller begins shyly. "My mom told me packing this stuff was my first test. Guess I failed."

"Yeah, well, my mom made me take so much that I had two extra bags to drag along." Macaroni smiles to his new friend who tosses back a beaming grin.

"How do you and Drake and James know each other?"

"Well, James is my cousin and we live next door to each other. Our moms are sisters and they bought a duplex together when my grandma left them some money after she died. So, he's like a brother to me—a bossy brother, too. Drake lives across the street, been there for our whole lives," Keller says quietly so James doesn't think he's telling family business.

"I've only got an older sister. She's bossy, too. She's even mean to all my friends. She wants nothing to do with me, or any of us, whenever they come over. So I understand. Slater's got a pretty bossy mom. Tobey, he's learning how to be the boss some day at his dad's pizzeria. So that's all the bossing around I know." Macaroni prattles on the way he does when somebody is willing to listen.

"Have you ever been camping like this before? You know, survival stuff?" Keller asks, wide-eyed.

"Heck, no. I'm only here because Slater was coming anyway and his mom convinced our moms it would be good for us, too. I could be swimming in the pool right about now; even washing my dad's car would be better than this," Macaroni says wistfully, worrying he will never make it to the end of the week.

"Dude, what's your camp name gonna be? I'm thinking about taking Owl because I'm pretty quiet, so most people don't even know I'm around, but I notice everything even when people don't think I'm paying attention. Like, I noticed you when you first came in dragging that wagon behind you. I knew right away we'd be friends," Keller says, truly meaning it.

"You're pretty funny, Keller," Macaroni says, happy to be making his first friend so quickly. "Hey, what do *you* think my name should be?"

"What about rabbit? They're nice. Maybe a little nervous, but they know how to run from trouble, is that you?"

"Yeah, I like it. I'll be Rabbit. Thanks Keller—I mean Owl."

Conversations like these take place between the other four pairs of campers. James and Drake are partners together. After fighting over which one will be Cougar or Rooster, James declares himself Cougar without even taking a vote.

Slater and Tobey keep looking back to check on Macaroni, worried about him fitting in with a stranger until they overhear bits of their conversation about their mothers, deciding those two will fit well together. "You know what my name is going to be? It has to do with the most feared animal in the forest, and not because it could tear you apart with its claws because it can't," Slater quizzes Tobey.

"Hmmm, not a gator because they don't live in the forest. Not a tiger, for the same reason. Is it a raccoon?"

"Oh, Tobey, that is so close. Want one more guess?" Slater asks, feeling generous.

"Not a raccoon, how about a porcupine? That would be awesome, you could just poke someone's eyes out whenever you wanted," Tobey laughs more wildly than he should because it isn't *that* funny.

"No, don't be ridiculous. I'm gonna be Skunk," Slater says with confidence. "It's perfect, right?"

"Dude, *that* is hilarious. Okay, then, I'm taking Porcupine so I can poke out people's eyes when I want to."

Suddenly, Bear stops the group to teach them their first emergency lesson: hand signals. "There are eight basic signs you need to know when silently communicating with your team in case you are ever compromised. Maybe there's a wild animal you don't want to alert, or maybe an opposing team is nearby and you don't want to draw their attention," he says gruffly. "You need to speak the same language in code that could mean the difference to your survival.

He teaches them how to move their fingers for counting zero through ten. He teaches them affirmative signs for *Yes, I understand, Follow me, Listen to what I hear, Look at what I see* and then the negative responses for *I don't understand, I can't hear you, I can't see.* Finally he ends with the active commands for *Crouch down, Hurry up, Don't move, Meet at the rally point, Stop* and *Freeze.* For the final mile before their first checkpoint, the buddies have been assigned to test each other, which they do jovially mimicking military operatives they have seen on the video games they have played their whole lives.

So far, so good. Three more tests before bed-down and they will be ready for their first team challenge tomorrow—finding food.

CHAPTER 16

Afraid of the Dark

"Hey, Mom, what are we doing while Slater's away?" Graham Hannigan asks eagerly. He is excited to have the house all to himself while his older brother plays with his friends on a camping trip for the whole week. He has never been away from Slater for this long, so it seems like he and Lynn should be doing something special to celebrate. If Graham only knew the real reasons behind Slater's attendance at survival camp, maybe he would feel a little sorrier for Slater. A soon-to-be fifth-grader really doesn't need to know a middle schooler's problems—at least this is what his parents decided.

"Well, my sweet, what is it you would like to do today? I'm all yours," Lynn says, snuggling up close to her little boy who has never given her an ounce of worry.

"Can we go to the science museum to see what new inventions they think we'll have when I'm old like you?" Graham asks innocently. His mother, on the other hand, is officially offended that her ten-year-old thinks she's already old.

"You never get tired of that place, do you?" she says with a chuckle.

"It's so cool, Mom. How would you like it if a robot could serve you breakfast in bed?"

"Actually, it doesn't matter who's serving; breakfast in bed always sounds good. Hey, how come I don't get that more often?"

"I know, maybe I should make it for you tomorrow! Okay, Mom?" he says brightly before thinking of an even better idea, "And then, we trade and you make it for me the next day." He likes the sound of his new plan a lot.

"Okay, buddy, let's see what you bring me tomorrow. If it's half as good as the Mother's Day breakfast I got, I might just stay in bed for the rest of the week, waiting to be served like a queen," she says, snapping up her keys, taking one more look in the hallway mirror and then setting the alarm. "Let's go, bud—off to the Imaginarium."

Whatever the engineer students can imagine at Technology Design Standard, they must be able to create with their team. Once it passes several mechanical tests to make sure it will work, Imaginarium features the design in one of their display rooms. It might take fifty years before these innovative creations become part of society, or they might not ever receive the funding required to go into production.

Graham loves eating at the restaurant on the third floor of the

Imaginarium. The best part is that the patron can self-select his experiences. You seat yourself instead of a hostess and instead of servers, digital screens the size of your face race along zip lines to promptly greet you and take your order. The image you see could be your favorite movie star, superhero, or animal. You select from the tabletop digital menu, asking you to announce your arrival and choose your theme. Graham loves requesting the hairy gorilla to take his order.

"Look, Mom," Graham squeals when the bags of food come swinging from the cable they are clipped to above. He reaches for his hamburger eagerly, while also pulling down his mother's salad tray inside its carton. "It's so awesome, I wish we could come back here every week."

"Well, celebrations wouldn't feel as special if they happened *every* week," she says with a wink.

The first checkpoint at Elmer Woods is quite welcoming. There is a large capacity tent in army green canvas so it blends into the woods. The cadet waiting inside of the front flap door is seated at a desk, reviewing inventory left over from last week's campers.

"Bear troop checking in," Bear says to the cadet whose name badge reads Crow.

"Checkpoint one, 10:30 a.m." he notes their arrival in the log. "You're making good time. Supplies needed?"

"I'll take two rows of tabs, ten Mylars, two cases of beef, thirty Bs and five rolls of duct." Bear reels off the typical laundry list he recites whenever he brings through a new group of campers.

Crow lays everything in front of Bear on the long conference table.

"The rule of three—" Bear begins seriously, "you cannot survive three *minutes* without air, three *hours* without shelter, three *days* without water, three *weeks* without food," he looks at his campers, who are stunned by his revelations. "In order to survive the elements, here are three bandanas for each person, providing many surprising uses from sun protection, to potholders, to toilet paper."

He passes them down the line with instructions to place them in their front pouches. "Iodine tablets, enough for each camper to purify two gallons of water if your canteens run low, drinkable after thirty minutes. A Mylar blanket for each one of you, the same kind invented by NASA to reflect body heat when the night air turns chilly, or as a cover from direct sun. It will keep you warm, but it can also be used as emergency shelter like a tarp if needed. Keep it folded and tucked away where it's easy to grab."

The boys silently follow his commands, unzipping and zipping protective pouches.

"This powder packet will be your dinner if you can't find food on your own—dried beef and potatoes requiring only a little water before cooking slowly over a fire. You get four each, so the rest of the week, you're going to learn how to hunt and fish."

The only other item that might be handier is the roll of duct tape each pair of buddies has to share.

Slater and Tobey look wide-eyed at each other. This sounds like the most fun they have ever had. Macaroni and Keller are wearing opposite expressions. In fact, Macaroni's eyes are welling with tears at the thought of possibly going three nights without dinner.

"Any questions? Good." He doesn't wait for hands. "We're moving out. Slater, since you're the only one who came prepared with a compass, pull it out; you're leading the way to base camp."

"Um, sir, I'm not real good at using it yet," Slater says timidly.

"Step one, get your bearings. Let the needle wiggle until it settles itself facing the marking for north. The compass will naturally move toward north every time because the Earth acts like a magnet. Do you boys know your directions?" He gives a quick test, which they all pass. "The river runs north to south. The lodge is south of us now, about ten miles. If you ever get lost, having a target in advance will help you establish your bearings. Step two, always study a map before you hit your trails. Today, you've got me, but any other time you go exploring, have a sense of your point of entry."

Bear lays out the map of Elmer Woods, which is zoned in different colors for each of the ten hiking trails.

"These paths don't cross even though they all start from the lodge. At one point, each group will need to locate a water source. We've got rivers, streams, falls, and a lake. The final challenge for each team will be to make their way through the goal posts made of tree trunks and then find the river to lead them back home within seven days' time."

Slater leads the group with Bear's careful tutelage. The boys keep practicing hand signal commands and mostly everyone, except for Keller, is able to remember. Macaroni patiently repeats the same motions another fifteen times until his partner finds his confidence.

It takes them the rest of the morning before they reach base camp. What the boys expected would be another tent filled with another checkpoint, perhaps a few other tents with a kitchen and a place for showers, is not what they imagined. They are quite surprised to discover there is no one waiting for them here—nothing but wilderness and heat from the sun's rays.

"Welcome to base camp. This is where we set up for the night. Who's hungry?" Bear asks, but something about his tone makes them suspect he's not cooking.

"I'm starving."

"Yeah, me too."

"So am I."

The group has been free of whining until now. "Listen, ladies, if you brought a snack, now's the time to power up. If you forgot to follow the packing list for that part, too, then I've got some beef jerky, but it'll cost you fifty points against the group. Any takers?"

The boys all look around at one another, eyeing who will be the first to put the group in jeopardy of earning fewer points than the other teams. "Hey, it's only fifty points, we'll make it up some other way," James pipes up, seeming overly confident about his predictions for their future. "I'll take some, Bear," he says, holding out his dirty hand.

Bear hands him one stick of jerky. "It's fifty points per piece, mate." James looks like he could cry. He is so hungry he would happily saw off his own hand to chew on his fingers.

"Wait, does anybody have any snacks they want to share?" James, the same kid who was willing to make enemies within the first sixty seconds of their arrival is now hoping one of these dummies will give up some of their survival food.

Slater and Tobey look at each other, holding the same thought. They know they have extra food, their mothers saw to it. But they don't want to share with James any more than anyone else he offended does.

"Well, Bear, I guess you better charge us the full one hundred points because I'm gonna need a second stick."

"Dude, you can't just go making those decisions for us about group points. You didn't come prepared, so it should be you who suffers, not us, man," Slater tosses out.

"Yeah, James, you should have looked at the packing list," Tobey echoes.

"Hey, you guys don't know anything. He had it but we got hungry on the long drive out here and ate our stash, that's what it is," Drake says, standing up for James.

"Well that's still on you; we shouldn't be punished because you ran out of food," Slater says spitefully.

"Men, I hate to break it to you, but unless you figure out a way to work together as a team—to solve this problem—I am taking points away from you for every minute that goes by. I'm starting my stopwatch now and taking twenty points for every minute I have to wait. Go!"

Over the squawking of boys calling each other names and challenging each other to dirt throwing matches, one person is able to reason with the group. "Guys! Guys! I know what we can do. Let's put all our snacks into a big pile and then divide it evenly so we don't lose any more points. I think we're gonna need those points if we get real desperate. What do you say?" Keller shouts with his thin little voice.

He dumps out the contents of his pack to show the granola bars and baggies of trail mix with dried fruit. Everyone looks at Bear who is still staring at his watch and they follow suit. Within thirty seconds, ten greedy boys are now emptying their pouches and packs like Halloween pillowcases turned upside down after a night of trick-or-treating.

There is a heaping mound knee-deep of list approved snacks as well as the *special* treats moms packed like contraband, with love notes attached to baggies of homemade cookies and mini-loaves of lemon bread.

"Quick, dealer gives five, luck of the draw," Keller yells, meaning everyone can grab five items and then return to their spot in the circle. They eyeball how much is left in the pile. "Dealer gives three, luck of the draw."

They continue grabbing, building their own personal stash, pleasantly surprised with some of their new loot. Keller was tired of his mom's oatmeal raisin cookies and now he is perfectly happy to have a few packs of Oreos instead. It goes like this for the next two minutes until there is finally nothing left. Everyone has an equal amount and kids are willing to offer trades for the favorites they lost in the shuffle. "It's only fair," Slater says.

By the time their lesson on establishing a new civilization has been put into practice, Bear finishes his count at five-minutes. "Your team owes me one hundred points. But I think you just learned a valuable lesson that is going to help you earn more points when it comes down to team challenges."

While they rest for a few minutes and snack on whatever they like, they anticipate setting up their tents to be the next task.

"What do you notice about this clearing? I want you to tell me in a word what we have here to make shelter."

Some eager hands shoot into the air.

"Trees," Tobey says, pointing out the obvious.

"Yeah, we've got trees. You see any trees with hollowed out trunks here? Did anyone bring an axe? No and no. So, how are these trees gonna help you survive? They're not. What else have we got?" Bear says, deflating their egos.

"Leaves."

"Bushes."

"Sticks."

"Grass."

"Bingo, grass. Who said that?"

"I did," Drake raises his hand proudly.

"Boys, I'm going to teach you how to make a grass hut for shelter if you are ever without a tent or a cave or any other kind of dwelling. People have died from too much cold or too much heat from direct sun exposure. Don't let it happen to you. Now, since we've established we don't have an axe—I don't either, we don't need one—look around. What do we have that is sharp?"

Some boys have pocketknives, while others agree that a stick can be sharp if the end is carved like a spear.

"There are rocks around here. You will want the ones with blade-like edges."

Bear gives each pair of boys a job to do for this team challenge. "If you get this hut made within the hour, I will give your team a thousand points. Shelter is *that* important. For every minute you go over the hour, I will take away one hundred points," he says treacherously.

The look of panic can be read on every boy's face. "Don't worry, I'm a good teacher," he lightens up with a little half-smile. "There are five stages of building a grass hut." He pulls out a brown lunch sack where he has drawn each step with pictures. In only a few seconds, the boys fully understand the end goal and in a few seconds more, Bear has assigned each duo their role.

Macaroni and Keller get the job of clearing the land by removing rocks, debris, and smoothing the dirt to make a nice floor.

Slater and Tobey must gather enough clumps of grass to circle the hut three times and then they need to tie those clumps together in thatches.

Drake and James have the difficulty of finding long enough twigs they can use to create the frame. These need to be thin with the ability to bend, and they must be tall.

The other pairs of boys rely on pocketknives to slice reeds from fallen branches or long leaves they cut into thin strips to use as twine for bundling.

"There is a natural order to things here. The frame needs to be ready first. Can't have idle hands. If your job is done, help Slater and Tobey because tying all those grass bunches together is time-consuming, but they can't even begin if there's no twine. So everybody, work fast, work together, and be aware of what your teammates need." Bear steps away, sets his stopwatch and yells, "Alley-oop!"

Within twenty minutes, James and Drake have secured the first long sticks used for framing the hut. Macaroni and Keller have finished clearing the floor and are now joining in with Tobey and Slater to tie grass bundles. They pass these off to Duncan and Reuben who tie them to the horizontal shoots above the base of the frame along the second tier—like a bunch of hula skirts hanging on a line to dry.

In another fifteen minutes, the whole team begins to feel encouraged by their progress. Next, everyone works in an assembly line rhythm, tying thatches together and securing bundles to the third level. Before the final skirt is finished, Macaroni and Keller create a spear out of one long twig to hook the loop created in the grass dome. Slater is given the honors to lift the dome gently, placing it atop the hut so no sun can peek through the roof's opening.

"Time's up. Looks like we just earned ourselves a thousand points, comrades," Bear says with a big grin. "I haven't had a team do this well in a few weeks. That was no small feat; now get inside and leave your packs out here."

The boys all shuffle in through the opening on their knees since they forgot to make the door any taller than two feet off the floor, but once inside, it's perfect.

"Check this out," Slater says, admiring all their work.

"It's so cool," James agrees, showing off his framing as he runs his hands along the twigs. "I can't believe we made a grass hut."

They are all equally amazed, proud, and exhausted. But they are also cooler now that they are out of the sun. Bear uses a stick on the floor as a writing wand in the dirt. He draws the river and asks the boys to identify—from memory after seeing the map for the first time only two hours ago—where the lodge is, where the lake is, where the falls are, and where the first checkpoint was located. Now that they can all see the same thing, they can rely on each other's recall if they ever lose their map.

"Show me where our trail ends," Bear challenges them until most of them are pointing to the correct spot. "Okay good. Now, before it gets dark tonight, I want you to establish zones around your basecamp for a latrine, a fire pit for cooking, and food storage— never, ever store food next to where you sleep unless you want to be awakened by a two-thousand-pound bear scratching at your back for the tuna pouch you brought to bed with you."

The boys all look terrified by the image. "Are there really bears in these woods?" Macaroni asks completely petrified.

"We're in nature. There are all kinds of animals around us. Many of them won't even come out until night, so that's when you've really got to be on your guard. But, sure, there are bears in this forest. Usually, though, they are deep up in the hills, and I haven't seen one down this low for a couple years," Bear says, hoping to calm their nerves. "But you can never be too careful. The less human they smell, and the less food that humans leave out, the better we all will sleep. That's another thing about the human smell; if you cut yourself, blood is going to be the first thing to attract a bear. So, we need to keep a gallon of water to clean any wounds and wash away any blood from rags. In fact, this brings me to lesson two: first-aid."

The boys learn how to tie tourniquets in the rare case one might be needed to help stop blood from gushing. They learn CPR and how to clean wounds before applying duct tape to close the skin. They practice making slings using their partners as patients. They learn signs of a concussion and how to make a stretcher using tree limbs and duct tape.

They are ready for someone to start bleeding.

As nightfall approaches, the boys have become an organized unit. They have made a fire pit to boil water for cooking their packets of dry food, cleaned their mess kits using dirt to absorb the sauce, and rinsed any trace of food with precious amounts of drinking water—bears smell everything. Responsibilities have been assigned to each person, with a checklist so nothing gets overlooked. After Slater inspects the camp for their human footprint—evidence of human debris or dung that was not properly buried in the latrine zone—he confirms to Bear that campers are ready for bed-down.

Even though they all brought personal tents, everyone wants to sleep inside the grass hut together instead. It is a tight squeeze for them to lie side by side, but they find a way to get into comfortable positions, despite looking like a jumbled mess.

"James," Slater whispers. "James." He pushes at James' shoulder with his leg until he hears a faint grunt. "Did you remember to hang *all* the backpack snacks onto the bear line?"

"Yeah, Slater, I got it," James says, annoyed to be awakened.

"I saw some kids eating from their stashes after dinner. Did you double-check that you collected *everything?*" Slater asks, fearing the worst.

"Well, I didn't see anybody," James says, sitting up straight now. "What am I supposed to do now, wake everybody up to ask?"

"Dude, we can never be too careful; that's what Bear keeps telling us, right?" Slater says, allowing his imagination to run wild. "Let's scope it out with our flashlights, you want to?"

"Not really, but I also don't want to be the one to cost the team anymore points—and food on the bear line was my responsibility," James says, knowing the importance of getting this right.

"Let's go," Slater says, pulling his feet out from inside his sleeping bag.

Both boys army crawl through the opening in the grass hut before hopping around outside because of the sharp twigs beneath their feet, stabbing at them mercilessly.

They do not speak, not even to whisper. They know the first rule of survival is to survey the scene and to not give away your position to someone or *something* that might intend to bring you harm. So, they wait—flashlights hanging at their sides in the OFF position.

James gives Slater the hand signal to begin moving with caution until, suddenly, he gives the jarring motion to freeze. Slater, only two steps behind him, now holds still, like a statue—without even adjusting his second leg to gain better footing. The moonlight shining above reflects the ten pairs of yellow eyes forming a cluster seven yards ahead.

"Dude, I think those are raccoons," James whispers real low.

"I kind of *hope* those are raccoons," Slater tosses back, not wanting to tango with anything more ferocious.

"I'm gonna shine the light and see if they disperse so we can check our site," James says, lifting his floodlight.

"No, wait, what if they charge us?" Slater says nervously. "Let's do like they do in the movies when they have those gun fights—go back to back. We each point our floodlights while slowly turning around in a circle. That way we always have each other's back, okay?"

"Yeah, I like it. Ready. Set. Go." Together the boys bring up their lights. James confirms a pack of raccoons who are not startled and do not move while Slater searches the ground cast in the beam from his flashlight. They move carefully, hoping for no worse surprises tonight.

"Dude, I don't see any leftover food pouches out here anywhere. The bear line still looks secure, so what are those raccoons doing hanging out over there?" Slater worries.

"I don't know. Should we go closer?"

"Yeah, I don't think that's such a good idea," Slater says, backing away even farther while James takes another step forward.

"Dude, they're not even moving. They probably can't even run that fast. I'm going to slide in just a little closer," James says quietly, inching ahead.

Eeeech, eech, eeeeech, eeeech. Suddenly, he has awakened the den. Their nervous calls alert the other forest animals. Owls hoot from high above. Creatures peering from behind trees zig and zag, darting out of harm's way now.

"Dude, let's go back. Come on, James," Slater says a little less softly now, frustrated by James's resistance.

"Okay, I'm coming." James heads in Slater's direction. "Hey, you want to really have some fun while we're out here?"

"No, I think I want to go back to sleep," Slater says truthfully.

"Let's scare the pants off the other guys, you want to?"

"Funny you should mention it. We had plenty of plans for scaring *you* guys before we got up here," Slater says, perking up.

"Remember where we found all those twigs for the frame? If we can find any with two prongs, then we can scoot them under the grass flap and pretend like we're Freddy Krueger scratching at their backs. They'll totally freak," James says, delighted with his plan.

"Okay, that's pretty good," Slater says, trying not to burst into laughter while imagining Macaroni wetting his pants.

They go scavenging with their flashlights, careful to avoid stepping on anything other than soft ground. The moon shines brightly enough that they only need to use Slater's flashlight.

Their search for the perfect sticks ends quickly. They each find a twig with strong finger branches at the end, excellent for scraping along thatch huts—and through hair.

They tiptoe toward the backside of their shelter, opposite from the entrance. They know where each person is sleeping on the other side of the grass wall, so they begin near Drake, Tobey and Macaroni. They must feel their way around, hoping to not poke a face by accident.

"Wait, we gotta be sure, dude, 'cause that'd be pretty messed up if somebody lost an eye because we didn't check to see what we were poking first," Slater says, sounding reasonable to James.

"Okay, you're right," James agrees, putting down his stick and crouching onto his knees to peek under the skirt of grass. "I can't see anything, gimme my flashlight," he says to Slater, waving his hand behind him when, suddenly, he feels both of his ankles propel into the air behind him after a harsh tug and a lift. "Whaaaaaaa! Put me down! Put me down!" James screams frantically.

In one fell swoop, he is seated on a tree hook next to his friend Slater, suspended by ropes and a net, trapped just like a big fish.

"The more you scream, the more likely you attract a bear. Is that what you want? You want to be catnip for a bear breakfast?" The tallest one is laughing at his own joke while the other five standing around him seem pleased with their work here tonight. Ten thousand points for the capture of two team leaders from another group will secure their lead when they make it back to the lodge in six days.

Both Slater and James are petrified. They don't know what to do, but they are both fighting back the urge to scream while the mean boys from Bridal Veil Falls scurry away in the dark.

"How did they even get here? I never saw them coming!" James says in a hush, in case they are still within earshot.

"Dude, they had war paint all over their faces. We never would have *seen* them anyway, they totally blend right in. *Who* are they? That's what I want to know. I want to get some revenge, don't you?" Slater says, getting more and more worked up as his feet become more tangled the harder he tries to kick his way out.

"Where is Bear, anyway? You'd think even from his tent thirty yards away, he would have heard this ruckus," James says, sounding agitated and feeling completely uncomfortable being sandwiched together like a yoga ball with his knees to his chest.

"Yeah, he gets to sleep in his *private* quarters while we get to hang out here all night until somebody wakes up—either from the sun, or from the sounds of our screams as we are eaten alive for bear breakfast," Slater says, trying to find the humor in this ridiculous predicament.

"Dude, I'm too afraid to wake the guys. Maybe a bear *will* come if it hears us making noise. You don't want to find out, do you?"

"No, not me. I'd rather just take my chances that my legs will fall to sleep in this pretzel position and then maybe the rest of me can," Slater says, willing himself to stay awake a little longer so he can plan his attack.

When Tobey and Macaroni awake in the morning, they aren't the first ones stretching and yawning. After a peaceful night's slumber in the hut that feels like a forest palace, everyone seems good-natured and excited to start day two.

"I'm starving. What's on the menu this morning?" Keller says enthusiastically.

"I don't know, maybe Slater and James are out making eggs to bring us all breakfast in bed," Tobey jokes.

"I've gotta go find me a log for sittin'," Macaroni says shyly, using his camper code the politest way he knows. He puts on his shoes and moves real fast to the opening of the hut where he squiggles himself through and then screams loudly. "Aaaaaaaarrrrghhhh!"

All the boys inside come pushing their way to the front and those who do not have a view, lift the skirt to see what has Macaroni so frightened.

"Help us! Help!"

"Hurry, please!"

Slater and James call endlessly even after their friends see them, rustling to get to their tree as fast as they can all move. The kids cannot believe their eyes.

"Who's got knives? Start cutting these nets. You guys got to lace your fingers through the top ropes or else you're gonna come crashing down," Tobey says to Slater and James, barking orders to the group. "Keller, take Macaroni and go wake Bear. Run as fast as you can!"

While the boys dash off to tell Bear what's happened, Slater and James fill in the rest of the team about the devilish prank from the Bridal Veil Falls team. "But, how do you know it was them?" Tobey asks, logically.

"They're so cocky. They didn't want us to see their faces, so they wore war paint. But, they wanted us to know it was them, so they wore bridal veils on top of their ski caps. That's Viper's group, too. I thought he was all about rules. We'll show them—"

"Guys, guys!" Macaroni screams, still panting from his run. "He's gone, Bear's gone!"

"What? What do you mean he's gone? He can't just leave us here," Slater says, bewildered.

"No, yeah, he did," Keller says, trying to catch his breath. "Read it; he left a note."

Gone fishing. Come and find me if you want some breakfast. 40° West, 25°North.

CHAPTER 17

Bear Attack

"What's your compass say, Slater?" James asks, waiting for Slater to solve this mystery.

"Dude, I don't even know. There's no numbers, just north, south, east, west," Slater says, shaking the compass hastily, wondering if his answer will magically appear, like in his trusty magic eight ball. "How are we supposed to find the *numbers*?"

He looks to the crowd of worried expressions staring back at him, their anxiety growing.

"Okay, who has the map? Maybe that's supposed to tell us something useful," Slater asks, masking his squeaking voice to sound as if he is in charge.

"Well, I only have the copy Bear gave each of us, but he's got the original he showed us with all the markings highlighting the different trails," Tobey says, unfolding his and spreading it across the dirt. "Does anybody have a clue what we're looking for?"

"Hey, guys, there's a point marked A circled here," Keller points out obviously, hoping he can piece together Bear's logic if his suspicions are correct.

"Yeah, that must be our starting point because he has multiple circles with different letters that look like a trail to me," Slater says, showing Tobey and James for affirmation.

"Okay, so these numbers around the edges of the map are coordinates for us to follow. The lodge looks to be latitude 37 degrees north and longitude 91 degrees west," James says, using his fingers to trace the lines.

"Yeah, and the one circled B must be for our first checkpoint tent," Slater says more excitedly, using the end of a leaf to point out the direction they have been heading.

"If we continue to follow this river—" James says before he gets interrupted.

"Hey, this is us, we're right here," Keller shouts, pointing to the spot James was just about to get to before Keller jumped in. "It's a grass hut, just like what we made, that's us," he says, dancing around. "We're not lost."

"Dude, of course, we're not lost. But, now we know what the rest of the trek looks like," James says impatiently.

All the boys peer over the map being held in place by dozens of dirty-nailed fingers. Their eyes follow along the White Feather Falls trail they remember Bear pointing out yesterday. A circle around the letter C is probably the final checkpoint, appearing to be about ten miles from where they stand now. If they are reading the map correctly, they have to reach the falls by day four, in order to cross beneath them, and circle back along the other side of the river to follow it south before returning to the lodge.

"So, if we're here, then Bear must be that way, straight ahead— maybe a mile, I think," James says, sounding only half sure.

"But what if you're wrong?" Slater says, wondering what their back-up plan will be.

"If I'm wrong, we're making a fire and heating up one of our dinner packets to eat for breakfast. I'm starving. Who's with me?" James asks.

All the hands shoot into the air—Macaroni's being the first one.

"It's only a mile, we'll find him. If we don't, we double-back to this same spot. He'll find us. He's gotta come back for his stuff sooner or later, right?" Tobey says logically.

"Hey, are we gonna run into Viper's group? Where are they supposed to be today?" Macaroni wants to know.

"Yeah, we're gonna find them tonight. When they least expect it, they're gonna get something to remember us by, that's for sure," Slater says menacingly.

"Okay, first food. Then, revenge," James says, laying out their priorities.

They walk through the untouched forest, creating a pathway of snapped twigs and bandana remnants torn into tattered rags they tie around thin tree limbs to mark their way back in case the map is wrong—or, in case *they* are wrongly reading it.

Twenty minutes of careful hiking feels more like twenty hours.

"Hey, what's that noise?" Macaroni whispers to Slater in front of him.

Slater leads with the hand command for *stop, listen to what I hear.* All the boys behind him stop moving at once. Faintly, off in the distance, they hear the sound of splashing, gentle movement against the soft ripples of water.

"We must be getting close. Bear should be fishing in the stream just ahead," James says with certainty, turning to Tobey and Macaroni who are right on his heels.

They creep forward, hoping they are not met with a different surprise instead. They approach from the back to spy on a man dropping his lure into the stream, sitting against a boulder, sipping on coffee with his free hand. Suddenly, his fishing line starts to bob, splashing that coffee all over the front of his shirt. "Well, don't just stand there, come and give me a hand, boys," Bear calls out to them without even turning around.

"How'd he do that?" Slater whispers to James.

"Beats me, I thought we were doing a pretty good job of sneaking up on him," James says, snickering.

The group rushes forward to help tug on the fishing rod, but Bear pushes them back with one arm saying, "No, I got this—what I need is a new cup of coffee." They all laugh easily at his relaxed demeanor. "You boys made it here faster than I expected. I've already caught a dozen fish, but there's plenty more where these came from, so I'll keep fishing and for anybody who wants to join in, grab a spear and do it the old-fashioned way—the really old-fashioned way, like when Neanderthals roamed the earth."

Bear hands his reel to Slater, after getting assurances that Slater knows how to handle a rod. "Yeah, I've done this, like, a million times with my Grandpa Bruce. I totally got this, Bear," he says with pure confidence.

"Okay, while Slater's roping in what will be our second helping of trout, who's making the fires? I want three fires set up so we can get breakfast going soon. You guys hungry?"

"Starving," the kids say collectively in varying degrees of shouts.

"Okay, I want to see the fire action I taught you last night. Three teams, one prize for the first team who gets flames: waterproof matches. You know how to turn your regular matches into waterproof matches? Dip the heads into wax from a candle and let them dry. When you need them, just pick off the wax before you strike. Works every time, campers," Bear says, imparting knowledge every five minutes, his own personal goal. "Ready, split into three teams; on your mark, get set, go!"

Tobey, Macaroni and Keller have no problem with the first step. "Gather up as many dry leaves as you can for us to put into a big pile. Leaves burn, you know," Tobey says, winking to Macaroni in front of Keller.

James and Drake search for sharp sticks they can carve into spears for fishing the way Bear suggested; while Duncan, Reuben,

Colby, and Zach compete in two teams to make fires of their own. Everyone is hustling, exactly what Bear likes to see from young men—especially before six in the morning.

Along with Keller's help, it should come as no shock that Macaroni and Tobey make fire before anyone else. Their reward of one pack of waterproof matches is shared between them, each boy taking four matchsticks for his own personal supply. Their other reward is they get first pick from the catch of the day. While they are cooking trout using their mess kit frying pans, the other two teams are staring closely at sticks that refuse to smolder, willing them to ignite with all their might.

Just when Tobey, Macaroni and Keller are enjoying fried fish for breakfast, the other two groups are finally getting their smokestacks to spew forth flames. No matter—their tummies needed some extra time for the queasiness to wear off after they watched Bear chop off the heads of several trout and rip open their guts to fillet them with his hunting knife.

"Bear, uh, we wanted to tell you something," Slater starts off now that everyone is mostly finished with their trout.

"What's that, camper?"

"Last night, when James and I went to check the bear line, we got attacked by Viper's group. They threw a net over us and strung us up on the tree limbs, telling us not to yell or bears would come eat us," Slater finishes, sounding sheepish for having to admit out loud he couldn't defend himself.

"I think my first question is why am I only hearing about this now? Why didn't you yell anyway for me to come get you?"

"I believed we might get eaten by bears," Slater says, bowing his head.

"Me too. They were pretty convincing and it was so dark and we already had seen a pack of raccoons and all the animals started making noises, so we froze," James says, making more sense of why they were so helpless.

"Guys, I'm really sorry that happened to you. Must have scared the holy business out of you," Bear says sincerely, before bursting into a gut-splitting laugh. "Imagine, you two hanging from the trees, all crawled up into yourselves thinking you were bear bait." He slaps his knee and throws back his head, while the rest of the group watches Slater and James start to steam.

"Hey, there were, like, a dozen of them, we were completely surrounded and they had war paint all over their faces. They were acting crazy," Slater says, justifying their decision to not scream for help.

"Besides, we didn't know if they really were gone after they left. They could have been lurking in the bushes, waiting to see what we would do, and then what would they have done to us if we disobeyed?" James adds, hoping this will get their leader to calm down and take them seriously.

Bear howls, unable to control his fits of laughter until Slater is boiling mad.

"Hey, Bear, you're supposed to be out here to protect us and instead you're just laughing at us like a big jerk—"

Bear flips onto his side quickly and Army crawls up the bank to grab at Slater's ankles before Slater can even finish his sentence. When Bear sits on Slater's shins, pinning his arms to his sides, Slater starts yelling at the top of his lungs. "Get off me! Get off!" Slater says, struggling to break loose. "My parents are gonna have you fired big time—you won't be able to work anywhere again."

James and the other guys have no idea how this escalated so quickly. Half of them are up on their feet now, while the others are still figuring out where to put their pan of food so it will still be safe when they return.

Bear says not a word. He is calm and unresponsive while Slater wears himself out. "My dad's the D.A., you know. You're gonna go to jail for this, Bear. Get your fat butt off me!"

Bear just looks at Slater, coming closer to his face, staring him directly in the eyes without even blinking once.

"You guys, help me, don't just let him torture me like this. Get him off!" Slater keeps squealing.

"Don't even move an inch. None of you is to take one step toward your friend here, not a single move—just observe what happens next."

Slater is so hysterical, he is practically crying.

"Bear, get off him. This is too far," Tobey says authoritatively.

"Not one word from you, camper. You are not in charge today. You haven't earned it," Bear says, continuing his laser focus on

Slater. "You're mad now, aren't you? I take your freedom from you and suddenly, you're kicking and screaming. But, why didn't you do a thing to protect yourself last night? You afraid of the dark, or something? Where was all this energy last night when the crazies were tying you up in a tree?" Bear says, goading Slater so that all his adrenaline surges through his body.

"I hate you so bad, Bear! I am going to get you for this. No job. Ever," Slater hisses, feeling foolish for appearing so weak in front of the others.

"Slater, take that energy and do exactly as I say right now. Use your left leg, point your knee upward, then quickly turn it on its side and get your foot on the ground," Bear says, feeling some shifting beneath him. "Now, buck your right hip into the air and twist your body to your right side real fast, taking me with you," Bear says calmly.

In some version of a sideways somersault, Slater has broken free of Bear's hold and is now sitting on top of Bear in the coolest wrestling move he has ever performed.

"Dude, you have two choices right now, stay on top of me and torture me, but know that I will be reversing this position really quick since I already know all the moves; or you can jump up to run for help. What your instincts should be telling you is to run for help—but your pride and your bruised ego are gonna make you want to beat the living daylights out of me," Bear finishes with a grin. "Am I right?"

Slater keeps his laser focus on Bear while he controls his

breathing, enjoying this vantage point of being in the position of power. "You guys think I should beat the crap out of him?" Slater says loudly to the crowd, who all know this is just his anger talking. There is no way Slater can overpower this man.

"Slater, just get off him. It's okay, man," James says, understanding his embarrassment.

"What's it gonna be, bud?" Bear asks sincerely.

"I'm getting up, but no tricks, all right?" Slater says, not sure about trusting Bear after this.

"Gentleman, give him a round of applause," Bear says enthusiastically to Slater's friends. "There is nothing scarier than being surprise attacked from the back, especially in the dark of the night, and worse, feeling completely helpless to do something."

He puts his arm around his shoulder and continues.

"Seriously, Slater, any one of us would have reacted the way you and James did last night. Part of my job is to prepare you against that from ever happening again, whether it be at school, or after some night dance, or coming home from the movies, even if it's five years from now. What you learn here this week is going to stick in your mind—and your body will know what to do whenever the time comes," Bear says, full of congratulations and awe at Slater's strength here today.

"So, you weren't being a jerk?"

"Oh, I was being a jerk—a big fat jerk. I was trying to get you mad so you would forget your fear. Fear paralyzes us. Anger I can work with," Bear says, smiling at the crowd.

"Well, how come you didn't act this way toward James?" Slater asks through narrowed eyes.

"Oh, I could have," Bear says, with a wink toward James. "But you seem to have a bit more fire inside you. Thought it might be easier to show the class our first self-defense tactic with your help."

Now Slater starts to grin, looking a bit more relaxed.

"Ready for some more moves? That is, if I'm not fired?" Bear says good-naturedly.

"Oh, yeah, sorry about that," Slater says.

"Hey, you swing with what you got. You have a mouth on you, that's for sure," Bear teases. "You've got some brains, too. Now we just gotta figure out how to put them to work together for your advantage."

The boys all volunteer to be the next victim until they learn all the moves in Bear's arsenal. It takes them the entire morning to get the basics and when they break for lunch, they return to their grass hut.

"I like what you've done with the place," Bear says seriously, pausing to look at the entire site destroyed in front of them.

"What happened?" Macaroni says, not believing his eyes.

They all look at the same thing when Drake speaks first. "Dude, check out our hut."

They solemnly move forward inch by inch. If a war had taken place here, it would not look any different. The grass thatches that were so carefully laced together with twine made of reed and strong leaves have been torn apart, strewn around the entire campsite as if wild banshees had cast spells across these grounds.

Their backpacks have been ransacked, depleting most of their belongings. The food that was once safely tied up on the bear line—cut now—has been ravaged by raccoons, or other animals.

"My food!" Macaroni screeches. "What are we going to do for the week? How are we going to survive?" He starts to make sounds like he is stifling his tears until he can no longer hold them back. "I want to go home, Bear," poor Macaroni wails while Keller, Tobey and Slater try to comfort him.

"Dudes, I'll let you in on a little secret—life is full of disappointment. You can't always control the good or bad things that happen to you; you can only control your response," Bear says evenly. "You're mad, you're upset and you're hungry, too. What are you most mad about? Tell me right now."

"Someone came into our place and destroyed what we worked so hard to build. That hut was a masterpiece," James says, everyone else nodding feverishly.

"Someone stole all our food. We shared our food with each other and even did trades to get back the stuff we really wanted. And now we have nothing." Macaroni cries more deeply.

"Where's our clothes and stuff? I want my stuff back," Slater says, desperately scouring through his pack, looking for it. "My compass is gone. Who took it, Bear? Who came through our camp and stole all our stuff?" His voice, on edge, cracks a bit, a hint of tears about to come from his eyes, too.

"Slater, you had your compass this morning. Check the side pockets of your pants," Tobey says, reminding him softly considering the stress of the day.

Slater pats down his cargo pockets, feeling for the small tin shape through the bulk of his hook-and-loop closures. "Yes!" he exclaims overjoyed. "It's here," he says, pulling out the familiar compass to hold in his hands. "Still, I want the rest of my stuff back, Bear."

"Guys, there's only one way to get your stuff back," Bear says, giving it to them straight.

"How?" James wants to know.

"Take it," Bear says, walking toward his tent, motioning behind his head with his hand for them to follow.

CHAPTER 18

What's Mine Is Mine

It is perfectly unsurprising to Bear that his tent remains completely intact. This is usually how the plan goes—other teams only
pick off a couple targets from within a rival group, never their
commander. So, he has full confidence that this agreement has
not been compromised. His soft bed is rolled, tied and standing
in the corner of his tent where he left it. His supply duffle is still
zipped next to it. When he opens it up to rifle around inside, he
sees that everything appears to be in place just like it was when
he inventoried his list last night.

From inside his shirt pocket, Bear pulls out his map with all the
markings they are used to looking at by now. But this time, the
boys copy the markings onto their own maps, matching Bear's.

This way, if anyone gets separated from the group, they all have the same information.

"Part of survival is avoiding the element of surprise. Anticipate the problems you might encounter before you encounter them, then prepare your response ahead of time," Bear says, passing around his canteen to share his water. "One thing you gotta know is this was planned. Viper has a senior team of boys who have been through this camp at least twice. They know these woods by now, and they sort of earn this rite of passage to scare the wits out of the newcomers—"

"What? You knew we were gonna get pinned to the trees?" James shouts.

"You knew they were gonna steal all our stuff?" Slater yells. "What kind of a camp is this?"

"Where are they now? Do you know that, too?" Drake asks threateningly.

"Are you gonna help us get our food back tonight?" Macaroni asks hopefully.

"Guys, I couldn't tell you about this part of the plan earlier because danger never gives a warning; it just comes at you. To survive, you must always be thinking, always be anticipating for what can go wrong and measure how prepared you are in this moment—at all times," he says, facing the scowls.

"Bear, you coulda told us *something*. Like, hey, maybe you guys should take turns guarding the hut tonight," James says boldly.

"In order to see what skills I needed to teach you, I had to first see how you would react in a scary situation," Bear says, hoping he is getting through to them.

"How do we know whose side you're really on, Bear?" Slater says, challenging him.

"You're right, how do you know if you can trust me? We just met. So, you gotta pay attention to what your gut says. When you get a feeling someone's lying to you, your gut will tighten. When you get a feeling someone's looking out for you and has your back, your gut will relax. So you gotta ask yourself right now, what's your gut say?"

The boys look around at each other, wondering what their friends think, unsure of what to know for certain. "What do you say, guys? Do we trust him?" Slater asks, putting it to a vote.

Keller and Macaroni raise their hands first. Bear is the only one who knows this forest and probably can fish for them if they never find their own food again.

Tobey, Drake and the other boys slowly put their hands up too. James and Slater are the last ones. They look at one another, trying to read each other's minds and then make the motion that they are better off trusting their commander—because this could go horribly wrong if they can't.

"Okay, from here on out, I'll tell you what you *need to know.* Everything else, you gotta kinda figure out together. That's the only way you're gonna learn how to survive," Bear says, sounding ominous.

"Well, here's something I think we *need to know,"* James starts out. "Are they planning a second attack on us before the week is over—not just Viper's group, but anyone?"

"Yeah, what else is in store for us in this little game you guys have rigged?" Slater asks, not liking this one bit.

"Yes, prepare for it. Before the fifth night, when we are deep up the trail, there are going to be some traps that you could easily fall into if you don't know what to look for," Bear shares quietly. "So, I'm going to teach you what to look for and how to set your own."

"Are these guys trying to hurt us, or what? Sounds like we're being hunted or something," Slater says to the group, before turning to look at Bear.

"Of course you're not being *hunted*—you're being *tested*," Bear says seriously. "You gotta remember, how do we know you're prepared with the survival skills we're teaching if you don't get a chance to use them, right?" he says logically. "Don't your teachers ever give you tests about the stuff they've lectured? Well, this is like your survival school. You gotta pay attention to everything I show you if you want to make it back to the lodge with this team. If anybody catches you and brings you over to their side, well that's just a victory lap for them—plus a five-thousand-point value for capture, along with a steak and lobster buffet on the final night—for *them*, not you. If you get captured, you better hope you have one last meal packet in your backpack because that'll be dinner."

"Well, considering we don't have any of our food now, we better hope we find the stuff they stole from us before then," Tobey says, seething before the rest of the boys chime in.

"So, do you know where all the teams are right now?"

"Did they hide our stuff somewhere nearby?

"How are we gonna take our revenge?"

"Will you show us some traps now so we can get on our way?"

Bear is peppered with questions from the boys who keep shouting over each other as their nerves start to get the best of them.

"How are we ever going to make it through this week?" Keller asks, the only one brave enough to say out loud what everyone else is thinking.

For the rest of the afternoon, Bear plots the course of where the other teams are probably camping tonight, and then he teaches night maneuvers for sneaking up on them after first making sure there are no watchmen.

"We need to do the same. Think like a unit. Assign rotating shifts for who will guard our campsite while everyone else sleeps. How will you camouflage yourself so you blend into your atmosphere? Use what's around you. Those guys wanted you to know they were from Viper's team, so they wore their bridal headpieces, but you want to be invisible—you'll have more power and can instill more psychological fear if the other team has no idea who you are," Bear explains.

"Yeah, that's totally what they did to us—right, Slater?" James says, feeling duped.

"Oh, yeah. Total fear. They made us believe bears would eat us for breakfast if we made any noise at all. They messed with our minds. Oh, I can't wait to give them a taste of their own medicine," Slater says, rubbing his hands together, after gaining new-found confidence from the traps Bear has shown them how to dig.

"Okay, you know how to secure your perimeter tonight, and you've studied your maps, so you know the markers in the forest. It's time to canvass the land, then determine how you can bed-down safely tonight," Bear says. He wants them to be clear on the instructions before they make camp somewhere new.

They walk nearly ten miles, making the distance much quicker with emptied backpacks. "Viper's unit is probably right about here, guarding the food they have stolen from us and whichever other teams they were lucky enough to ransack," Bear says, pointing to a circle drawn around Parrott Cove. "This is the only cave between our two trails. It's small, but cool inside, so it's a good place for storage. They will probably have two guards posted all night, the rest of Viper's team will be sleeping further down the hill," Bear says, pointing another thirty yards away.

The boys imagine which one of them is going to be *brave* enough to surprise the guards and which one of them will be *strong* enough to hike out the food they steal back. Nobody wants to volunteer for either job.

"We gotta see the cave in the daylight to make our plan," Tobey says.

"I think Viper's team is probably too close to it by now and you'll be spotted for sure," Bear warns. "You've gotta trust that it's a regular cave and figure out your plan from there."

"Okay, we can't climb the hill in front of their camp, and we can't come in from the north or the guards will see us walking right towards them," James says, thinking this through out loud. "Can we access it from the backside and walk along the top to drop down the lip of the mouth?"

"Bingo," Bear says encouragingly, "now you're thinking."

The boys strategize from here and the more they talk, even Macaroni and Keller are feeling encouraged. "I think this might work," Macaroni says, willing to support whatever the group wants if it means getting back his food.

"You know, I can't go up there with you," Bear says, tucking himself in behind the small grove of trees away from Viper's camp. "You've gotta prove yourselves on this one."

"Yeah," Slater says, wishing it was different, knowing how much the gang needs moral support.

"Just keep an extra eye out for Keller; he's probably your most vulnerable target," Bear says with a parting reminder, as if Slater needs one more thing to worry about.

"Because of his size, yeah, I know. He reminds me of my brother. I'll watch him extra carefully," Slater says, staring across the grounds to the rest of the guys.

By the glow of the moonlight, ten adolescent faces exchange stares with one another, mirroring images with mud smeared over their exposed skin. On their heads are wreaths made out of leaves weaved together, sticks tucking into the side of their headbands with more foliage encircling inches above their hairline. They wear only the darkest clothing they still possess from the few items not stolen. They huddle now, speaking in low voices, assuring each other they have planned for everything.

"Macaroni, are you cool?" James asks, checking in after his near meltdown earlier when his band of leaves for his camouflage helmet kept falling apart.

"Yeah, I'm okay," Macaroni says, projecting confidence that is still shy of sounding like he means it.

"Dude, we're not gonna let you get captured," Tobey says, reassuringly.

"Yeah, we all go in together, we all come out together," Drake says, echoing their motto.

"All Bear can do is watch. He's hands off on this one," Slater says, getting ready to give the final Go signal. "Are we ready?"

He looks at every boy—every comrade—to be sure they feel him. They need to know this is the time to have each other's backs.

"We're ready," James says, his head nodding. "Let's do this."

Their campground has zero evidence they were ever here this evening, in case Viper—or any other team for that matter—comes looking for them again. They were sure to keep their packs out of sight by climbing trees, one at a time, hiding them high in the crotch of the branches—where the boys plan to sleep later. Any earth they disturbed was scattered beneath bushes a few yards away—the holes they dug, covered by leaves, the first step to building good traps. They learned to minimize their footprint the way Bear taught them. No food means no crumbs left behind, which really means no wrappers, no smells, no camper stamps.

Their middle of the night advance toward the cave carved into the hillside, with a path trailing up its dome like a dirt ramp, goes faster than expected. Nature made this part easy. The hard part will be crawling across its roof, surprising the two guards posted at the mouth's opening, getting what they came for, and getting out without retaliation from Viper's sleeping unit.

There are no words used—only well-rehearsed hand signals between Slater and James, who are leading the way. When they crawl, Drake and Tobey crawl too. When they stop, there is nothing but immediate silence. It's as if they are one long centipede, all arms and legs moving in synchronized steps.

James inches forward on his belly, choosing to wear only his long-sleeved dark t-shirt and his darkest underpants. He didn't want his cargo pants pocket loops to get caught on any twigs and he didn't want to make a sound with their brass buttons scraping against the rock shell. Since he took tumbling in elementary, the group decided he would be the front man—the most agile to glide and roll.

James peers over the edge of the dome, holding his breath, moving so slowly a snail might pass him by. He scouts all points to be sure the rest of his team is in place. He sees Macaroni and Keller make it to the tree line—the one Bear advised would be about twenty feet from the mouth. He slithers back again, indicating with his fingers there are two guards at the mouth, one of them squatting on the left side where he points beneath him. He calls the play they practiced with his silent fingers for the Go signal.

In one stealthy move, both James and Slater drop from the cave roof five feet above directly onto their assailants, riding them unevenly piggyback style before knocking them clear to the ground. They straddle them with their thighs, quickly covering their mouths with their hands until Tobey and Drake, only two seconds behind, rappel in using Bear's rope secured to a tree behind the cave to break their fall. Swatches of duct tape are used to mute their screams, while belts secure arms to their sides—an old trick of Slater's he happily shared with the group.

While Tobey and Drake manage step two, Macaroni, Keller, and the rest of the boys revel in step three—seizing the cave. They grope around in the dark, stuffing everything they can get their hands on into Bear's sleeping bag. Within two swift minutes, ten boys have raided their enemies' refrigerator tucked away yards from where they sleep. Slater and James carry the head and feet of the mummy bag while the other boys scout the trail back to Bear.

They are in and out so quickly they can hardly believe the hours of planning it took. Nobody says a word. They only lift their feet in a syncopated rhythm—the centipede storming softly away from the scene of the crime.

When they make it back to Bear's tree, he speaks with hushed excitement. "Any trouble?" He doesn't expect them to say anything different from what he witnessed through his binoculars.

"All according to plan," James says proudly, throwing his head back to Slater. "Right, man?"

"Even better," Slater says, watching Tobey and Drake strong arm one of the captured kids, while Macaroni and Keller flank the smaller of the two.

"Nice work; that ought to be ten thousand points and a steak and lobster dinner fit for kings. That is, if they don't steal these guys back—or worse," Bear says, stroking his chin.

"We already thought about that, Bear. So, we decided we want to move out tonight, no sleeping. We can get at least six hours ahead of Viper's group and maybe even push in front. We want to be the first ones to the lodge," Slater says, acting the part of mastermind.

"Yeah, and if you guys know what's good for you, you'll enjoy the food and our pleasant company and not make any more trouble for us. Got it?" Macaroni sneers boldly to the victims still bound, hardly presenting any threat at the moment.

The two boys nod their heads in agreement, happy to enjoy the food from Bear's team since they know there will be nothing for them on the last night. Shamefully getting captured means no lobster and steak rewards will be shared.

"Okay, then, let's move out. When I saw you coming down the hill, I started gathering your packs from the trees. I'm ready; let's go," Bear says, more alert at two a.m. than he has been in weeks.

They high-tail it out of this part of the woods, putting significant distance between them and Viper. They only stop to rest for the first time at eight a.m. when they check out the loot they scored inside Bear's sleeping bag.

Some of the food is recognizable, but there is even better stuff. Huge Ziploc bags hold barbecued chicken drumsticks by the handful. Others contain slices of meatloaf, dried salami, and beef jerky. They find tins of cookies and dessert bread loaves and dozens upon dozens of dry food packets along with military rations of canned food. They find tuna in cans with easy pull tops and a couple jars of peanut butter. There is enough to feed them easily for the rest of the week if they continue to fish for their breakfasts.

"You guys might actually like hanging out with us after a while," Tobey says to the two captives, who promised to remain silent in exchange for having the tape gently taken off their face after the first ten minutes.

"Whatever you say; we didn't like it over there that much anyway," one of them, named Vincent, says.

"Why is that?" Tobey asks curiously.

"One of those kids is crazy, we think," the other one, named Tim, says.

"Crazy, how?" Slater asks, wondering what else they should be preparing against.

"Mmmm, I don't know, maybe you'll find out before you make it back to the lodge," Vincent says, laughing maniacally at Tim in a high-pitched squeal, rolling onto his back and flopping around from side to side.

Slater and Tobey and James all look at one another, wondering if they just made the worst mistake of their lives.

Viper's group awakens at six a.m. to a sharp whistle blowing in one long emergency signal. The unit scrambles to fall out from their sleeping bags and tents into their shoes, racing to where Viper is standing up the hill in front of the cave.

"Anyone care to tell me what happened here last night?" Viper seethes.

"What's wrong, Command?" the kid called Cobra wants to know.

"Take a look for yourself and then do a head count," Viper says, stating the obvious.

All that's left inside this ramshackle of a cave is a note written in a hastily-penned scrawl on a dingy white under shirt.

What's mine is mine.

What's yours is now ours.

Eat dirt.

Catch our dust.

CHAPTER 19

Home Sweet Home

There is no slowing them down. Bear's team charges hard until lunch when they break for their first real meal. They don't even bother to fish because fish bite in the morning or evening, not usually during the day when they know they are more likely to become a lunch snack for some hungry angler. So, the boys are forced to eat from the rations they haul from Bear's sleeping bag. They disperse anything not requiring a fire to cook. The last thing they want is to help Viper track their smoke signals.

They shove globs of peanut butter by the fingers-full into their mouths, washing it down with water they still have in reserves. They empty cans of tuna one after the other, then relieve themselves in the woods, burying any signs they were here beneath scattered leaves covering their nature holes.

They move again, making it to the great turnaround point marked by two fallen trees, cresting at the peak of the hike thirty miles from where they began at the lodge three days earlier. Their fear of getting caught drives them to push onward. When dusk finally comes, they scale the tops of each other's shoulders to reach the crotch of the trees where they collapse into sleep. Bear stands guard below for the first watch. When the second shift is due to take over, there is no stirring—the boys are snoring with little hope of waking them.

"What the heck?" Bear peers through his binoculars, assessing what he has just spotted miles behind them farther down the trail they just hiked up. Urgently, he starts shaking the dangling legs attached to Slater, Tobey, James and Drake. "Guys, wake up. We gotta go. We've been compromised." He speaks with a rush of words, loud this time, hoping the others will become more alert with his blaring calls for everybody to move.

"What's going on, Bear? What time is it?" Slater asks, the fog still not lifting from his head.

"Guys, I fear we're about to have some visitors very soon. We gotta make a break for it," he says, stuffing his things into his pack, jangling ankles still suspended from trees. "If you want to be the first ones back to the lodge, we need to go—now. Your new little friends here have put you at great risk by leaving a trail of breadcrumbs straight to you," Bear says, throwing a sneer and a look of disgust at Vincent and Tim, who are already awake and feigning wide-eyed innocence.

"What? You thought we were just going to let you *take* us without any consequences?" Vincent roars in a voice bigger than his small frame might suggest he had the lung capacity for.

"Yeah, this is even better than what we could have anticipated, you dummies," Tim says, snickering at Bear's group, fully alert now.

"But how can breadcrumbs be followed at night? It's late, man, we should just sleep for a few more hours, I'm so tired," James says, still clearing the blurriness from his vision.

"Take the binoculars, look behind you down the hill. You see what I see?" Bear directs Slater, who gasps, handing them to James, who jumps out of his tree immediately to grab at the end of the sleeping bag he has been responsible for carrying so far.

"Slater, take the other end, let's move, move, move!" James yells feverishly.

Everybody jumps down from their perches, and laces up their boots, grabbing for anything they don't want to leave behind, scrambling to make haste out of these woods.

It only took two experienced juveniles held captive, uttering five words to scare the living daylights out of Bear's team—*glow-in-the-dark goo.*

"They've done a good job of laying markers for us," Viper says to Cougar, analyzing the small putty drops of goo made into balls smaller than the size of marbles.

It has been easy enough to follow Bear's team by daylight—the tramp of footprints stamped into the earth is a dead giveaway. But at night, it is so much harder to know if any shortcuts have been taken, which is why Viper's team has rehearsed for every scenario, including capture, and how to aid in your own inevitable rescue.

Viper has taken pride every year for the past six years in the fact that his teams rule the forest. Scoring the most points assures him of that steak and lobster feast he considers a given after every expedition. With so many returning campers this week, he thought for sure his team would be doing the capturing, not the other way around. But his unit knows that even the best men can be caught off guard once in their lives, so they all carry glow goo for this very reason.

The fact that Bear's team was smug enough to pick off Vincent and Tim is really only a relief to Viper because those two were a pain in the rear. They constantly compared the wealth of their parents to each other. They made sure to point out their grade point averages for each trimester and list how many awards they received. When the tie was still not broken, they would continue to bore the rest of the team with their long schedules of after-school activities they participated in, sometimes *three* in one day—and that they still had homework that kept them up until *two in the morning.*

Viper figured it wasn't his job to shut them up—he'd leave that to the rest of his unit. Unfortunately, he trained them all so well to operate as comrades who always looked out for each other that the other guys figured it'd be bad for morale if they made a stink out of hearing one more braggadocious story from Vincent and Tim. When they went missing, Viper's team took an hour to break camp—instead of only the seven minutes it should have taken.

"One loss is bad enough, but there's no way we want the reputation for two captives stolen from us in the dead of night. No way," Viper snarls. And when he says "we," he means "he"—*he* doesn't want to become the laughing stock of Elmer Woods.

"What should we do with these little urchins?" James asks the team about Vincent and Tim, implying they should just be left behind after giving away the team's position.

"Yeah, after we fed you guys and everything. We coulda been a lot meaner to you, too," Macaroni says, trying to sound tough, but his dimply knuckles and round face don't allow him to be too convincing.

The boys huddle together away from Vincent and Tim's eavesdropping. "Dudes, they're trouble. We shoulda known that from the beginning. What would happen if we just left them here for the Viper team to take back? We know they're following the goo. Those little deceivers, trying to act so innocent to us this whole time," Slater says with disdain, but secretly admiring their trickery.

"Something tells me we shouldn't do it. I bet we could get in a lot of trouble for abandoning kids out in the forest. What if there really *are* bears?" Keller says nervously.

"Yeah, I'm with him, we better not. But bringing them with us is only going to mean more problems. Besides, I don't really feel like sharing from our stash with traitors, do you?" Macaroni says wisely.

They stay in their huddle for a few minutes longer, Vincent and Tim staring at their heads jerking side to side and then bobbing forward rapidly as if they have all landed in general agreement. "You think they're talking about us?" Tim asks Vincent in a whisper.

"What else?" Vincent replies with a snort.

"What do you think they're gonna do to us?"

"Nothing compared to what Viper and the guys are going to do to *them* when they finally catch up to us," Vincent says arrogantly.

"Uh, Bear, we need you over here for a minute," Slater calls, waving his arm for Bear to come.

Bear leaves his post where he has been babysitting the two con men. "Don't even think of running. We've got kids who run track here—they'll flatten you within your first thirty-seconds out."

They have no intention of leaving. They are waiting for the drama to unfold and the only way this happens is when Viper shows up. Then the Bear team will be sorry.

"Oh, we're not going anywhere, Bear," Vincent says tauntingly.

"What are you guys thinking?" Bear wants to know what Slater's plan is now, throwing a glance over his shoulder at the two captives laughing wildly together in front of the tree where they stand. "They are so smug. They can't wait to see a war break out between Viper and me—I mean, our *teams*," Bear clarifies.

"We want to keep going. We can make it back first if we get a clear head start," Slater begins, locking eyes on each of the other guys who have already been consulted. "We want to make a clean break from the breadcrumbs, and who knows how close Viper's group is. We're gonna go it alone, Bear. We think we can do it. Will you stay here with Vincent and Tim until Viper shows up to reclaim them?"

All heads nod slowly that this is a group decision—unanimous. But what they don't know is how Bear will react.

"Guys, you're kinda my responsibility. I'm not supposed to just leave you here in the woods," he starts out reasonably.

"Well, how would it be any different if you broke your leg, or fell into a ditch and we had to go back for help?" Tobey asks legitimately.

"Well, hopefully, not all of you would leave me to my peril. Bears like the smell of broken bones, too," he chuckles.

"Okay, yeah, some of us would stay, you're probably right. But what do we do? We should go now, but we can't just ditch these guys in the woods—can we?" James asks, smiling vengefully.

"No, we can't—at least we *shouldn't*," Bear insists.

"How 'bout this: We only go twenty miles. The way we figure it, we could be to the lodge a day ahead of schedule if we keep trekking until sundown tonight. But we'll stop just before the final checkpoint and wait for you before hiking in the final ten. That way, no one has to know we ever got separated—"

"Except Viper and all his boys," Bear says, knocking down another suggestion.

"Come on, Bear, we're trying to make a break for it. Just let us go. Babysit these guys for a few more hours; Viper can't be that far behind, right?" Slater asks, sounding believably confident that he and the guys can pull this off. "We don't even care about the five-thousand points per capture, we just want to get back to the lodge before they try to steal one of us."

Bear thinks about this for a minute too long, which the boys take as a signal that his silence means he might be convinced. They throw out a few more solid reasons why he should let them take this chance, overpowering his thoughts with their solid rationale. "Bear, you said it yourself: this is our test. How else are we gonna prove we can survive if you hold our hands the rest of the way?"

This kind of logic is what he trained them to be ready for—how can he say no?

"Wait for me a mile before the checkpoint. You stay together, and remember everything I've shown you," Bear says cautiously. "I'll return these yahoos to Viper. If all goes well, I should see you before nightfall."

They have only known each other four days, but suddenly they feel as close as family ever could. They high-five Bear and get on their way. James and Slater take the lead, with Tobey and Drake bringing up the rear, sandwiching Macaroni, Keller and the other guys in between.

The weather is accommodating, but their appetites passed ravenous hours ago. They are numb and grimy with dirt and baked in sweat. They look like wild barbarians, hair so gritty it sticks straight out. Faces still heavily darkened by the mud smears to hide their identities in the night now serve as protection from the sun.

They walk in silence, while listening for the urgent approach of strangers whipping through the leaves, hoping to ensnare one of them for their victory prize. They ignore their fatigue. Pure adrenaline drives them forward. They will bathe in the river when they know they are safe, and they won't feel safe until they see the markings for the last checkpoint.

"Viper," Cougar says, looking through his high-powered binoculars, allowing him to see up to three miles ahead, "Vincent and Tim are sitting in a tree straight ahead of us."

"Their team must be worn out; they're finally sleeping—and in the daytime—what a gift for us," Viper says, getting ahead of himself.

"No, there's no one else around. It's just them," Cougar says quietly. "Here, have a look."

Viper sees two babies straddling the limbs of a tree where they are passed out in the shade of its branches. Behind them, only his good friend, Bear, stands watch.

"I can tell you one thing, we're not gonna be listening to their report card rundown for the next three days," Viper says, shaking his head before spitting at the ground.

"Okay, let's stop here," Slater says out loud, pulling his map from his pocket. "Are you guys reading the same thing? Are we only three miles from the checkpoint already?"

They confer with their own maps, thinking it odd they could have already traveled seventeen miles. "Well, considering we've been walking and jogging for several hours, it makes sense to me," Tobey says, grunting as he plops down on the forest floor.

"I'm so tired all of a sudden," James says, laying the sleeping bag down, hoping for some deli sandwiches to come crawling out of it. "We should eat. Let's eat as much as we can. We're gonna be at the lodge so soon, and we'll get more food then," he says, swiftly throwing out the remaining of their rations.

"Okay, let's at least be smart about this. Macaroni, you and Keller take Colby and Reuben with you to fill all our canteens in the river. We'll stay here to guard the food and set up our sleeping pods in the trees, okay?" Slater says, giving instructions as a force of habit by now.

"Yeah, we wait here for a little while, take a short rest, then move a couple miles closer to where Bear said to wait," James says, sounding like *he* is the one in charge.

"Yeah, that's just what I was saying, James," Slater huffs.

"Dude, attitude," James throws back.

"Hey, guys, let it wait until Bear gets here. We can't have any distractions. We gotta be vigilant. You never know when Viper's team might be coming up from behind some tree. We get water, we have some food, we take a short rest, then we move, like we *all* agree," Tobey says, sounding rational.

When Macaroni and his helpers return from the river a few feet away, the other guys are sound asleep, having eaten only their fair share of the rations, leaving plenty for their friends to enjoy. Soon, Macaroni, Keller, and the rest are sleeping at the stumps of those trees, just too tired to climb up to the beds that were already made for them in the limbs. So sleepy, they stretch out—never feeling the boot kicking at their feet three hours later.

"Bear," Viper says cordially. They are, after all, best friends who golf together when they're not running these survival camps.

"Viper, you finally found us," Bear says, ribbing him a bit.

"Yeah, looks like my men here knew to lay a night glow for us to follow," Viper says, turning to his two campers. "Good work."

"Well, my bus already left, so I've got to hoof it outta here. I return your two recruits to you, fine young gents they are," Bear says, with a knowing glance to Viper.

"I'll take 'em. Bet they can tell us a whole lot of your secret plans," he says hopefully.

"Bet they can't," Bear spouts off, waving his hand over his head as his back becomes smaller and smaller in the distance as he runs through the trees, dodging and weaving.

"Hey, wake up!" Bear says, kicking at Macaroni and Keller who rock from side to side, mumbling inaudible strings of words he can't put together.

Splash!

"Aaahgggg!" Keller yells, waking abruptly from the nice dream he was having.

Macaroni has the same reaction—quite grumpily opening his eyes before smiling widely, shielding the sun to be sure it's not a figment of his imagination. "Bear! You're back!"

"Sorry about the water in the face, Mac, but you guys sleep like a bunch of logs," he says smiling at them. "Hey, guys!" Bear shouts up at the tree limbs, grabbing onto ankles, and clapping their feet against each other, "let's get a move on to the lodge. I ran all the way here, but Viper is right behind me, maybe two or three hours is all," Bear shouts happily.

The only way Bear is able to put so much distance between himself and Viper is the long-distance running he has done ever since he learned to run cross-country track in high school. A twenty-six-mile marathon only takes him a little over four hours—so reaching the boys seventeen miles in, took only the afternoon.

"Guys, let's go. We only have the last ten miles before we finish. You could be getting a hot shower and a warm meal at the lodge in about three hours from now if we hustle," Bear says, making it sound tempting.

Their bones are weary. Their throats are very dry. Even though they've eaten more today than any other, the lack of sleep and the panic that has sustained them are draining their energy. The final ten miles feel longer than all the combined miles they walked this week. But no one complains. No one insists on sitting down. No one cries. Instead, they follow each other's shadows. Like a centipede, they move through the motions in a single syncopation, in rhythm to the current of the river's call. All they can think about is home. Home sweet home.

"What's the first thing you're going to do when you get back?" James asks Slater.

"I'm gonna raid the fridge. My mom always has food. Like, good food, too. I bet she'll have lasagna waiting for me, and maybe some barbecued chicken legs, and I bet she'll have some chocolate cake with fudge icing. She knows what I like. Man, why'd you have to get me thinking about food?" Slater says, joshing his new friend. "Why, what are you gonna do?"

"Probably I'm gonna hang out with my baby bro. He's, like, three and he's my best friend. He imitates everything I do. It's hilarious, man," James says, smiling at the thought of it.

"Cool, does he talk yet?"

"Dude, he says everything I say. You should hear him, but he can't even pronounce stuff right, cracks me up. My mom says I better watch my TV when he's around because he copies that too. He comes into the kitchen, climbing into his highchair, and then pounds his fists down and asks, 'Where's my food, woman?'" Only it comes out sounding more like, 'Wes ma food, woo-man.' She does not like that at all, but it's hysterical," James says, laughing so much his eyes start watering.

Slater starts cracking up hard, too. He and James laugh until they can hardly stand up straight, holding onto each other's shoulders, the other one leaning down trying to breathe, pushing his hands onto his knees. Pretty soon, the rest of the group is talking about what they're gonna do when they get home.

Everyone has some variation on the same thing—pig out and spend time with family.

"What's the second thing you're gonna do?" James asks, waiting for the next golden answer to keep their fit of hysterics going.

"Put my damn door back on its hinges," Slater says, howling even louder. James throws his head back like he's never heard anything funnier before. Oh, if he only knew—Slater is dead serious.

CHAPTER 20

Trifecta

When Bear's team clocks into the final checkpoint, they are logged in at 6:23 p.m. Thursday night—twenty-four hours ahead of schedule. "You're the first team through, Bear," Rooster says, collecting the last of the supplies Bear didn't need after all. He returns only the first-aid duffel.

"Really? Now, that is a first," Bear says to himself, before turning to the guys to shout, "Hey, you did it! You're number one!"

Cheers resound, although their enthusiasm is replaced with shallow hollers when Bear reminds them there are still three miles between them and that hot shower. They guzzle cold waters, refilling their canteens under the spigots outside until they are frozen by the sound of crunching branches.

"It's them," Slater whispers to Tobey. "How'd they already catch up to us?"

"They must have run like we did. Dudes, we got to go," Tobey murmurs quietly, darting inside the checkpoint to alert the others.

Even the guys relieving themselves in the woods catch glimpses of Viper's team at the narrow part of the hill path, trailing single file toward the lodge. Bear charges to the front and signals for everyone to fall in, buddy to buddy this time, making sure they don't leave anyone behind.

"Move, move, move," his hand waves wildly while he silently mouths the words.

They jog the final three miles back to the lodge, making such good time they drop across the last checkpoint in twenty-five minutes.

The caretakers of the lodge are there to greet them with astonished looks. "Look who we've got here—we didn't expect to see you boys until tomorrow evening," Floyd says to Juniper, who puts down her broom.

"My goodness, you look like you haven't eaten for days," she says, walking over to hug Bear. "I've got steaks marinating for tomorrow's final farewell dinner. I suppose I could grill them now and get some more this afternoon to replace them," she says with a wink.

"Oh, Juniper, how would we ever get along here without you?" Bear asks, backing away politely so she doesn't have to smell his lingering stench. "We'll hit the showers, then I'll show them where they can bed-down tonight. Is the Tree House already made up?"

"You know it is. First team back always wants the Tree House, so I got it ready this morning. Go get the boys settled and your dinner will be ready when you come out to the kitchen," she says, revealing a small gap between her front teeth in her enormous smile.

Juniper and Floyd are the married caretakers for Elmer Woods. They're not the only ones seeing after the place, but they are the most senior couple that has been here from the beginning of this family business. Elmer—their son—was a fine officer in the military, with a long history of leading boys into battle, teaching them how to become men who would return home again because of the survival skills they learned under his command.

When he finished his service, Elmer wanted to extend his knowledge to summer campers so they could learn to think like soldiers even if they never planned for a life in the military. He bought this land twenty years ago and built the lodge that sits on it today.

What began with help from his cousins and parents has evolved into a high-demand profitable business. His family all loved the experience of being outdoors so much they decided to stay. Now that Elmer Woods is known all over the country, he can afford to pay them a nice salary and house them in the private cabins he built three years after opening.

"Thanks, June," Bear says, saluting his aunt.

"Use a little extra soap, baby. I can still smell you from here," she says, laughing warmly.

"Fellas, let's go. You get the honor of sleeping in the Tree House tonight. It's the first bit of royal treatment we extend to the first team in," Bear says, good-naturedly.

The boys walk behind him through the lodge, to the back staircase built along the outside wall, facing the river. They climb the steps made from knotty pine—its wood evenly coated in a golden glaze to give it a rustic look. When they reach the top, the entire floor expands in front of them, to show a thatched grass roof canopy, hovering above ten beds dressed in fresh white sheets and goose down comforters. Plaid wool blankets are draped across the end of each bed, right beside a modest chest positioned at the foot for personal belongings.

The boys take in the sight of the enormous terrace and can't wait to crawl into bed—after they eat, of course. Their fraternity bathroom is through an inside door that features the length of one wall with ten wooden stalls made of the same knotty pine. Behind each private door is a long gooseneck rainfall showerhead ready to greet them with all the scalding hot water they need to wash away the week's filth.

They waste no time, claiming their own showers, stripping off clothes they would like to burn, then standing on slats of teak wood, allowing the water to wash away the mud and debris.

The soap mounts on the wall generously dispense scented foam at the push of the lever, or shampoo and conditioner from aqua blue bottles. They lather with it, staying under the water for longer than their parents who pay the water bill at home would ever allow.

Realizing they have no change of clothes becomes no problem when they notice matching grey terry cloth robes already hanging inside each of their door stalls.

Across from their showers, they find an incredibly long aluminum counter with ten sinks all in a line. Stacks of towels in varying sizes are rolled neatly in the open cupboard beneath each personal washbasin. A miniature grooming pouch supplies each guest with disposable toothbrushes wrapped in plastic, a packet of floss, along with a tube of hair gel and a wide-tooth comb tucked inside.

"Did I die and go to my mom's beauty spa?" Slater says out loud, wearing a wide-eyed grin, the same as the other boys.

"Did I die and go to a fancy hotel?" James counters. "Quick, name a fancy hotel," he says, trying to think.

"I don't know but this is about as good as what those dogs got in that one movie," Macaroni says happily.

"Yeah, this just can't be beat," Keller says, slipping his feet into a cushy pair of one-size-fits-all terry cloth slippers in matching grey, like the robe.

"Bear, are we supposed to wear our grimy clothes after *this?*" Drake asks, wondering about his putrid-smelling pants, shirt and stiff underpants.

"Nah, you guys are gonna be treated like kings from here on out. Juniper left linen bags in the hall. Grab one, write your name on the tag, then stuff all the clothes you want washed inside. It should be ready after dinner. We've got like thirty machines in the laundromat here."

"This place is so cool," Macaroni says, totally impressed.

"We've got another little surprise for you waiting on each of your beds," Bear says, still smiling.

When the boys finish scrubbing their faces, polishing their teeth, and combing their hair, they find a lounging outfit inside each of their footlockers. Each heather-grey, thick-cotton T-shirt reads, *"I survived Elmer Woods."* On the back, their name appears across the top, just above *Bear Team.* The drawstring pants are in a charcoal gray and feel extra soft against their fresh skin.

Some of the boys keep their robes on over their lounging clothes before they all head down for their private feast. Juniper's kitchen is not so much a kitchen as it is a cafeteria where the boys walk through a long line, selecting as much as they like of everything she has prepared. They choose from baked potatoes, mashed potatoes, macaroni and cheese, and an assortment of steamed vegetables. They grab at baskets of warmed rolls, continuing to the end where freshly grilled steak is still sizzling. For anyone wanting a different option, Juniper also keeps vegetarian lasagna on hand, all heated, oozing cheese and dripping in her homemade tomato sauce.

When the boys grab their drinks and head to their banquet table, they walk right by the dessert table, planning to save room for their next plateful.

"Boys, put down your forks; we're gonna say a proper word before we eat," Bear begins solemnly. "I want to commend you for the grit you showed here this week. I would estimate you've experienced nothing harder in your lives thus far, and I want you to know you are among the top teams I have had the pleasure of guiding through Elmer Woods. I'm grateful we made it back safe and sound. Bless this chow. Now eat," he says, raising his glass of milk as they follow his lead.

After the clanking of silverware and the quiet inhaling of food can be heard for the span of a few minutes, another sound interrupts their peaceful eating altogether. The rustling of people and jangling of emptied canteens alerts them to Viper's presence.

"They're here," James says slowly, before having a chance to finish swallowing.

"I hope this don't get ugly," Drake says, gulping his milk.

The rest of them stay real still at their seats, planning their next move in case it does get real ugly.

"Bear, you dog," Viper says in a booming voice, leading in his posse of disheveled looking troopers.

"You certainly look like you ate our dust. Good night, man. I've never seen you look worse," Bear throws back to Viper in a gloating manner.

They give each other a hug as Viper mutters under his breath for only Bear to hear, "If I had to listen to any more of that *'No, my GPA is higher on account of my college math class,'* I was going to have to hurl myself into the river and float back, brother."

Bear pulls away stifling laughter beneath his breath. "Dude, hit the showers, then come join us. We probably won't eat it all. June says we're eating the steak for tomorrow night's celebration, but she'll get some more later. It's so good, man," he says, sitting back down to finish.

"Hey, Bear team," Viper shouts assertively, startling everyone at the table. "Good job! You guys are the first team to ever beat me back. I think you may have just given Bear a whole new purpose for living," Viper says, razzing his younger cousin.

"Go on, get outta here, you're embarrassing me," Bear says, waving a fork at him in a gesture of appreciation.

"Yeah, we're gonna go get cleaned up. But seriously, nice work out there," Viper finishes, leaving the Bear team to eat in peace and to scratch their heads, wondering why they feared this guy the whole week long.

"Dude, he's not so bad, right?" Slater says to Bear.

"Remember what I taught you on day one? The biggest trick to survival is psychological warfare. Everybody plays his part—victim or survivor. You just gotta know what you're made of," Bear says, finishing his last lesson for the week. He knows better than to give away the family secret that, indeed, Viper is not so bad a guy. Especially considering that his cousin, Viper,—and Elmer Woods—are one in the same.

There haven't been many conversations between Slater, Tobey, and Macaroni that didn't involve some memory of their experience at

Elmer Woods. They used to talk about it in front of Chicky when they first got home nearly two months ago, but then they stopped since he started acting like he was being left out.

Summer flies by with regular secret meetings held between the boys in their favorite gazebo at Sugar Ridge Park. Today's meeting promises to be the juiciest one of all.

"So, you know how I got these side jobs and everything?" Slater pauses unnecessarily because all his friends know how much busier he has become earning money from practically every senior citizen and single mother in the neighborhood. "Well, I was over at Charlotte Rigby's house, helping her mom unload her garage full of boxes, and you'll never guess what I found," he says, pausing now in the very right place for dramatic effect. "Go on, guess."

"I don't know, some of her old stuffed animals?" Macaroni offers weakly.

"Naaaahhh," Slater says, sounding like a buzzer for the wrong answer on a game show. "Guess again."

"I know, her most embarrassing school photos," Tobey says, hoping he's right. "Is that it? I want to see them," he starts laughing, getting way ahead of himself.

"Dude, worse than that," Slater says. "You're never going to believe me."

"Just tell us already, will ya," Chicky says impatiently.

"Her diary!" Slater says triumphantly.

An audible gasp can be heard collectively. "No way, what's it say?" Macaroni asks excitedly.

"Where is it? Do you have it here? Let us see it," Tobey says overeagerly.

"Dudes, you're missing the point. I *saw* it but I couldn't actually get to it before her mom said she had been looking for that box for two weeks—"

"You mean you got us all excited for nothing?" Tobey grouses.

"Not hardly. It got me thinking, I bet you-know-who also has a diary," Slater says with a gleam in his eye.

"Who, Sibley?" Macaroni asks nervously.

"Yeah, I bet she does, and I bet there's a way we can maybe find it, too," Slater says, hatching a new plan for them.

"Count me out; my sister would kill me if I ever read her diary and I don't want to end up dead meat from Sibley White. I bet she would take a lot of revenge out on all of us. She's got weird parents. Who knows what's going on inside that house," Macaroni says.

"Dude, she's probably not as weird as you think. In fact, I've met her parents, they're cool," Slater says, defending her to his friends even though she's nowhere around to see him do it—just one more thing he won't get credit for doing right.

"Hey, I'll help you if you come up with a good plan that doesn't get us caught," Tobey says, mostly because he's been bored this summer just working at his dad's pizzeria.

"I can help you until school starts, but then I gotta stay focused. That's what my grandma says," Chicky says obediently.

"I don't have it all figured out yet, but I'm thinking about it," Slater says, leaning back and folding his fingers to rest across his chest as he looks up to the tops of the pine trees above their gazebo. "Boy, what I wouldn't give to know what she's written in there."

"Hey, Mom's taking us back-to-school shopping. She wants us downstairs in ten minutes," Graham says, poking his head into Slater's room.

"Uh, no. You can go, but I hate shopping. Just tell her I want some new jerseys and jeans. Oh, and tell her I want the new shoes by Taiko," Slater says, lying back on his bed, reading a car magazine.

"Come on, don't make me go alone with her. She's gonna make me try on all these colorful shirts and I think she mentioned pink last year. I know she's gonna get me something to make me look like the Easter bunny. You gotta come," Graham says, pleading his case.

"Hey, I got a better idea. Why don't you tell her we'll wear whatever she picks out without us, and you can stay here to help me with my master plan," Slater says, sounding like he is up to his sneaky old ways.

"What's your plan? I want to know," Graham says eagerly.

"First, go tell her. Make it sound convincing, too. Don't get her mad or suspicious, Graham. Don't blow this," Slater says menacingly.

"Okay, okay, I got it," Graham says, slinking out of Slater's room to play out the scene Slater practically scripted.

"Let's go find your brother," Lynn says to Graham, who was not quite as convincing as he was supposed to be. "Slater, are you saying you don't care what I come home with; you're going to wear it to school—no complaints?" she asks, narrowing her eyes, hardly believing her ears.

After years of wishing for a little girl she could dress, she is finally getting what she's always wanted—sons willing to let her pick out their clothes for the first day of school.

"Okay, I'm going then," she says, turning back with a grin. "You boys are going to look even more handsome this year, if that's possible."

"Thanks, Mom," Slater reels off casually.

"Yeah, thanks, Mom," Graham copies his brother.

Her taillights are fiery red when her foot is on the brake. They spy their usual way, through the slats of Slater's shutters, watching patiently as she puts her foot on the gas, shifting into gear. Once she turns the corner, they check downstairs to be sure she hasn't left behind her purse or her phone, or anything sitting on her errand table by the front door.

"I think the coast is clear," Slater says, feeling amped up about finally putting his plan into motion.

"What are we going to do?" Graham asks, following Slater out to the garage for his toolbox and then through the house and back downstairs to the basement, where he drops off his tools on the bottom step of the staircase.

Graham keeps yammering about how it's dark down there and

recalling the time Slater locked him in the basement and he had to crawl up through the laundry chute like Spiderman. "Hey, you're not planning on leaving me down here again, are you? That would be really mean, Slater."

"Graham, quit your whining already. I need you for far more important things today," Slater says, heaving something heavy away from the wall where it's been tucked for the last year.

"No way, uh-uh, nope, can't do it. Slater, you're gonna get in even bigger trouble," Graham says, backing up slowly, marveling at how strong his brother has gotten since he returned from that fun-sounding camp.

If Graham only knew what really went down that week at Elmer Woods, he would never be able to sleep again. He'd have nightmares haunting him for the rest of his life.

"Dude, just be quiet and help a guy out for once in your life," Slater says, wrestling with the girth of an unwieldy door that tilts side to side while he awkwardly balances it behind his shoulders. "Pick up that end, and don't drag it on the ground. I don't want my door all scuffed up because you're clumsy," Slater says temperamentally, huffing and puffing.

"Oh man, you're gonna get me into trouble, too. I'm telling Mom you made me do it. I completely protest against this idea for your own good, Slater," Graham blathers while Slater grunts.

"Come on, Graham, two flights to go, hold it steady. I'm doing the heavy lifting here," Slater says through gritted teeth, not realizing how heavy a door really is. "Just save your strength and keep your trap shut."

"Gee, Slater, you're really nice. I'm helping you against my will. The least you could do is be appreciative. Would a little kindness kill you?" He sounds more and more like their mother, who has been overheard muttering the same beneath her breath ever since Slater returned from the woods.

"Yeah, okay, Graham, let me think of a few nice things to say to you while I'm sweating this thing on my back," he says sarcastically.

"That's it. I'm dropping my end. You're mean, Slater, just plain old mean," Graham says, his voice becoming high and tinny the way it gets right before his feelings are hurt and he begins to cry. Even Slater can't stand the sight of Graham in tears.

"All right, all right, I didn't mean it, I'm sorry. Come on, Graham, you don't need to cry about it. I'm just hot and this is harder than I expected. I'm taking my frustrations out on you," he says, sounding sincere. "Promise, I am," Slater finishes, beads of sweat dripping from his forehead.

"Okay, Slater, but you owe me something for this, something nice," Graham says, not sure what he wants just yet.

"Okay, I guess I do. You sure you've got your end really good now?" Slater asks, happy to be deflecting those crocodile tears.

"Yeah, let's go."

It is surprising that a soon-to-be seventh-grader can navigate a bedroom door all the way up two flights of stairs and position it into place with the expert help of his soon-to-be fifth-grade brother holding it steadily. It is even more surprising that this twelve-year-old boy is able to perfectly align the hinges on his doorframe, drill the screws back into the holes from where they were removed, then hammer the long golden pins to secure the door in its place—just as good as new.

"You did it, Slater! You actually put your door back on. Dad's gonna kill you, but still he's probably gonna be blown away that you did this all by yourself—well, with some help from the kid," Graham says, congratulating himself.

"Thanks, kid, now scram," Slater says rudely, before doing what he has longed to do for an entire year—slam his door shut.

Back inside his private sanctuary, Slater does nothing more exciting than return to his magazine, studying about the first car he plans to have in his driveway when he is old enough to drive—maybe even sooner at the rate he's saving. Working for the neighbors is earning him plenty of money to stash in his account.

Power. Money. Fame. It's all he's ever dreamed of—his personal trifecta. Oh, it is going to happen, too—he can feel it in his bones.

FROM THE AUTHOR

Thank you, dear reader, for burning through these pages of *Menace-Book 3* with Slater Hannigan and his friends. Here is a sneak peek at what lies ahead for all of them in the next book called *Malice-Book 4.* —*Stefania Shaffer*

CHAPTER 1
Starting Lineup

"It's here, Slater," Lynn Hannigan calls through the house, skimming through the pile of mail deposited through the gold mail slit with its metal flap on the bottom half of the front door. "Your schedule for Everly is here. Oh, and look, Graham, your welcome letter is here, too," she calls to an empty house.

She peers through the sliding glass door off the kitchen, watching Slater introduce Graham to his fitness camp. "You gotta work all the muscles and hold for at least four minutes, then when you get good like me, you push your leg straight back behind you like this," Slater says, demonstrating new calisthenics for today's muscle workout lesson.

"My arms are shaking; how much longer?" Graham asks, holding his plank for nearly a minute now.

"Dude, there's no way you're gonna get strong unless you can suck in your gut and tighten your butt," Slater says, bending over Graham, shouting for him to breathe.

Something about his experience at Elmer Woods and having Bear for a role model has really taken hold. Slater is into lifting weights now. The belly blubber he carried around all through elementary and into sixth grade has melted away. He does one hundred sit-ups every morning and every night, powering through just as many push-ups in his next set. He has grown two inches since his birthday in April, but his dad says his own growth spurt didn't even come on until he was a freshman in high school. Slater is determined to get a six-pack before high school, so he follows the conditioning routine he learned from Chicky who learned it from Reginald Washington.

"Ugh!" Graham says, collapsing to the grass. "I'm done," he says, rolling onto his back and stretching out his arms.

"Dude, you're soft," Slater taunts. "You've got girlie arms. Is that what you want—little, tiny girlie arms for the rest of your life?"

"Just you wait, Slater. One day I'm gonna be bigger than you; Dad already told me so," Graham says, letting Slater get the best of him.

"Boys, come inside, you he-men. I've got mail for you both," their mom calls from the slider. When they cross the threshold, she is sure to compliment them on their new muscles. "Wow, so big and strong—who needs spinach when you can spend an afternoon at Slater's boot camp?"

"Feel *my* muscles, Mom. I'm already bigger than yesterday," Graham says, flexing as much as he can, hoping she can find his bicep more easily than the last time he asked.

"Oh, yes, very firm, honey," she confirms, squeezing it gently between her index finger and thumb. "Pretty soon, your dad will be losing his wrestling belt in your next match," she says, smiling before turning to Slater. "Honey, you are working like a champ; good for you. You'll never be sorry about staying healthy and and fit. By the way, care to wrestle me with my girlie arms right now?"

He knows better.

She tears open the letters coming from the Everly District. First, the one for middle school students and their parents.

Dear Everly Middle School Families,

Welcome back to what we expect will be another fruitful year full of nice surprises and support to keep your learning goals within reach. I hope you have enjoyed a restful summer and are ready to apply all that you have learned in the past, maintaining a thirst for all that is still in front of you to be taught.

I believe routine is important, but adding a fresh approach can do wonders for a learning environment. Every fifth year, I direct my administrators to take on new challenges of leading a different school within our district, so the following changes have now been implemented. Please make our principals feel welcomed on their new campus.

Esther Bookman Elementary Principal, rotating in from Christopher Columbus Elementary, **Mr. T.C. Uliuli**

Christopher Columbus Elementary Principal, rotating in from EMGATS, **Maureen Templeton**

Everly Middle School Principal, rotating in from Esther Bookman Elementary, **Bill Daly**

Everly Middle Grade Alternative to Traditional Scheduling (EMGATS) Assistant Vice Principal, rotating in from Everly Middle School, **Miriam Horowitz**

As for changes impacting student matters, last year's pilot of the No Homework policy was so successful with the mandatory tutorials attended by all students that we are opting to continue this for a second year. Again, students new to Everly are required to meet three times a week, while seventh and eighth graders meet twice on Tuesdays and Thursdays. Please avoid scheduling extra-curricular activities for your child on these days, as per our agreement last year.

Your child's schedule is enclosed. Any questions may be directed via your electronic school account portal. Replies will be returned within 24 hours. The front office will resume regular hours three days prior to school commencing.

To all our Everly District students and families, we hope each one of you will have a wonderful year ahead!

Cordially,
Delcia DeMarco-Bradley
Everly District Superintendent

"Wow! What a change. You get your old principal again, Slater. What do you think about that?" Lynn asks, quite relieved.

Bill Daly was never anything other than a pussycat for Lynn to deal with during Slater's elementary school years. She much prefers *him* to Miriam Horowitz—last year's new principal who sent Slater packing to EMGATS after that horrible episode of plagiarism. It was a first-time offense over one little thing.

"Mr. Daly? He's cool, I guess," Slater says nonchalantly completely uninterested in who the leaders of the schools are going to be. All he cares about are the classes he will have with friends.

"Well, I think it's a smart move. I wonder what the new principal at Esther Bookman will be like, hmmm," she says, thinking aloud while she skims the letter for Graham, realizing it says the same thing.

"You think he'll be nice, Mom?" Graham chimes in, wondering if he's going to like his new principal the way he has liked all his teachers.

"Oh, he's going to be very nice to you, my sweet. Who wouldn't be charmed by those dimples," Lynn says, looking down at her soon-to-be fifth grader. "Slater, let's look at your schedule."

He rips it from her hands and holds it on the counter, forcing her to look over his shoulder. "What? Why am I in Reading Support again? I don't need that stupid class. I got by in English last year, so I want to take something else. What electives are they offering? Mom, see if you can sign me up for band; I want to learn to play the drums," he says eagerly.

"Well, I prefer to not be listening to drums being banged upon in my home," she says half-seriously.

"Mom, I'm not kidding. I'm not taking Reading Support again; it's a dumb class."

"I'll see what else is still open. A lot of these classes might already be filled," she says cautiously.

"Even I know better than that," Slater says smiling broadly. "You always find a way to get what you want when it comes to your kids."

"Yeah, like a door back on its hinges? I think not," she says, reminding him of the fuss she put up after discovering he rehung his door without their permission. "You're still on my list for that one," she says, pretending to be more miffed than she really is. "You're just lucky Dad and I were already discussing putting it back on in time for the start of the new school year," she finishes, narrowing her eyes, trying not to laugh when he narrows his right back at her.

The first day of school at Everly Middle Grade is met with many smiles between friends all reunited again. Chicky decided to return to Everly—even though he says he liked EMGATS a lot—when he found out a certain someone was also planning a move back to Everly.

Marilyn Washington has laid out her plans since the beginning of her fifth-grade year. She knows what she wants to do when she gets older, and she knows how to find the right people who can help her. Chicky has no idea what he wants to do with his life, but he certainly likes watching Marilyn swirling around so full of confidence. Besides, all his buddies are at Everly, so it's not like anybody thinks he followed her over, which he would deny a thousand times if anybody suggested it.

Reginald Washington, the student body president of Everly Middle Grade, graduated in June and got an invitation to play varsity at Everly High. His all-city coach trained him well, and with his stellar grades, the high school coach is willing to take a calculated risk that this kid is going to put Everly on the map with a winning season.

Sibley White has still not carted herself off to the all-girls prep school she so imagined for herself. She is relegated to absorbing everything the Everly teachers can impart upon her with their knowledge, and what they don't know, she can research for herself.

So, it is in the first class of the day when the blessed reunion of old and new friends occurs. First period is for Literature and Composition, two classes rolled into one extended block period. The class stands at attention in the hall, waiting patiently for the door to open. There is a hum in the air, anticipating this one more greatly than any other class on their schedule today. When the door swiftly pushes open promptly in time with the bell, all the kids fold their arms around their books and grin widely.

"Number one, you'll find your seat labeled against the right-hand corner of the room; number two, please follow behind. The seating chart is posted in large letters on the board, positioning you alphabetically by last name. Please read it accurately, then quietly find your seat," the teacher says without needing to repeat her directions. The children file in accordingly and never say a word. They stare straight ahead transfixed by the familiarity of her routine, wearing pleasant expressions on each of their faces.

When she is assured they have managed to arrange themselves in the correct seats, stuffing their collection of personal items within the perimeter of personal space beneath their seat, she begins with a thumping of her cane to capture their attention, as if she did not already have it. They soak up the image of her: the grey fuzzy hair, her hand-knit sweater tied around her shoulders with two strands of yarn, the tails of their bow bouncing with two yellow pom-poms, and spectacles atop the bridge of her nose, a familiar perch, indeed.

"Good morning, I am Madame Wilson, ancient as time, decrepit as a mummy's crypt, but retirement is for the birds, dears. I will not rest until I have shared my love of learning with as many of you creatures as my life permits," she says dramatically.

Slater, Tobey, Macaroni and Sibley all feel like they are together again in fifth-grade when they first met Madame Wilson as their substitute. She ran that class like a drill sergeant and while they were afraid of her at first, she became one of their fondest memories from the entire year. In fact, they were sad they never got to see her again.

After she finishes her greeting speech, she spies a hand in the air. "Yes, dear?"

"Madame Wilson, several of us were in Miss Burbank's fifth-grade class when you substituted at Esther Bookman Elementary and on behalf of us, I just want to say it is an honor to be in your class again this year," Sibley White says, happy to see the nodding heads bobbing enthusiastically in support of her remarks.

"Well, then it should be my great pleasure to teach you lads and lassies this year everything I know. I have been at this school for two years now, and I am quite enjoying the older children. It's not something I ever considered after a forty-year career with the youngers. But, I find the more the mind is engaged, the more life we must live, and I have not finished living mine yet. So, we have much to look forward to this year, children."

Chicky is staring in disbelief at his buddies who are totally buying into whatever this teacher says. He has no idea what happened between them in fifth grade, but he will find out everything after school today when they meet in the gazebo as planned.

Charlotte Rigby is also in attendance this morning. Her Australian accent is still intact, even more so after spending her summer Down Under seeing her grandparents and old friends. She is ever so happy to reunite with Sibley, her true best friend, even though they managed to stay in touch for all the weeks they were apart.

Second period is science with a brand-new teacher named Mr. Ferrari, who looks like he could own one. He is young and sporty, but beyond that he is smart, like super, super smart. He is funny and what the kids will find out this year is that Mr. Ferrari teaches like he drives—fast. Every day is a new concept, and he makes it more exciting than they ever expected learning could be. He rips apart TV episodes to discuss crime science and what's in the blood, and what can be learned from DNA and fingerprints. He keeps students hanging on his every word.

The rest of the afternoon rolls through the usual classes with the best news of all: the entire cluster of friends travel together for the *entire* day. Whoever thought of this scheduling convenience should be thanked, if it were up to Slater and his crew. Perhaps, some of the adults on campus might have different feelings closer to the end of the year—but, alas, that is still so many months away.

At Esther Bookman Elementary, a new group of students is being swept into their fifth-grade teacher's room. "Good morning, children, I am so excited to welcome you to your last year of elementary. We're going to have so much fun learning about how to build a better society after we study what our forefathers had in mind when they imagined forming a more perfect union." The teacher looks around the room, smiling at every child until she sees one slightly familiar little boy.

Graham Hannigan has the Hannigan handsome gene, all right, but his features are softer around the eyes, and his dimples make him utterly darling. His hair is sweetly polished with gel holding it in place and he sits straight in his chair, unlike his brother who used to rock in his seat, despite the fact that the chair was always attached to the desk.

She hopes for the best from this Hannigan. His teachers have always had such positive things to say about Graham. *He loves to help organize the bookshelves. He is an excellent reader. He likes to make new friends at lunch, so he rotates tables—he's precious, Dana, really.* Her friends give her every assurance that this will be unlike any other Hannigan experience. The other teachers have never once had to call home to Lynn Hannigan, so they don't know the mother apart from stories Dana Burbank would tell in the lunchroom about the brother, Slater, and his shenanigans when she had him.

"Part of what I would like to do with you this year is to have you experience what it is like in real life to run a society. Sometimes it is not easy to be a leader, but it is such a valuable lesson in life to learn how to listen to other people's opinions, finding out what's important to everyone, and then making decisions that help your society," she says brightly. "I want us to select a person who will be our leader this year, our class president."

All the eyes in the classroom are aglow at the possibility that they might be put in charge, given some power to make decisions the way they would like things to go. But, of course, this is the risk a society faces when someone is not willing to listen to the interests of the people.

"Before we can even discuss the responsibilities of the class president, we must first establish the rules of our society and what we feel will be important for us to all agree to this year. This includes behavior expectations, privileges, and actions to be taken if someone goes against our society's values. We should write it all down in our own constitution, just like our founding fathers. What do you think? Are you ready to get started if I give you some guidance?"

Miss Burbank's explanation is met with enthusiasm from her new students. They are able to sort themselves into small groups, and as she listens in on their productive conversations, she is impressed with their level of thinking and sensitivity toward others. It is one of the best first days of school she has ever had.

Much like she has always done, she has given each student their own chart, along with different colored markers, one for each child, to share his or her ideas. When they have finally narrowed down their top five governing principles, and their top five punishments for going against these, the class votes on the top ten that become their constitution.

The list includes familiar items like no homework on the weekends and no stealing from each other, but it also includes new language like *compliment your classmate whenever you work together, ask for a work pass when an assignment gets too hard with a maximum of five per month, include a fifteen-minute rest after lunch before learning starts again, hold class meetings every Monday morning and every Friday afternoon.*

"My, these are very specific. I like that," she says encouragingly. Miss Burbank can tell this is going to be a very gentle society to teach this year.

Once they have settled on the final ten laws, it is time to outline the criteria for what is needed in a class president.

"Think of the person you feel you can talk to, you can trust. They'll really listen to your point of view and ask you why what you want is important to you. They are not going to share your private thoughts with everyone else because they value your friendship.

This should be a person who has a wide range of friends. Ideally, this person hangs out with more than one group so everyone feels represented. This person should like to work and establish a good relationship with the teacher, since I will act as the judge whenever there is a tie that needs to be decided. Your class president should be a good organizer but a person who also wants to get other committees involved and be able to delegate tasks for them to perform. Your class president should be able to inspire you to be your best this year and learn your strengths so these can be incorporated when we do class field trips, or parties, or are in charge of a campus cleanup or anything like this. Any questions?"

There are no hands going into the air. She wonders if they understand what she has explained in the simplest way she knows. "Really? No one needs any clarification? No one?" She looks around the room at their sweet faces and folded hands. "Does that mean we're ready to vote?" She is met with frantic head nods. "Okay, and don't forget, it's okay to vote for yourself. Don't be shy if you want to try something new."

She distributes one card per student with the instruction for them to write the name of the person they believe embodies all these characteristics for class president. When she counts them minutes later, there is no need for a tie-breaker. "Gosh, I've never seen an entire class unanimously agree on any one thing before. I am happy to announce that you have voted as your class president, Graham Hannigan. Congratulations, Graham!"

Dear Reader,

Did you enjoy Menace? Is your heart still racing? Are you wondering what will happen to our fine friends in the next book? Oh, it is delicious. But I am sworn to secrecy.

But you don't have to keep Menace a secret from the world. In fact, would you be willing to go straight to amazon.com to write an honest review for the author? She is competing against all of those other books you read and is hoping to get your friends interested in reading all about Slater, Macaroni, Chicky, and, of course, me.

It's pretty easy. Just go to: www.amazon.com and then type in Stefania Shaffer.

Find the book, write a review, add some stars and then, snap, you're done.

As for me, I have already cleared a special spot on my shelf for all four of the new books in the Mischief series. See you in the V.I.P. Club!

Yours truly,
Sibley White

P.S. To become a V.I.P. member of the Mischief-Makers Club sign up for my newsletter at www.MischiefSeries.com.

You will be first to find top-secret giveaways and previews of new releases from future books.

Kids visit: www.MischiefSeries.com

Parents visit: www.StefaniaShaffer.com

All books by Stefania Shaffer

Fiction for Middle Grade readers:

Heroes Don't Always Wear Capes
Mischief Series: Mischief-Book 1
Mischief Series: Mayhem-Book 2
Mischief Series: Menace-Book 3
Mischief Series: Malice-Book 4

Non-Fiction for Adults:
9 Realities of Caring for an Elderly Parent: A Love Story of a Different Kind, a memoir
9 Realities of Caring for an Elderly Parent: The Companion Playbook, accompanying workbook

53986225R00192

Made in the USA
San Bernardino, CA
04 October 2017